It's the End of the World, My Love

It's the End of the World, My Love

•

ALLA GORBUNOVA

TRANSLATED BY ELINA ALTER

DEEP VELLUM PUBLISHING

DALLAS, TEXAS

Deep Vellum Publishing
3000 Commerce St., Dallas, Texas 75226
deepvellum.org · @deepvellum

Deep Vellum is a 501c3 nonprofit literary arts organization
founded in 2013 with the mission to bring
the world into conversation through literature.

First US Edition, 2022

LIBRARY OF CONGRESS CATALOGING-IN-PUBLICATION CONTROL NUMBER: 2022942742

ISBN (TPB) 978-1-64605-210-3
ISBN (Ebook) 978-1-64605-236-3

Cover design by Sarah Schulte

Interior layout and typesetting by KGT

PRINTED IN THE UNITED STATES OF AMERICA

CONTENTS

IV. MEMORY OF HEAVEN

I.

AGAINST THE LAW

IT'S THE END OF THE WORLD, MY LOVE

When I was a child, what scared me the most was the end of the world. I was afraid of change in general. It seemed intuitive that changes would largely be for the worse—changes for the better were not likely. I was surrounded by nice things, and it was nice being among them. In the morning the sun filtered in through the bedroom windows, which faced east, and lit up the orange drapes. It was a nice sun and they were nice drapes. My nice grandfather pointed out the nice stars in the evening sky and, in the spring, the budding leaves—which were also, as you may have guessed, nice. Summers at the dacha, I would wake up in a joyfully expectant state of ease, and my friend Nadya would come over, an inevitable deck of cards in her pocket. Even then it was obvious that it would be best never to grow up. "Someday you'll understand that happiness is anticipation," my father said once.

One of the adults I knew said that children could have a kind of complex consisting of a fear of change and the desire for everything to remain as it is. I certainly had that complex. And the end of the world was the manifestation of the most frightening change of all. There were also some terrible facts of a cosmic nature to consider. My grandfather had told me about entropy, and I understood that chaos increases exponentially, and the universe is moving toward its death. Then, at school, we were shown a movie about the impending death of the sun. There were simulated shots of how the sun would become huge and red, then parts of it would start falling to Earth, then Earth would catch on fire, and then the sun would finally die. After the movie ended, just to be sure, I went to my teacher and asked: "Lyubov Mikhailovna, when will the sun die?" Lyubov Mikhailovna apparently didn't know and asked another teacher, who said it wouldn't be for a long time, not for millions of years, and I was somewhat calmed by this temporary reprieve.

I had another reprieve, too, though this one wasn't as long. As a very young child I'd heard about a prophecy made by Nostradamus, according to which the end of the world would come about in 1999, brought on by a star called Nemesis, meaning "vengeance." There was an exact date: August 11. So I counted the years: in 1990 I told myself, "It won't happen for a while, a whole nine years," in 1992, "a whole seven years," and so on. Another time, somebody having frightened me yet again, I asked my grandfather what he thought about the prophecies of Nostradamus, and he told me that everything would be as the Lord God wills.

Another version of the end of the world was the Second Coming. Also as a very young child, I asked my mother whether there was a God, and Mama told me there wasn't. Some time went by, and I asked Mama again whether there was a God, and she told me there was, because in the meantime she'd become a believer. During perestroika a lot of literature appeared on the shelves that hadn't been available before; Mama started reading all kinds of esoterica and as a result of her reading came to the conclusion that God existed after all. Well, fine—if He exists, He exists. Thus I also became a believer. Once, Mama and I were taking a stroll on the avenue, walking west by the neighborhood library, and the sun was setting, the sky was flooded with brilliant crimson-gold light, and Mama said, "It looks just like Christ in His Glory is about to appear in these clouds." So, overall, everything pointed to the end of the world happening any minute now. It was basically closing in on all sides.

One summer at the dacha, Sanya started teaching me and my girlfriends magic. Sanya and I had a romance going. He said that the world would end next year, the year 2000, and that the final war would happen then, too. We were going to fight in this war, all of us together: me and Sanya, Yurik, Nadya, and Nyuta. Later I'd learn that Russians have been expecting the end of the world and the final war for hundreds of years, in the most varied, wild, and ridiculous sectarian variations. So in the nineties we had this, too. The war we were going to fight in was, for some reason, the war in Afghanistan, which really hadn't ended. But at the same time, it was going to be the war that marked the beginning of a new world, in which Earth would merge with another planet, its magical double, home to dragons, elves, and gnomes. And at the same time it would be the final battle of Armageddon. We were all preparing to really go to this war and to die there; Sanya had already ordered special military uniforms for us. Sanya badly wanted to join the army, but they wouldn't take him, because he started telling the admissions committee that he did magic. They didn't believe him and said, "Make something happen, then." He made it so that one of the women on the committee got a headache, but they still wouldn't believe him, and gave him a diagnosis of schizophrenia. My grandparents had no idea that I was going to go to war and die, I couldn't tell them that, but I felt extremely sorry for them, and for all my nice, familiar, and beloved things. I began to see them as already lost forever: here they were, my nice washbasin, some nice bushes of meadowsweet, my nice grandfather watching TV, my nice cat who'd come out to lie in the sun. Each day I lived through became, for me, my last day at home before the war.

I was thirteen, and it was a nice summer. Sanya and I went on walks in the woods and once accidentally sat on an anthill; we rode around on his old motorcycle and I burned the platforms of my boots putting my feet on the exhaust pipes; at night we sat between the roots of an ancient, enormous oak, drinking Black Monk wine; Sanya came to see me after work (during the summer he worked in the village as a plumber), and hid behind my stove from some friends of his who were looking for him, Gapon and Master, about whom there was a joke going around that they'd drunk a little too much brake fluid. Jealous, he'd come along when I went to visit lanky Andrei. It was a beautiful summer of waiting for the war and the end of the world.

Then I went back to the city, to school, to the eighth grade, and Sanya promised to visit me in a month and to call, but time went on and he did not appear—and by late October I found out that he had actually been in the city for a while, had apparently dumped me, and was now dating Nyuta, though by that point he had already half dumped Nyuta and was with Nata, a school friend of Nadya's. Such was the end of my first love and that strange, unforgettable fairy tale, and also the end of my childhood and the world.

I began taking a lot of walks by myself, skipping school, writing poems, and it was astounding to me that everything in the world went on as before. Up until the very beginning of spring I waited for the war to begin. I started seeing Yurik, who was officially Nadya's boyfriend, just to stay in the friend group, so they'd take me to war with them. Yurik told me that in our past lives we had all fought in Afghanistan and died there. I had been a military pilot and crashed my plane, Nadya was a nurse, Nyuta was a sniper, and not one of us had survived. The world I knew, my childhood world, continued to dissolve: I looked around our tiny kitchenette with its red-and-blue linoleum, where I'd sit and talk on the phone with Yurik, and at the painted roosters on the serving boards, the old Lysva electric stove, and I thought about my grandparents, who sat in the next room distressed by these calls with Yurik; I thought about my entire life up until then, perishing before my eyes, how Mama and I had gone to Sochi when I was ten, how I once had a caterpillar that I fed rose hip petals. All around me, things were terribly vulnerable, they were melting away and crying out to me for help, but I had to accept that by going to war, I would destroy them—had already destroyed them, in fact, by making the decision to go. I was in terrible despair, because I really had made that decision, and it had strained my soul to its limit. That fall and winter I said goodbye to everything. I wandered by frozen rivers and dark trees, rode the subway aimlessly, hung out at the train station from which we usually left to go to the dacha, walking the platforms, and went a few times to the neighborhood of high-rises by the bay where I had lived for the first three years of my life, to throw myself from the roof of one of those buildings, but it was either the case that the entrance to the roof was locked, or that I couldn't even get into the building, or that I stopped wanting to do it. At night I listened to the radio on my headphones, to rock music, and I wrote poems. There was something new hatching inside of me, tearing my heart to bits, but it couldn't quite hatch all the way. Among the concrete fences of industrial districts I wandered in darkness, hoping that I'd be raped and murdered by some drunk. Around this time I started drinking a bottle or two of Baltika 9 beer a day.

Spring came, and nobody went to war. We said it had been rescheduled, maybe, or made up some other reason. Then Nadya broke up with Yurik, Sanya broke up with Nata, and gradually we all stopped seeing each other. Nata, whom I saw a few more times, started working as a salesgirl at the market and living with her alternating boyfriends; after ninth grade Nadya studied sewing and pattern-making, worked at a photography studio, became an accountant, got baptized, lived for a long time with a common-law husband, then married another guy and had a son; Nyuta initially shaved her head bald, dropped out of nursing school, hung out all over the city with all kinds of people, hitchhiked around the country, and managed to get diagnosed with "dromomania," wanderlust syndrome—but then, pretty early, around eighteen, she got married and had a child, then was divorced, and now works as a surgical nurse. Yurik was divorced several times, quit drinking for his health, and now assembles furniture; Sanya, too, got married and then divorced, and also works somewhere, and God bless him, honestly, but I still remember how we lay in the pine forest holding hands, and there was so much that bound us together that even now, for me, it belongs in the category of things that can't be spoken of. After all, all of us, ages thirteen to nineteen, died in the war that never came.

I've stopped being scared of the end of the world. I've begun to love it. I've come to know its ways: when it comes, it passes by very quickly, and all that's left for you to do is shout something senseless in its wake, and when it doesn't come, some people dread it while others expect it and believe that when it arrives, they'll be able to exist within it forever, but then they find themselves in front of the TV with a bottle of beer. It comes and doesn't come simultaneously. And you look on in astonishment as the whole world crumbles, but the most frightening thing about that is that everything stays the way it was. The same trees, streets, houses, people. And a child's fear that the world will end is just a joke when you understand that there's not going to be any more end of the world, nobody's coming to unlock the crystal jewel box of the world in all its unbearable eternity. All my little life I tried to protect the world, to save it, to keep it from dissolving like clouds and seafoam, but the world tricked me and turned out to be solid, quite solid.

My father once said, "Happiness is anticipation." To which I might add: happiness is the anticipation of the end of the world. I know now that the end of the world is the border and the break, the fulfillment and the miracle, and its function, like the function of borders generally, is to exist and not exist at the same time; to happen, so that you give yourself over to it and perish, and never to happen, and nothing else would ever be enough. The end is not outside but at the very heart of the experience of the world, and Apocalypse is only one of its names, since the end of the world is also its beginning. I want to live at the heart of the end of the world. I continue to learn to love it. To recognize it under new and different names in the company of new people, to be on time for it, to work hard to expand it over the space of life. And no matter how oppressive the solidity of the world becomes, and how variously all of us, the young magicians of that summer, meet our deaths, all of us are—or at least I am—a little bored in the world, because after the floods ended, boredom came, and "the Queen, the Witch who lights her coals in the clay pot, will never want to tell us what she knows, and which we do not know."

AT THE MARKET

I spent the summer after eighth grade getting wasted on top of the crates at the market. Whenever I stop by our village market now, years later, buying fruits and vegetables from the booths and meat and berries from the stands, it occurs to me that I'm in one of those places in the world where I was once completely happy. I feel this most acutely if I happen to pass by the market at night, after it's closed, and I hear young voices, laughter, cursing, singing along with a guitar, the roar of motorcycles and mopeds taking off through the market gates, and I know there are young guys riding the motorcycles and mopeds and driving their girlfriends around, and they're all drinking and kissing there on the crates, and they're playing cards, and I think that they themselves must not know just how happy they are.

In my day, same as now, teenagers hung out at the market at night. It's a convenient spot, right in the center of the village. Only the stands used to be configured differently, milk and beer splashing down on them, pig blood dripping down. Enormous squinting pig heads lay on the counters, and in the middle of the market, surrounded by the rows of stands that lined the perimeter, stood a storehouse where household goods were sold. Bats lived in the storehouse. Then the storehouse burned down—people said it was the local mafia who torched it. Directly behind the market was the yellow wooden village hall, which also burned down, likely for the same reason. In the mornings the milk churn would arrive from the nearest town and stop next to the hall. To this day in the village square there's a central store, and behind the fence there's a spot where propane cylinders are sold. There's a rusty sign nailed to a pine tree that says NO TRESPASSING, and when the market gates are open, you can see a paved area, some gravel, an old tractor and a few parked trucks, a storehouse, rusty canisters, a huge wire coil abandoned there for some reason, plyboard structures, garages, a pile of logs. By the market's main entrance there are a few booths. Back then I knew everyone who worked the booths: elderly, blue-eyed Aunt Lyuba; cute, twenty-seven-year-old Natasha; lively, dark-complexioned Alia.

Aunt Lyuba's daughter was raped three times, and then she married a rich guy. He gave her a large allowance, she started shooting up and spending all of it on drugs, and then she died. Natasha had a daughter, too, a little girl, and Natasha sewed gorgeous dresses for her. Natasha also had a husband and a lover. We never saw the husband, but the lover was a local guy, Ivan. He had been shell-shocked during the war, and occasionally, when he drank, something in his head shorted out, and he became deranged, launched himself at people, and was liable to kill someone. Ivan spent his days at the market on some unknown-to-us business, and then at night he'd fool around with Natasha. In the evenings, her husband spied on the two of them from the bushes; once he jumped out and started a fight, and then at home he beat

Natasha, and afterward she came to work with a shiner. Alia was young and bubbly; she'd make eyes at the guys and giggle with us.

The market lived its own life, concealed from the view of the casual visitor. On weekend mornings the stands disappeared beneath endless cottage cheeses and sour creams, clothes and knickknacks; in the second half of the summer there were mushrooms and berries that had been picked by little old ladies in the woods. Beginning at midday the stands emptied out; only Beard and Aunt Panya stuck around until evening. Aunt Panya sold sundries: biscuits, chocolate bars, chewing gum. She left the market at night, dragging her cart, in her invariable wool leggings. Sometimes her ancient mother would come to sit with her. Beard was a weird, vague guy who never said anything about himself, only hinting that he was some kind of important retired mafioso who ran everything around there and knew some very serious people, thieves-in-law. He talked constantly about having sex with underage prostitutes, his favorite kind, and he wanted to go into business selling local teens for sexual services, meaning, first of all, my friend and me, and he pitched this idea to us pretty often. At the market he would sell, or often just give away, watered-down vodka. He had a son, a kid who was about eleven or twelve. When the son got older, as Beard told me a few years later, they started visiting prostitutes together.

The local whores also showed up at the market occasionally: they were unattractive young women who drank, dreary and destitute, toothless and diseased. Sometimes they fucked the half-savage local guys who were always hanging around the market on the lookout for booze and an easy way to make money. They usually stood around Beard's spot, and he poured them his diluted vodka. One of these guys was Buggy, tall and thin as a rail, dressed in rags, with an earthen tinge to his skin. His long gray hair hung in clumps around his perpetually drunken face, and there was a bald spot at the crown of his head. When he was drunk, he liked to say dirty things to me and my friend. Uchkuduk, an old man who looked Asian, was supposed to have been a professor before the drink got him. He was harmless; when he was drunk, he'd stretch out by a fence somewhere and grin, muttering to himself. Grandpa Au was a less frequent visitor; he looked like an alcoholic forest sprite with his cloud of beard and shaggy gray hair and clear, piercing eyes. Another rarity was Rickshaw, always driving around in his "kopeika" sedan. Bad-tempered and exasperating, he would either grossly come on to us or insult us, calling us whores. The most obscene, cursing like he was still at sea, was Ivan Sevastopolsky, who had been a sailor. Ivan served at Sevastopol and got his nickname that way. He had a ruddy, rugged face, and when he drank his eyes went from gray to watery blue. Sometimes a tall, fat, balding man stopped by the market; people said he was Jewish and had once been an important scientist, and they treated him with a mix of derisive pity and sympathetic respect. Once at the market, he would inevitably pull down his pants and show his ass. He couldn't help it, because he had long ago lost his mind. Sometimes people egged him on, saying, "Show us your ass," and he would, following which they'd laugh at him and chase him off, and then later they'd say, "Yes, he was an important man once."

Probably the strangest thing of all was that my friend and I hung out with these people. I was fourteen, my friend was fifteen. In the mornings we'd leave our houses and head to the market, where we spent entire days. Beard treated us to free watery vodka, and we sat on the market crates, played cards, and chatted with the men. I was thin and delicate, while my friend was more robust and well-developed, and guys inevitably hit upon the subject of which one of us they preferred: the more refined characters liked me, while others, Rickshaw for example, said that I didn't "even have anything to squeeze," and clearly favored my friend. We knew everything about everyone: who made money on the side and where, who had a busted carburetor, whose wife was cheating on him, who'd gorged himself the other day and how he had behaved. And we were also almost always drunk, or a little buzzed, and I rolled around in the local ditches regularly. We wore bright makeup bordering on vulgar and dressed provocatively. The "normies" our age steered clear of us, a lot of people thought we were whores, and one guy who was about twenty came up to me once and asked, "Is it true that you're a nymphomaniac?" In reality I was a virgin and a difficult teen, the "girl with a gaze sharper than a dagger's blade." I was being raised by my grandparents, and my grandmother was incredibly strict and held me in an iron grip until the last. The system of restrictions in my family bordered on the absurd: for a long time I wasn't allowed to go out on summer evenings, and when I finally was allowed, the length of my outings was shortened in tandem with the sunset, which came earlier and earlier. In the city I was forbidden to go out after four in the afternoon or for longer than one hour, and when I walked down the street, my grandmother, standing on a stool, watched me from the kitchen window, although she watched my forty-year-old mother and thirty-year-old uncle in the same way. I was constantly threatened with psycho killers and strangers in cars who kidnap little girls; they wouldn't let me go into the stairwell of our building alone; I had the gold and silver medals of my forbears shoved in my face, their diplomas with honors, their advanced degrees. It was understood that there was a certain "path" a person ought to follow: school, college, perhaps a graduate education, then starting a family, having a child, working with others at a job that you went to every single day except weekends and vacations, and after all that came retirement, and then it was time to die. I didn't want to live like that. My family loved me and wanted what was best for me, but there was one issue—I was clearly somehow not quite right. And then, in the summer of 2000, my rebellion manifested as this whole story with the market. At the end of the day, the market was really how my friend and I came to know the world. We came to know it poetically. The market was like a beautiful ballad, the finest and cruelest poetry of this very specific society of "strong ties," populated by drunks, criminals, and whores, and in all of this I saw a kind of enchantingly "real" life laid bare.

I was in love then with an alcoholic and a bum, a fully grown, twenty-eight-year-old man, exactly twice my age. I was drawn to the feeling of wild, boundless freedom that I felt when I was with him. I wanted to save him. He had a broad and blissful smile, and it may have been the smile that made him seem somehow American; he wore his hair long and on his shoulder had a rudimentary tattoo of a wolf. We called him Willy. Willy lived in a container at the dump and had an eighth-grade education. He had lost his housing in the city in some kind of nineties scheme; his mother and uncle lived in a village house with a tiered garden, but they had thrown him out: he didn't get on with his uncle because of his drinking, and the uncle looked down on him as a sloth and parasite. He'd been working from the time he was fifteen and had held dozens of jobs, like the hero of a certain kind of American novel: he had been a metalworker, a machinist, a courier, a driver, a fishmonger, a bootlegger—an underground vodka peddler during Gorbachev's anti-alcohol campaign—a successful makeup salesman, and even a hired killer, as he confessed to me once while drunk. He said that he'd only killed bad people, total bastards, and that whenever he received an assignment he would first learn everything he could about the intended victim, watch the person for a while, and only then accept the assignment or turn it down. But then he repented and threw his gun in the river, traveled to a monastery to beg forgiveness from God, moved to the country, and started drinking. Willy was an autodidact with broad and scattered knowledge; he was convinced that the education system existed to standardize people and make them fit for society and that everything a person really learns, he has to learn on his own. He didn't really like other people, considering himself an aristocrat and a genius; he loved nature and thunderstorms and Erich Maria Remarque; he'd been married three times and had a seven-year-old daughter with his first wife. Willy could travel through different dimensions, but he was being hunted there, and he kept falling into the terrifying lower depths and asking me for help. The celestial realms he visited resembled beautiful, otherworldly cities that he would describe to me when we sat on the crates during thunderstorms and kissed. His father had also suffered from alcoholism and had worked as a first mate on seagoing ships; he loved women and finally sailed away to be with one of his women for good, abandoning his wife and son. Willy's ancestors were of noble blood, and in old photographs they stood next to members of the royal family. The happiest period of Willy's life was the time when he worked at a cosmetics company and seduced a pretty coworker, stealing her away from her family; together, they started their own business. Young, energetic Willy bamboozled the male customers and enticed the women, carting makeup around the district in his car. Things were looking up: Willy got himself an aquarium full of exotic fish, bought a telescope to gaze upon the stars, and got into astronomy, but then his wife left him for another man, he started drinking, lost everything, and moved in with his mother in the village. None of the other guys who hung out at the market had as good a head on his shoulders or as deft a touch as Willy: he could tell what was wrong with an engine just by the sound it made.

A few days after the incident near the market wherein five thugs from a nearby town tried to drag me into their car and rape me, I realized that I was in love with Willy. He was lying near the market stands in a stupor, his pants soaked with piss, and I looked at him and thought that he was unlike anyone I had ever known. We talked for hours about the things we had in common. I thought it was a little annoying that Willy ended everything he said with "fucken," but I quickly got used to it. He told me about a time when he climbed up to the roof of his house during a storm to take pictures with his Zenit camera, and about how in the "days of his youth"—he was always referring to the "days of his youth," because he considered himself to have lived through a lot by then—he'd stay in the forest for days, catching fish, picking mushrooms and berries, and living like a real man of the taiga. He knew the local woods like the back of his hand, and he showed me the path to the Black Lakes. He told countless tales about himself in the old days, probably making up a good deal, but I took it all for the honest truth and saw before me not an alcoholic village hustler but a daring cowboy, the hero of many an adventure. "My greatest flaw is bravery," he'd say, though once, when we were hanging out on the crates, we were approached by an elderly guy with a red face and swollen veins; he didn't like something Willy had said and hit him with his belt. Willy bore the blow, and everything was sorted out peacefully. The younger boys called him a bum and laughed at us when Willy, in his piss-soaked pants, and I, garishly made up, in heels, walked through the village hand in hand.

One day I came to the market, and Willy wasn't there. Beard called me over and said, "Want to see a video? I filmed it yesterday when you weren't here. It's your darling Willy showing his ass."

"What?!"

"The mafia guys were on him, he owed them money. They said, 'If you can't pay, show us your ass.'"

"And he did?"

"What else was he gonna do? They made him, so he did it. They nearly screwed him, too."

"You know, I don't want to see that," I said.

"Right, and I wasn't gonna show it to you, I just called you over to tell you, showing you is too mean. I feel bad for you."

"Why do you let Willy drink? Why do you give him vodka?" I once asked Beard.

"There are different paths. Vodka is a path, too," Beard said.

Willy and I were going to get married, but our relationship was completely chaste, we didn't do anything but kiss. At first I didn't even want to do that, but Willy brought me to tears talking about his lost soul, how I must not love him since I didn't want to kiss him, and that meant we would have to break up, though he couldn't live without me, and so he had no reason to live. I cried, and then we started kissing.

"Grandma, I have a boyfriend," I told my grandmother. "He's a lot older than me."

"How old is he?"

"Twenty-eight."

"Well, that's all right," my grandmother said, "I was afraid he'd be forty. He doesn't drink, does he?"

I lied: "No, he doesn't drink. Just on holidays." Then I brought drunk Willy home to meet my grandparents. He talked drunkenly and at length, seated at the table on the veranda. My grandparents listened to him without saying a word, stone-faced. I kept lying and saying he didn't really drink, he'd just had a little before meeting them, to calm his nerves, but everybody knew the score. I was unshakable in my decision to marry him. My poor grandmother called in to some TV show, a program on which they were discussing the problem of alcoholism, told them our story, and asked for advice.

Willy got stitched to quit drinking. He disappeared for several days and then turned up sober, with flowers. He went back to his mother and uncle's house, promising me that he'd find a job in the city, rent an apartment somewhere near me, and then I'd get older and we'd be married. In the meantime, he took a job with a construction crew, building cottages. In the garden of their house, by fall, there bloomed astounding, majestic chrysanthemums and asters, and every day Willy brought me a fresh bouquet. We were very happy. We believed in our future. In our love. We talked endlessly about the most personal things and marveled at how much we had in common and how well we understood each other, almost without speaking a word. We kissed in the sun and in the rain, among the flowers and the apples, sober Willy smelled like some pleasant brand of eau de cologne, his cheeks were clean-shaven. He would hold me very tightly and say that soon I "could be plucked"—like a berry, or a flower.

I loved Willy, and I would always remember him. I missed him after we went back to the city, where he had promised to follow me in a week, start settling in and looking for work, but he didn't come. Another few weeks went by, and there was no word from Willy. At the very end of October, my grandfather took me to the dacha one last time. My friend went, too, and we immediately set out together to look for Willy. I felt afraid. Near his house we ran into his mother, who said, "I don't know where he is." We went to look for him in the village, walking as far as the Saucer—a small, deep lake, surrounded by the forest and Bald Mountain. There were no people around, the leaves were yellowing, I was looking out at the lake, at the tops of the pines, and something irreparable about the world was becoming clear to me.

On the way back from the lake we were overtaken by a wasted Willy. When we had come to his house he'd been home, passed out drunk, and his mother couldn't bring herself to tell us that he was drinking again. He dropped to his knees before me. He said that he'd fallen off the wagon, that tomorrow he would get back on, and that everything would be the way that he and I had dreamed. I forgave him. We went to light a bonfire outside. In our part of the world in October, the Milky Way is clear in the sky. We stood beneath the stars, chilly and shivering, warming ourselves by the fire, holding each other for the final time, and talking for the final time about the things that bound our hearts together: our love for the stars and for fall, the silence of October, our dreams of boating down the Vuoksi River.

The next day I went back to the city, and Willy disappeared from my life. Later he told me, "I decided then and there that I didn't want to ruin your life." Slowly, I got used to living without him. Slowly, I came to see that it was better this way. Not until the following summer did I feel ready to date again. I dropped out of school, having suffered through a year of arguments with my grandparents, and enrolled at a vocational school where I never even showed my face, instead spending my days and nights crashing with various informals, hanging out with different crowds, hitchhiking around. Years passed, and I think I was already married and studying philosophy at the university when I received a visit from Willy.

He showed up in his own car, with his broad, blissful smile, and told me he that he hadn't wanted to ruin my life and that he had remembered me all these years, and that when things were really rough for him he would look at my photograph and pray. He drank for years, drank blindly, until he nearly froze to death, beaten senseless on the village highway. Then he stopped, quit drinking, and didn't even miss it anymore; he was working as an electrician in the village and making good money, about a hundred thousand rubles a month. We started spending time together. In the summer we drove around the district together in his car, to the confluence of the Smorodinka and the Volchya rivers, to the fields in the west; he got into trading, started making money and explaining to me what Forex is. He showed me the beautiful, professional-quality photos he took of local nature. But our conversations had become limited, not the same as they had been before—they felt a little forced, because we could no longer talk about the things that brought us together. I had changed. I saw him differently now. But a sense of gratitude remained—gratitude for our only summer together and that genuine, unworldly intimacy that had been possible between us then and was impossible now. And gratitude for the fact that he had let me go, and joy that he had made it out and was still alive, and constant worry for him.

Almost twenty years have passed. Much has changed at the market. Aunt Lyuba, Natasha, and Alia no longer work in the booths. Natasha's husband took her farther from sin, meaning farther from Ivan, and Aunt Lyuba and Alia have also gone somewhere. Beard doesn't sell vodka anymore. Grandpa Au died one winter during the frosts. Buggy died a terrible death beneath the wheels of a tractor trailer. Now I'm just one of the market's visitors, I'm not part of its secret inner life, I know nothing of the dramas that unfold within it, the lives taking shape and falling apart, but I remember, when I look at the old wooden crates, how I lay on them and looked slantwise, from beneath the roof, at the sky, Willy was next to me, and a shot of vodka and a deck of cards, and no matter how strange, antisocial, and unacceptable it was—I was free, and I was happy.

TECH

After ninth grade I went to study at a vocational-technical academy: tech. I wasn't planning on actually doing any studying there, but I wanted to be enrolled somewhere in order to reassure my family that I wasn't just out wandering the streets. In reality, of course, I planned to be out wandering the streets. My folks had a difficult time accepting my decision: I lived through a year of arguments and psychological pressure in the form of the gold and silver medals and honors diplomas of my forbears; they shouted at me, they pleaded with me, they threatened me with the big bad techies at the academy who would torment me, but I had made up my mind.

I was driven to this decision first and foremost by the family atmosphere—the hypercontrol exerted by my grandmother, which bordered on the absurd and led to inevitable revolt. I was also influenced by my boyfriends at the time: they were usually uneducated, laborers, plumbers, security guards, loaders, and two or three of them had admitted to me that they were also hitmen. From them I acquired the notion that the education system exists to standardize people, making them fit for society, and that the much worthier path was to be a loner and self-taught. In general I felt that I stood in opposition to society, the existing order, the Demiurge of this world, and all those kinds of things.

Throughout the ninth grade I skipped school, rode the subway during classes, wrote poems, and wandered around the city with my friend Nadya. We met and started hanging out with some street musicians, Grisha and Dima, who played in the underground pedestrian crossing at Gostiny Dvor. We both developed crushes on Dima and would stand in the tunnel for hours, listening to their simple songs and flirting.

At the start of summer I began preparing my application to tech, passing almost without my noticing it the comically easy entrance exams, scoring one hundred out of one hundred possible points, and gathering various certificates of eligibility. One of the required certificates was from the skin and venereal diseases dispensary. I was standing at the bus stop and waiting for the bus to the dispensary when a young man at the stop across the street noticed me. We made eyes at each other, and he came over to introduce himself. "Where are you going?" was the first thing he asked. "To the skin and venereal diseases dispensary," I said. He was floored. Thus our romance began.

He came from a little Ukrainian town, he was twenty-seven, though he looked younger, and he had a shock of dark, wavy hair and huge eyes that changed colors. He'd once studied at the military academy but was expelled, now worked with his brother laying floors, in his spare time played music. Let's call him Lyonya. We started having long conversations on the phone at night, taking walks in the park and kissing, and there, in a gazebo on an island in the middle of the lake, he confessed to me that we couldn't have sex—he had some kind of insurmountable issue. He had lived with a girlfriend for seven years, and everything was fine, but ever since they broke up he could no longer do it. He asked if this bothered me. I said it didn't bother me, but if there was anything I could do to help in this regard, I was ready. I would go to his place and attempt to help, we'd roll around and make out, but as soon as we were about to get down to business, he'd push me away and withdraw into himself. Beneath his pillow I found porn magazines. Periodically Lyonya had depressive episodes, he'd disappear for about three weeks and stop calling me, then call and apologize, saying he hadn't been well.

During one of his disappearances I went to Black River (the main hangout spot for informals, where I went all the time) and there, in the rain, on a bench in the square, I drank wine with a very good-looking nineteen-year-old guy. He was a student at the university philosophy department, his name was Sasha, and he was over six feet tall, an informal intellectual who wrote for the *Limonka* newspaper, a member of the National Bolsheviks and a producer for a rock band that later became fairly well-known. After that I stopped answering Lyonya's calls when he finally reappeared, and for a while I was with Sasha.

We walked around Petersburg, and he bought me a thick volume of Nietzsche; we went to Pavlovsk, and he told me about the National Bolshevik Party and the contemporary goth scene, we fed squirrels, took pictures, sat on a bench, and he put his head on my lap; I stroked his hair, and he said it was better than sex. He knew that I planned to study at tech, and he probably thought I wasn't very bright, a typical techie. Still, something good was taking shape between us, but by fall he disappeared. I took the subway to wander around Yelizarovskaya Station, where he lived, sulked in the rain, and hoped I would run into him. Half a year later at Black River he told me that our relationship had ended because his ex-girlfriend, for whom he still had feelings, had reappeared, and he got back together with her. He said he had a "body memory" of her, and it was a really powerful thing.

In September classes started at tech, and at the same time I was kicked out of my grandparents' apartment. My grandmother said she couldn't live with me any longer because I was out of control, so Mama and I were sent to live with my grandmother's sister in a different apartment, where, in principle, we had always been officially registered. In this way I was rid completely of any parental authority and found myself at long-awaited liberty. My mother never attempted to, and couldn't have if she tried, set any limits for me, and my great-aunt was—to put it mildly—not overjoyed by our move, grumbling and saying nasty things, so I just tried to run into her as infrequently as possible. She was an unhappy, seriously ill person, an old maid with some form of schizophrenia that resembled bipolar disorder, and I felt sorry for her but tried to keep my distance.

Tech was spread across several campuses throughout the city—near the Narvskaya, Petrogradskaya, and Vyborgskaya stations—but most often lessons were held near Frunzenskaya, in a rundown, yellow-white building only reachable after a long walk through courtyards strewn with autumn leaves. In these courtyards there were bushes where exhibitionists regularly hid and flashed their dicks. But overall I went to class very rarely; you could count on your fingers the number of times I showed up. Yet I remember the atmosphere perfectly. It was much stricter than at my old school, there was a deputy headmaster and a head craftsman, and a bulletin board where the surnames of truants appeared three times; the fourth time there would be a notice of expulsion. There were a few different departments. The most prestigious one, where I was enrolled, trained tour operators. The others produced marketers and merchandisers and prepared people for hospitality work; the department that accepted the lowest score for admission was the one that trained cooks. Kids from the culinary department would gladly tell you during smoke breaks how they spit into the food they cooked. My department consisted almost entirely of women and had only two men.

There were many girls I befriended right away. Zhenya was a beauty with a thick, light brown braid who had actually been a star student at school, but the circumstances of her life had made it necessary for her to think about earning money and learning a trade. Zhenya wrote poems and told me that there was a new prize for talented young poets called the Debut Prize, it had even been announced on TV, and she was going to send in her work. I thought then that maybe I should send in my poems, too, but somehow I never got around to it. Alina was a very cool chick, and for a while we hung out together. Dasha was a model and an orphan; she lived with her rich adult patron and had been his lover nearly since she was a child. Many of these girls had interesting life stories, a lot of them had had to grow up fast and think about their futures; they were far less childish than the girls at school.

As for the teachers. The biology teacher never said a word about biology; she told us about energies, yetis, Atlantis, and all kinds of esoterica; later, in one of our textbooks, we found a photograph of her—it was unclear how it got there—naked in the woods, wearing a flower crown and hugging a tree. The elderly teacher of Russian language and literature was very stern. At school I was used to being the best student in both of these subjects, accustomed to the fact that my essays were always declared superior and read aloud to the entire grade. At tech we were assigned an essay on Ostrovsky, and I wrote an excellent paper, as far as I could tell—bold and strange—and received, to my enormous surprise, a score of three out of five. Meanwhile, the girls who had written "correct" essays got fives.

But what I remember best is, of course, Ksana. The very first time I was walking to the academy from the Frunzenskaya station, she caught up to me and asked if I was going to tech and if I could tell her the way there. She probably asked me because I was dressed in informal gear: a Rammstein T-shirt and a brown fringed cowboy jacket; Ksana was wearing a KISS T-shirt and a green fringed jacket. Ksana had tan skin, green eyes, and black-green hair, since she dyed it with a black dye that had a green tinge. Ksana also had enormous and unbelievably gorgeous breasts, which she bragged about and showed off every chance she got. Ksana was extremely beautiful in general. One of the most beautiful women I've ever seen in my life. She was beautiful in a way that was at the same time completely childlike and completely whorish, and the effect was unbelievable.

Whenever I actually showed up at tech, I showed up to see her. She listened to Nightwish, so I started listening to Nightwish. We both got into goth culture and dressed only in black. I bought combat boots and started doing my makeup like Marilyn Manson. We smoked and drank together in the tech courtyard during classes. Ksana was wild, she was direct, she was fucking cool. She was afraid of nothing; she had so much power and life, so much daring, so much energy. We would meet at tech and leave to hang out until nighttime at Castle Rock, a basement rock music shop in the courtyards near Moscow

Station. In those days I listened to Tiamat, EverEve, Lacrimosa. A lot of the people we hung out with listened to death and black metal, but I wasn't into that. Ksana also sang and had a very powerful voice, like Tarja, the singer of Nightwish; sometimes she'd get so drunk that Margo and I—Margo was another young goth and regular at Castle Rock, which we called Crutch for short—carried her to the subway; other times I'd be the one who was wasted, and Ksana and Margo carried me. When the three of us walked down the street or rode the subway together, people looked at us with fear and accusation. Once someone shouted, "Three Marilyn Mansons!" There was another girl who always hung around with us, a redhead in a purple leather jacket who looked like a little fox; she was a devout Satanist, but when she wasn't hanging out she sang in a church choir. There was a couple, Snake and Death, who were also enrolled at some technical academy; a nice guy called Perv, who hit on me; tall and skinny Solitaire, who tried it with me, too. None of them had graduated, many were also techies or didn't study anywhere at all, but there was one single fantasy: the university's philosophy department. Guys who considered themselves brighter than the rest, Perv and Solitaire for instance, would say periodically that they were thinking about enrolling in the philosophy department. It was generally thought to be a place worthy of informals and rebels. Once I silently snuck up on Perv, and for my silence got the nickname Stealth, so that's what they called me after. The clerk at Castle Rock was Andrei, who felt toward me some combination of love and aggression. We smoked weed behind the garages on Staronevsky, and he'd move in such a way that it seemed like he wanted to hit me, but it was clear he wasn't exactly indifferent toward me.

It was a time of constant partying, music, intoxication. Hanging out there, I ran into all kinds of people: harmless hippies and psycho punks; by Katya's Garden I kept occasional company with gay underage prostitutes; at the Pipe we drank with homeless guys who were just passing through. Sometimes actual criminals and murderers turned up. One guy with a mean face told a story at Black River about how he had just killed a bum, and everyone kept drinking and hanging out with him as though nothing had happened. Another guy who was always there, Bear, was white-haired and had a little potbelly, and I thought he was in his forties or fifties until I found out that he was actually quite young and had come back from Chechnya; his whole company had been killed, he was the only survivor. There was also Arrow, who used to be a roadside whore; she had a boyfriend who beat her, her face was always busted up. She was an alcoholic by then, but men liked her, and once she drunkenly told me who she really was. "I'm a Valkyrie! A real Valkyrie!" she confessed. "Can you believe it, a real Valkyrie! I can fly! I'm writing a novel about it!" And as Arrow was telling me this, her blackened, swollen eyes burned with such an unearthly, northern flame, that I understood once and for all that she was telling the truth—she was a Valkyrie. Another person at the Pipe was a hippie nicknamed Elena the Terrible, who said she was carrying a dead baby in her stomach and that the baby was decomposing inside of her, making her sick, but for some reason she couldn't see a doctor. There were a lot of people who shot up, the teenagers were largely from broken, dysfunctional families. Along with some punks who were passing through, I ate at the city dump. My future was disappearing before my eyes. All was not well with me, either, but sorting out what was going on in my mind and what was happening to me was beyond what I could manage.

Bold, beautiful Ksana was only into long-haired blonds. She lived with her boyfriend and her grandmother. The boyfriend was studying law at the university and would occasionally turn up at our hangouts and drag Ksana home, and sometimes her grandmother would show up and also try to take Ksana home, but Ksana would run away, and her grandmother would run after her and try to hit her with her umbrella. Then Ksana broke up with the law student and started messing around with some other guys from the scene, naturally also long-haired blonds. Once, at the Crutch, when we were drunk, I told Ksana that I had never kissed a girl before and I wanted to try it. We tried it and afterward sometimes kissed when we were drunk. Ksana was rowdy, she liked to provoke, she cursed loudly and made indecent gestures, she called all guys "sausages," and if she ran into a real moron, she'd call him a "moodle." She was basically my dream girl made flesh.

Neither one of us was long for tech. By the end of October my surname had appeared two or three times on the bulletin board with warnings for truants; any day now I would be expelled. It began to dawn on me that I couldn't handle studying there. The philosophy department was another matter. I was beginning to be bored by the monotony of my life: drinking, crashing somewhere, the scene, every day the same thing, and it seemed like this would go on forever. As though a ceiling of some kind were hovering above my life, and in a short while there would be nothing I could do about it. Ahead of me was just a steep downward slope. I began to want an open horizon, I wanted not to know what would come next. It was shocking: I wanted to learn. No one was putting pressure on me now, and of my own free will I decided that I wanted to go back to school. Though not my old school, left forever behind in my former life, in the dank courtyards through which day after day, throughout the long years of my childhood, my grandmother walked me to my first morning class and we saw how in the blue gloaming the streetlights went out one by one. I wanted to go to a new school, where I would have a new, independent life. I left tech, and after an interview with the principal I was accepted to one of the schools in our neighborhood, a completely fine, unremarkable school, though with an intensive focus on French, which I didn't know, but that's just one of life's little things.

Ksana also left tech: she was sent to a special academy for difficult teenagers. She ran away, acted in some kind of porn film made to be sold abroad, got pregnant by someone and had the baby, and we fell out of touch. I know that now she lives with her husband and son, works as a merchandiser, and frequents the gym. And that she's still amazing. Whereas I went back to the classroom. The classroom was quiet, bright, and calm. Chalk lay by the blackboard, potted plants stood on the windowsills. Children sat all around. As a group they were innocent and infantile, pinkly white and well adjusted; their hearts had not yet awakened. I sat at my desk dressed in black and wearing goth makeup. I wrote essays, sketched triangles, solved logarithmic equations. I often skipped class and did whatever I wanted, but it was easy, very easy, for me to learn. I didn't know what tomorrow would bring, and I believed that it would be something incredible: long years of youth, a happy adult life, love and friendship, learning and creativity. Ahead lay two more years of school and the philosophy department.

MEMORIES OF MY FORGOTTEN BELOVED

I've forgotten my beloved, but I'm trying to remember him. Whom did I love so much when I was young that I tried to kill myself? I remember that he had long hair and he was very tall, nearly six feet four inches. I don't think he had a human name — instead he was called the King of the Gnomes, the King Beneath the Mountain.

He was a perpetually expelled then reenrolled student, until one day he was finally kicked out for good; he was into role-playing games, he was a metalhead, and he was twenty years old. I remember that he studied math at the university, though he had an aptitude for history. His childhood had been spent in Kazakhstan at an apiary, and his mother sent him honey and cheese from there that she had made herself. I remember the taste of the honey and that cheese — it was rich and fresh, we took bites as we drank tea in the warmth by the stove in the wintertime village of Berngardovka, where he and his brother lived in a house that could be reached by walking along the village road that ran through the forest from the station. Now I wouldn't be able to find the house, I could get to the woods, but where to go from there I don't remember. I do remember the forest at night, the innumerable cold evening trains from the Finland Station, and the morning trains back; I remember the little flowers by the platform in spring, and how in the summer we ran around in the woods playing some kind of shooting game. At Berngardovka they'd shot Gumilyov, my forgotten beloved's favorite poet, and he told me about him, standing on the Berda (that was what we called Berngardovka) platform in winter, saying that Mayakovsky was a punk, but Gumilyov was a real role-player.

He sang beautifully, my forgotten beloved, he had a pleasant and powerful voice, and he played the guitar. He and his friends had a rock band that kept breaking up and then reappearing from the void; they didn't play anywhere, they only practiced, and their lyrics were written by my boyfriend's best friend, a young writer, they worked together doing construction. In my beloved's room there was a Manowar poster, but his favorite bands were Blind Guardian and Crematory. I've said that they did construction. And I really do remember something like that. They climbed tall buildings, worked on scaffolding; once my beloved got an electric shock and nearly fell off. When he finally bid farewell to the university, all he had left was this job as a scaffolder at a construction site. "Well, we're not stokers and we're not carpenters, but we don't have any deep regrets," he liked to say.

He had eyes that were both blue and many-hued, and, if I remember correctly, he was uncommonly beautiful. He had a leather jacket, obviously, and later he gave it to me. Today it hangs on a hanger in my front hall. It's not the right size for me, of course, and it's so worn out that my mother wanted to throw it away, but I told her, "This is all I have left of him." Actually, there's also a photograph, in which he's very young, standing against a background of green grass and train tracks and smiling, and there are some sheets of paper on which he copied out a quote from LaVey's Satanic Bible and drew an upside-down pentagram, and also a few pieces of paper on which he taught me, a tenth-grader, logarithmic functions.

I think I remember our first meeting rather well. It was the day after my sixteenth birthday, at Black River, on Halloween. He told me that he had said to Sigvald, "I want a woman," and Sigvald put me before him. But he told me the same exact story years later about meeting his future wife, that Sigvald put her before him, and so I wonder if it's possible that I'm remembering it wrong, or maybe Sigvald really did put all of his girlfriends before him; at the end of the day, that's not so surprising, stranger things have happened. I hung out all over in those days and dressed like a goth. But not only like a goth, I dressed like a rock 'n' roller and like a hippie, too. I listened to heavy stuff, I liked Tiamat, Lacrimosa, Nightwish. I was in tenth grade at school, as I've said, but I hardly ever went to class. That Halloween, along with an elderly painter I had met in the street, I went to a party at some club where I drew phalluses on everyone, claiming to be the painter's assistant, a body art specialist, and I tried drinking some guy's blood out of curiosity. To go with the blood I also had a lot of cocktails, and then went on to Black River (where many informals were hanging out). That's where Sigvald put me before him. Before my forgotten beloved. Or, rather, at that moment, my beloved-to-be. And we hit it off. He took the subway with me to make sure I got home, and it was obvious even in the subway that we were falling in love. We said a lot of nonsense, talked about drinking blood, flirted, and our eyes were already aglow with an otherworldly shine, and then I waited: would he call or wouldn't he? Then I remember that we met and walked over the Liteyny Bridge, it was raining lightly, I wore a long black coat and rivulets of mascara ran down my face. He did most of the talking, all about submarines, he loved military history. I also remember: I had a facial, my face was completely broken out afterward, and he came to my house while there I was with my spotty face, without makeup, in a bathrobe. He picked up a guitar and started singing to me about the dragon ships of the Vikings. I lay on my bed, and he sat at my feet and said that he was thinking about leaving Petersburg and going back to Almaty, and I felt the fear of loss, afraid that he would up and leave when everything was only just beginning with us. He never did leave, and we had our fling.

From there on everything in my head gets a little mixed up. Trains, bleak light, darkness, the winter, the village, cheese, honey . . . And long walks around Petersburg, often eating shawarmas together, going out to clubs at night to see Irish folk rock bands: Rowan Tower, Reelroad, Darts. I remember that at a club called Milk I first saw some people doing traditional Irish dance. And I remember that at another club I first took note of the crowd: hippied-up, attractive young people, apparently students, well-dressed, long-haired, smoking weed. I got to know the folk scene and understood that these people were very different from the ones I usually hung out with at Black River and the Crutch. I hung out with techie informals, kids from dysfunctional families, while these clubs were frequented by intellectual informals, among them young artists, poets, musicians. I was pleased and flattered to feel that I belonged with them as my boyfriend and I sat listening to music played by people he knew, his friends, people he spent time with, and I was proud to be his girlfriend. I was too shy to share my own work with anyone then, except for a couple of girls I was friends with, one of whom said that they were the best poems she had ever heard, but I certainly couldn't show my poems to my boyfriend, I would have died if I tried, I just mentioned, occasionally, that sometimes I wrote poetry, but he wasn't particularly interested. Generally in our relationship he was the one who talked, while I listened, admired, and adored.

Hanging out, parties, crashing for the night—everything danced and spun. I was brought along to visit a real young writer, and I was a bit like mute furniture, like a pretty schoolgirl with her cool, twenty-year-old boyfriend. In the evenings I called Mama from payphones to tell her that I wouldn't be coming home, and we'd take the train out to Berngardovka. We rang in the New Year together, 2002, walked around the city with our friends, drank champagne, my beloved got drunk and shouted out "Happy New Year!" to passersby. Then we hung out at his friends' apartment, sang songs, had a good time together. Once, my beloved forgot about me and didn't call for a week. I started trying to find him through friends; he called, apologized, and said he had just gotten busy and forgot to phone. Then, closer to spring, I noticed that the way he treated me had changed. He started constantly cracking rude jokes at my expense, as though he were purposefully trying to offend me; he barely noticed me when I visited him, in the mornings he sat down in front of his computer to play Civilization, forgetting about me completely or even hinting that it was time for me to go. I accepted all of this without a word, thinking it was the way things should be. Once, at his place, I found Herman Hesse's Steppenwolf, read it in one sitting, and fell in love with it. At the time I was reading and memorizing poems by Rilke and getting into Nietzsche. My beloved was an admirer of Richard Bach and supplied me with his books, which I liked, too.

The way it ended I remember only in bursts. Endless slights, cruel jokes, neglect; at Black River he flirted demonstratively, right in front of me, with a girl who dressed in green and whom behind her back he called "that green broad." I don't remember whether he announced the end of our relationship or simply disappeared, or if he disappeared for a long time first, then told me over the phone it was over . . . I think that there was such a moment, a statement of the breakup, but I've honestly forgotten. I don't remember the words he used to say it, what his voice sounded like. Usually you remember these things for life, but I've forgotten them. I think that I suffered, that there was extreme pain, and then I took that mountain of drugs: Phenazepam, Dimedrol, Phenibut, some others, there were so many pill packets, I don't remember, and I don't remember wanting to die, only wanting to sleep, not to be, and somehow I had a feeling that I knew what my life would be like and I didn't want to live it. There were broken eggs, I remember that. I think I went to the kitchen to make an omelet; an egg broke and fell. Then I passed out for three days. I was practically in a coma. But not entirely, because they told me later that a friend called and I picked up the phone (the phone was next to the bed) and said, "Misha, go fuck yourself," and hung up.

I woke up on the fourth day as a deeply deranged person. For a long time everything ran together in my head, days stuck to other days, people morphed into weird chimeras, and the actual reason for my poisoning was forgotten for good. Memories of my forgotten beloved began to appear again as though through a curtain of smoke. It was like it had happened to me—or maybe not to me. The first thing I did when I came to myself was head to

Crutch, approach some people I didn't know who were hanging out there, demand that they find me drugs, fall unconscious into a ditch, then get up and stumble off. They remembered my visit there for a long time.

I saw my beloved many times after that, we fucked, there was some inching toward being together again, but all of it was slowly fading away. I remember sitting with him behind the railroad tracks by a muddy river, after we had broken up, just chatting, and he said, "It's strange, I have the feeling that I'm courting you again." I remember that his friends left us alone in their apartment overnight in hopes of getting us to reconcile, and we had a nice time together, but it didn't fundamentally change anything. I remember that after some summer music festival in the courtyard of the Petersburg Electrotechnical University we walked—it was the middle of white nights season—all the way to Berngardovka, and it was a totally blissful, unforgettable hike, and I stayed there with him for three days. When we were walking to Berngardovka that night, he told me that he had been horrified to think that I could have died after swallowing all those pills.

He was already sleeping with someone else by then. I was falling in love again, too, but I kept holding on to him, I couldn't let him go completely. Finally, I remember that after a night together we were sitting at a courtyard playground, and he read me his friend the young writer's short story and then said that I was young, I had to have experiences, explore, not cling to the past. And I was looking at him then and feeling that a wonderful, unknown future was calling to me, and I let him go, easily, precisely at that moment, that morning at the playground. And the following day I left to hitchhike around with my new love.

After the pills everything in my memory becomes hazy, shrouded by smoke, hidden by thick, thick clouds. So this is all I've been able to remember. But maybe I've made a mistake and remembered something wrong: something that didn't happen, or something that happened, but not to me. I've forgotten my beloved, but I'm trying to remember him. Maybe the one I'm trying to remember never existed in this world, the waking world. He comes from the world the body dreams, the world of the soul, the world in which we exist alongside music, and spring, and the true, innermost beloved who lives here. In the depths of the soul dwell lovers who love each other eternally. And it's an error to confuse the forgotten beloved for any of the lovers I knew in reality. Sometimes the forgotten beloved appears in the guise of one or the other of those "empirical" lovers, the one I loved at sixteen, or the one I loved at thirty. He waits there, beyond the limits of memory, he has no name, he belongs to no era, for a face he has the deep, dark forest, on his head grow flowers and grasses, in his mouth is the sea, the sun shines in one eye, the moon in the other.

I've forgotten my beloved, and the one with whom I went hitchhiking is no less my forgotten beloved than the one who drove me to poison myself with pills at sixteen. I've forgotten my beloved, but I'm trying to remember him. I think he knew how to assume the forms of animals and birds. I think he fought in a war and was wounded, and I found him and helped him heal. He tore through the jungle to come to me. He flew on a dragon's back, he freed me from imprisonment, and I bore him seven sons. He kissed me in a high castle, he woke me from sleep, he resurrected me from death. He found me as a pauper and made me queen, ruler of the world. By my side he was a besotted teenager and a white-haired husband, he was short and tall, thin and fat, beautiful and hideous. His beard was like a blackbird's beak, his horns were like a deer's horns, and his neck like a crane's neck. I've forgotten my beloved, but one day I'll remember him, I will definitely remember him, and we will fly away from here forever.

UNDER THE BRIDGE

By the eleventh grade I was finally ready to show my poems to the world. The nation should know its heroes. I'd been writing poetry since early childhood, and by eleventh grade I had amassed an entire oeuvre. Only it was unclear to me where, exactly, the poems were supposed to go, and how they were supposed to get there. So I went in search.

I looked up the literary organizations—LITOs—located in the city and visited a few of them. The impression was not encouraging. At one LITO, at the Lensoviet Palace of Culture, there were mostly pensioners making little pencil pluses on each other's poems, next to the lines they liked. They picked my poems apart this way, too, then offered to pay a bit of money so that one of them could be entered in a contest in honor of·the city's founding. At another LITO, they were reading long reams of poetry in the style of Brodsky and heckled me when I read free verse. The third LITO was more or less all right; the people there were attentive and kind to me, a nice older poetess was in charge, and I met and drank vodka there with some ex-Baptist.

The fourth LITO was a club for children and young people called Daring, and that's where I met Marta.

I went to Daring about three times that year, and the first few times I only heard about Marta. She didn't come herself, but everybody talked about her, about her poems. After he heard me read my poems, the man leading the seminar immediately said, "Do you know Marta L—? You absolutely have to meet her!" Marta was Daring's shining star and its enfant terrible, and I really wanted to find out what it was she wrote. At the club itself I felt out of place: the other kids seemed arrogant and knew a lot more about contemporary literature than I did; I didn't know how to talk to them and felt shy around them all. There was one eighth-grade girl who wrote five spectacular poems a day and by ninth grade quit writing forever, and a girl who wrote terse, refined short prose and later was admitted to the Literature Institute, where she flunked, and a pregnant girl who wrote amazing essays, and a person who used masculine pronouns and dedicated poems to Beethoven. They were arrogant, cruel, and beautiful, but the most arrogant, cruel, and beautiful of all was Marta.

It was the third time that I came to Daring when I finally saw her. I saw an extraordinary creature: talented and devilishly proud, behaving outrageously and conceitedly, openly mocking everyone and beloved by everyone, complicated, affected, clever, and, possibly, tender and vulnerable inside. She read her poems, and I really liked them; then I read my poems and she said she liked them, too, and invited me to a café after the Daring session. The café was her favorite one, by the Liteyny Bridge, later we would go there together often. The café had soft green lighting, wooden tables, and abstract paintings on the walls. That first time, we talked about Rimbaud and Verlaine, Van Gogh and

Gauguin, Oscar Wilde and Lord Alfred Douglas. She was sixteen, also in the eleventh grade, and it turned out that we both planned to study philosophy. Both of us considered Rimbaud our favorite poet, and out of contemporary poets we liked Victor Sosnora. Though, admittedly, I didn't know any other contemporary poets and had only found out about Sosnora just before we met. Marta gave me her collected poems—a thin black book with a white square on the cover. It was a book of subtle, delicate, black-and-white verse, full of rainy cafés, lonely rooms, and the chords of a neighbor's piano. The poems contained evenings drawn out like a sip of cognac, an umbrella from a Pissarro painting, love and death, snow, the darkness of alleys, birds and kisses, wine and the sea, madness and lucid dreams, a veil of debauchery, a broken angel, Petersburg and faraway Venice.

I was writing a lot, writing obsessively. I was learning about the Silver Age, the Russian and European classics. I was falling for all the dead poets in turn: Mayakovsky, Yesenin, Pasternak, Tsvetaeva. I discovered Khlebnikov and fell in love for life. I was trying out writing in different styles and meters, from various classical meters to free verse. I wanted to be equally good in free verse and in rhyme. I wanted to give word to grass, tree, wind, animal, and nebula. I wanted each poem to be extreme, piercing, relentless. That year I identified myself with poetry the way I always tried to do later—with utmost dedication and exertion of soul, working not so much on the texts as on myself: on how I saw and felt, on my ability to catch and make manifest the ephemeral and the unfulfilled, the never-said, the not-of-this-world. It was a time of transformation of my child's poems into adult poems; a time of transformation of myself from a promising teenager into a poet.

My next encounter with Marta happened during the philosophy department entrance exams. Marta took my number and said that we would celebrate getting in with wine and an evening walk through the summertime city, but she never called. And then later we met as students; we were in different classes but started hanging out. We would go together to literary-ish events, like evenings at the XL Club, where Marta knew everyone and I knew no one. Marta liked crashing poetry nights, causing scenes and picking fights, and sometimes I would accompany her on these escapades. We both wanted to look worse in front of each other than we really were. We also both liked to fuck around, and how we fucked around is a story in itself. Marta went about it very elegantly. Whereas I filled this transgressive practice with complex spiritual significance. I thought it was an important alchemical event, a phase of the Great Work, a stage in the breaking of social conventions and norms, so you had to act as deranged as possible. This kind of derangement did not come easily to me, to some extent I had to force it, but I believed it was necessary for the liberation of the soul. Marta had a classmate named Max, a gay guy about five years older than we were, and they had a strange kind of relationship: they went everywhere together and were clearly very into each other but did not seem to be a couple in the usual sense. Marta liked gay men, and for my part I thought Max loved her. We often went out as a trio. Sometimes I thought that Marta treated me with arrogance and disdain; she betrayed any understanding that ever arose between us, she made jabs and snide comments in my direction, including about my poems. But I was drawn to her. Marta never showed up on time to any tests or exams, though she knew everything better than everyone. During an exam session she could be strolling and smoking outside of the department building, idly getting ready to go in and ace the whole thing, but somehow, in the end, she never arrived. She was above that.

That fall of my first semester, when I was just seventeen, the university held a contest for young poets, and Marta and I decided to enter. We sent our poems to the contest and both made it to the finals, though neither of us went on to win. We read in the finalists' reading that was held at the philosophy department. This was one of my first public readings. I wore a yellow cardigan and combat boots and tried to read as loudly as possible. To top it off I had my hair in two braids. After this reading I was approached by a wonderful contemporary poet who had been on the contest jury, and he invited me to take his special philosophy department course on contemporary poetry. In the spring I was invited to my first-ever poetry festival. And around the same time I met a writer and editor who offered to publish a book of my poems, which I had already put together (though that series never came to be). My path in literature began from all of this, and some publications of mine started to appear. But I wasn't happy, I felt extremely lonely and adrift.

In April Marta invited me to her birthday, we drank in a courtyard by Brodsky's house, got drunk and started kissing, and that night ended up at somebody's apartment and slept together. I had never slept with a woman before that. I remember walking, hungover, past the Fontanka River on the morning after, sunlight playing over the remnants of spring ice, and feeling so very strange: joyful, and a little scared. In the evening Marta sent me a text: "Should I forget everything?" I responded: "No."

After that we were together. We were Rimbaud and Verlaine, Van Gogh and Gauguin, Oscar Wilde and Lord Alfred Douglas.

We held hands, provoked people, kissed in public places, talked about poetry. In the half a year that we were a couple, after that first time we had sex exactly thrice. Once at my house, after getting drunk on cheap, bad Salvatore vermouth. Another time was before I went to Ukraine for the summer. We were getting ready to be apart for a long time, and we took the train somewhere in the direction of Sestroretsk. On the train we made out and scandalized everyone as usual, then drank vodka in the Wild-West-themed station café and went in search of the sea. For some reason we looked for it for a long time and in the end found a sandy, windy vacant lot by the bay. There was no one around, and I remember how we touched each other; it was cold, the wind tossed our hair into our faces, our hands were freezing and wouldn't obey, it was as though consciousness itself were tangled—we were extremely drunk. The sand was everywhere, it smelled of the sea, Marta's long, light hair was spread across the sand, and it was a kind of crystalline happiness.

Then I went to Ukraine: first with my mother to an Odessa guest house; from there to the village on the Dniester River where my grandfather lived, storks flew, and the reddish shards of the Trypillia culture were scattered all over—and from there, slowly, passing through Zhmerynka and Vinnytsia, I made my way to Kyiv. And I cheated on Marta everywhere, if you could call it cheating, because we had never settled on any rules or obligations, and occasionally I would get her tender and titillating texts. In Ukraine I was joyful and happy in a way that was rare in life, because I was traveling alone and roaming over the green hills.

Then I came back, and in the fall Marta and I had our last time. She came to spend the night with me, looking downcast, and it was obvious that what we had was ending. By that time she was already constantly blowing me off, standing me up, not calling, ignoring me, and becoming distant. It seemed that my growing fame was also coming between us. Marta was passionate and jealous when it came to poetry, and I think she was envious of my relationship to it. Whenever I told her about contemporary poets I had met or liked, she viciously mocked them all. She was a wonderful poet, but by that point had nearly stopped writing. For her, poetry had ended with growing up, with the beginning of her adult life, while I lived only through poetry. We both continued on, going in different directions relative to that moment when we were seventeen, standing before the gates of literature. I went the way of poetry, the way of go-there-I-don't-know-where, while Marta turned out to have a different, no doubt interesting and beautiful path. It was also maybe the case that Marta, in the labor of her life, in her self-conception, relied on the example of Rimbaud, who quit writing at nineteen; indeed one of the big questions we'd always talked about was why Rimbaud quit poetry. It's possible that for Marta, too, given the way she experienced poetry and the role of the poet, poetry had to break off at nineteen. And that night, our last time, she asked me, being uncharacteristically direct: "What do you think—could you fall in love with me?" And I don't remember what I said.

That night what concerned me the most was whether she had come. She said that she came a hundred times, but I had my doubts and couldn't figure it out. By then Marta was no longer in the philosophy department. She and Max had both been kicked out—they just hadn't shown up for the final examinations. Afterward Marta received a different kind of education and was very successful in the humanities, but, as far as I know, she didn't write poetry anymore.

When we were together we liked sitting under a bridge. Usually the Liteyny. There, underneath the bridge, we often spent our days, as though we were some kind of Parisian bohemians or outcasts. We drank without stopping, but I was losing my head then on something stronger than wine. We sat beneath the bridge night after night and watched the pale-lilac rings of sunset above the city. Sometimes we came to the bridge after the café—the one where we went to talk when we first met— had closed, and kept drinking, easing up a little. Max was invariably with us. We kissed as a trio: one long kiss for three. This delighted Marta. Sometimes she demanded that Max and I kiss while she watched. I would press him up against the wall and kiss him, then light a cigarette. Marta would put her head on my shoulder, and we'd look out at the water and the late-October sky, the Military-Medical Academy and the Finland Station. Our vision was clouded, and if you squinted or shut your eyes, you could see everything, including what wasn't there—see the Neva as the moon: a fine, beaten-silver landscape. And then it seemed we were in a spaceship, hurtling through the cosmos. Marta, it's the moon, can't you see? The three of us sat beneath the bridge and night crashed down onto our heads, the city boomed, and its lights were shining. Now I would put my head on Marta's lap. And I would see the sky, which looked so little like the summer sky over the Ukrainian village when I was rolling in the fields with the old village elder's son, and thinking that the village elder's son was beautiful, the grass was silver, and the earth floated in interstellar space.

That fall I had a reading at Platform, my first solo reading, and for an hour and a half, with determination that should have been put to better use, I recited my poems from memory, because

I thought that reading from a piece of paper was rude and didn't know yet that everyone read that way. After the reading I sat at a table with some important, grown-up poets, and they told me I was a big poet, and a waiter came and brought me a glass of wine—he said that it had been ordered for me and pointed out the table. I looked over and saw Marta and Max, they were sitting by themselves, they waved to me but didn't approach us. The wine was bittersweet. And we didn't see each other again.

BEFORE THE GATES

To the heroes of my dreams

In the kitchen there was fish stewing for the cat, I sat having tea with zapekanka.

At that time Mama had just broken up with Bob, bastard, dirtbag, sixty-four-year-old American millionaire. The head of international terrorism, as he claimed in his insane letters to her. "When I pay, I'm the boss."

Lyuska and I had been friends since first grade, but we fought constantly. Lyuska had a blond braid down to her butt and blue eyes. I thought she was materialistic. I was twelve and had never been kissed, unlike Lyuska, who'd mastered kissing over a summer in the village when she was eleven. She called it *suckage*. Yusya and I had also been friends since first grade. We didn't talk to boys, and the feelings that we might have developed for members of the opposite sex became, for Yusya and Lyuska, directed toward me. They were terribly jealous of each other where I was concerned—which one did I sit with, which one had I come up to—and would take me by the hands and pull me in opposite directions. All this suffering drove up Lyuska's blood pressure, and she had to be taken to the hospital.

There was also Marisha C., with her woolen tights and wispy, dirty-blond braid. Marisha's grandmother wouldn't let her out of her sight because her mother had been a baby having babies, as they say, and Marisha's grandmother didn't want her to suffer the same fate. Marisha took music lessons and karate and rose periodically to the top of the class, and after school her grandmother always carried her schoolbag home. Sometimes Marisha showed us love letters supposedly sent her by the boys in our class. At first we didn't believe the letters were real, but once she read aloud a letter from a smart, fat boy which said he beheld in her the incarnation of Russia's eternal soul. I believed her after that. Around the same time, in seventh grade, Marisha started telling us that she was a lesbian, or rather a bisexual, and that she had a girlfriend and a boyfriend at the same time. All she talked about were lesbians and gays, and she started listening to Boris Moiseev and Shura. The upperclassmen found out and started harassing her. After that there was a parent-teacher conference at which the issue of Marisha's homosexuality was discussed, and our deputy headmistress and math teacher Olga Vasilievna, a strong, wise woman, said that sexual orientation is each person's private business. At least that's what I was told she said, and I'm just telling you what I heard.

For my thirteenth birthday I was given a small amount of money, and I used it to buy a blank cassette tape and a pair of earrings. There were no birthday guests. In years past, my girlfriends had come over: Lyuska, Yusya, Natasha, Anya, Vika, Karina. Delicate Karina with the beauty mark by her mouth reminded me of Assol—like Assol, waiting for her prince to come, she believed in fairies and in Father Frost. I believed, too, in my own way, but I thought that unlike Karina I could tell the truth from the lies, whereas she took everything literally. Fourteen-year-old Natasha was my cousin thrice removed and my friend at the dacha. She was into *suckage* already, too. Little Anya was another dacha friend—my favorite—but two years back they stopped coming, because Anya's grandfather had divorced her grandmother and married a woman who wouldn't let Anya come to the dacha, and in general showed her true colors. There were four of us who were dacha friends—me, Anya, Natasha, and Nadya—but Nadya never came to my childhood birthdays. Over the two most recent summers boys had appeared in our dacha gang, and together we built bonfires in the forest behind the train station. Though I'd only really made it to one bonfire; when I was going the second time, standing on the rack of Nadya's bike, I ran into my grandfather, who picked me up off the rack and pulled me home by the ears. At the dacha, I wasn't allowed to stay out late at night; in the best-case scenario, during white nights season, I had to be home by ten. I had a little crush on Dima from Priozerskaya Street; he had a moped, and when we saw each other, we always said hello, though we hadn't officially met.

"They used to marry you off at thirteen in Old Rus'," my grandfather Andrei said to me over the phone. "I wish you a happy youth! Are you doing your makeup yet?" I was not doing my makeup or my homework.

In my past life, I had a brother, I thought, *but in this life he wasn't born, because Mama had an abortion.* But I didn't blame her—what would she do with another illegitimate child?

For many years I was in love with Sasha. Sasha was a guy, a teenager older than me, and an orphan, a boy of astounding beauty. Not a soul knew of my love for him. I don't remember a single feature of his face, but I know that I haven't seen anyone more beautiful to this day. I was eight, I often dreamed that I lay in a deep faint on the street by his house, and he picked me up, took me in his arms, and carried me to his home.

In sixth grade I saw Igor, who was in ninth, and I was shocked by how much he looked like Sasha. They were nearly identical, though Sasha had hair that was probably dirty blond, and eyes that were probably light-colored, while Igor was dark-haired and green-eyed. Igor was tan and Sasha was pale, but because he reminded me of Sasha, I fell in love with him. Mama gave me an encyclopedia for young readers, and there was a saying in it, "no better game than that of glances." We played that game for an entire year, never actually meeting, until he finished ninth grade and left the school. There were a few times when he approached me, probably to introduce himself, but in those moments I became terrified, my every look and gesture screamed *don't do it*, and he couldn't bring himself to do it, and then from a distance I would again send him looks of love. By the end of the year, I began to suspect that he'd leave our school for a technical college and that I'd never see him again. I had a dream that we were walking together, but he had to go somewhere else, and before parting he asked me if I wanted to be his lover.

In seventh grade Lyuska and Yusya started chasing after ninth-graders: Danya Izvozchikov, Andrei Yanovsky, and Ilya Nikiforov. I pretended to be interested in them, too, so that we would have something to talk about.

My father came to visit me the weekend after my birthday, bringing a Palmolive bath set—body milk, shampoo, and soap. The adults managed to spend three hours talking about the political crisis. My father said that his German colleagues had offered him a permanent job in Germany, while I thought to myself that it was wrong to leave, because Russia would save itself and save the world. *The earth has spun off its axis*, I was thinking. *Economics is fundamentally wrong. People have forgotten that they are brothers. Woe to us!*

I was reading the sacred texts of various traditions, philosophical and mystical treatises alternating with trashy esoterica, and in a large notebook I drew a map of three worlds: the material, the astral, and the spiritual, by which I meant the internal world. The material world contained planets, stars, water, air, earth, fire, and the ether, together with all the beings that lived there. In the astral world there were astral planets, stars, water, air, earth, fire, and ether, their guardians and all the creatures that lived there, and also astral doors, angels and archangels, people's souls, creatures of various kinds, egregores, and the Book of Knowledge. I drew the spiritual or inner world as a giant human head that contained separate sections for consciousness, subconsciousness, love, memory, inner beauty, talents, personality, a section for sexuality and family life, a section for genetic inheritance, a section for psychological trauma, a section for intuition, and a section I just called the Divine Spark.

Evenings I lay in bed while Mama, with her back to me, worked at the secretary desk. Our evenings were always like this, year after year in our shared room. The table lamp was lit. The windows were hung with dull orange drapes, and the red rug bloomed with flat black flowers. Next to me lay Dreiser's novel *An American Tragedy*. I wondered: does the Bible exist on other planets, and if it does, is it the same as ours, or a little different?

In the summer, Nadya and I were followed all through the village by a car, a yellow Zhiguli. The guys who drove it liked to threaten that they'd drag us into their car and take us out to the lake. We squealed loudly and ran from them, and Dima from Priozerskaya saw everything and afterward only had eyes for us and started waving at me when we met. Once, Nadya and I put on lipstick and went for a walk, and he and a friend passed us on his moped. They yelled to us: "Hello, beautiful!"

We spent every night by the pond on the side of the highway—we could watch all the guys from there: Zheka with his cigarette, Gray, Vanka, Number One and Number Two, and everyone else who hung out on the highway at night. We sat there playing cards. We had another source of entertainment, too—getting passing cars to brake. The two Nadyas and I once sat down on the highway in something like lotus pose. That's how we met the two motorcyclists, Numbers One and Two. Later, whenever they drove past, they always alternated between blowing us kisses and flipping us the finger.

I had two cigarettes, one of them partly smoked, and a lighter. Zheka had given me one of the cigarettes over the summer, Lyuska gave me the other one, and I bought the lighter myself. We decided to smoke Lyuska's cigarette in the entryway. Lyuska took three drags and I only attempted one but felt nothing, because we had to put the cigarette out immediately—someone had entered the building. At home I kept both cigarettes in a secret compartment of my old school satchel.

Lyuska, when she was back from the hospital, told me about a guy she met there who had tried to rape her, or at the very least kiss her. At school I heard a rumor that Yanovsky had invited Lena Bakhtina to his house to fuck. But when she came over, at the very last minute he couldn't get it up.

When I was left in peace, I filled notebook after notebook with poems.

If everyone saw each other as they really are, they'd beg each other for forgiveness immediately and rush to embrace one another, I thought. When I lay there listening to music, I was touched by a ray of light, and I wanted to sacrifice myself for humanity. When I didn't know what to do, I asked myself: what would an angel do here?

One summer, Mama, Bob, and I went to Nevsky Prospekt. We hired a taxi to make the trip, and at the end of the outing we were supposed to see *Swan Lake.* I was dressed all in white, in velvet slacks and a blouse; Mama was wearing athletic clothes. The taxi waited for us while we went to the parking garage at Konyushennaya Square so that Mama could change. On the way out of the garage I saw a long black car with a young man inside. He was definitely an adult—older than twenty, though probably under thirty. He was unbelievably handsome. The man stared at me without looking away, and I fell in love with him at first sight. We reached the taxi, and Mama and Bob started chatting with the driver while I stood outside and looked back at the man, glancing away from time to time. But he never stopped watching me. Then, still without breaking eye contact, he started to get out of the car. Seeing that he was going to approach me, I got scared—I was only twelve. I ducked inside our taxi and a few seconds later popped out again and saw that he was in back in his car, looking at me. Then Mama and Bob decided to let the taxi go, and we started walking in the direction of the man's car. I turned around one last time to see that he was waving to me, with a hand as beautiful and refined as the hand of a prince.

In seventh grade I was allowed to walk to school alone, but my grandmother insisted on going down with me in the elevator and walking me out of the building, and because of her I thought the entryway as a place of muggings, murders, and drug addicts.

In a hallway at school, Moshinkov from Grade 9 Class B said, "I want you," to Lyuska and burst out laughing.

Lyuska told me that her grandmother thought that Lyuska had slept with half the school, that Lyuska had slept with her own father, and that even I had a boyfriend.

Someone first tried to hit on me when I was ten years old. I was coming home with my grandparents late at night; we were returning from visiting friends and were walking through a subway transfer tunnel. I wore a jacket with a dressy silver skirt sticking out underneath, and my hair, which reached below my waist, was loose. I fell a little behind my grandparents, and a Georgian guy started following me, saying, "Young lady, turn around, I'll give you an orange." I turned and he said, "What a beautiful young lady!" Lyuska, when she found out about this, made me retell the story in detail for a week.

At the clinic they punctured a vein in my arm, but no blood flowed. They tried a vein in the other arm, and again there was no blood. They never did manage to get a blood sample.

I would wake thinking, "Time to get up again?" and fall asleep thinking "Time for bed again?" I thought I was bored with living, and I went on doing it out of a sense of responsibility and with hope for the future.

On December 14, 1998, the temperature outside was negative twenty-one Celsius. My grandmother was trying to force me to eat barley kasha, I was refusing because I had barley kasha every weekday and it was insulting to have to eat it on a weekend, too, and my grandmother slammed the door, saying, "Don't count on your grandfather and me, we're leaving!" A day before that, when she and I fought, she complained about me to my mother and grandfather and screamed as loudly as she could so that I would hear, apparently hoping that I'd break into tears and apologize: "That good-for-nothing won't listen to me! That smart-ass! She should be punished! Look at what you've raised!" Then I walked in and laughed in her face.

My grandmother would say about me, "I've never met such an awful child."

In my spare time I often paged through the family photo albums and invented stories and fairy tales to go along with the pictures. There was an entire photo series of nine-year-old me in ball gowns, with the hairstyles of antique ladies. Mama liked to make me into a doll: she put makeup on my face, worked my long hair into complicated hairstyles, dressed me in either blue bobbin lace or pink satin or gold and silver brocade. One of those dresses she'd brought back from France, another one she'd made especially for me, and a few others had once been her own evening gowns. She had extensions of golden curls that she would attach to my dark hair, and I also posed in her many blond wigs, with bare legs and in heels, with a cheeky expression and an apple in my hand. The "Pedophile's Dream" series. In the next few pictures I wore two velvet "business" suits, red and blue, with inappropriately short skirts, a puffy white frill on my blouse, and sparkly silver leggings. Mama had bought me these suits and told me to wear them to school every day. I was in second grade. The suits were cute, but I was embarrassed to wear them because of the short skirts, the sparkly leggings, and the frill. But there was nothing I could do, so I wore them, becoming even more alienated from my classmates, trying to ignore their teasing and the reprimands of my teachers, who forbade us from wearing leggings to school. I believed Mama when she said that the business suits were beautiful, my teachers were Soviet bluestockings, and the other girls were just jealous of me. I came to class like that, ridiculous, dolled-up, obscenely beautiful, sat at my desk, and gazed vacantly into the void. Then came photographs from the dacha: me in the gazebo, by the hedge, sunlit, me on my bike, me and Mama, me by the lake, me with Natasha and Nadya, then my grandparents, Uncle Alesha, Aunt Beba, Bedya, the Korablevs, the Bogdanovs, Aunt Lena, me and Mama at the botanical garden, at the park on Yelagin Island, my grandparents' wedding anniversary, New Year's at the Korablevs', Mama's friends, Mama and Sobchak, Mama and the deputy secretary-general of the UN, Mama wearing long earrings and gold, silver, low-cut, flowing dresses, my father and me on my tenth birthday, which was the day we met.

In the street plumbers flirted with me while Lyuska and Pyatkova walked a little behind and heard everything.

At the turn of the millennium I predicted the end of the world, the planets forming a cross in the sky, and the king of horror coming down to resurrect the great king Angolmois, who would rule.

We rang in the coming year, 1999. We listened to Yeltsin, the striking of the clock, watched *Little Blue Light*. I drank a glass of champagne and a glass and a half of dessert wine. Before New Year's I waxed my legs for the first time, or rather Mama did it for me, and it was the worst physical pain I had ever experienced. I scratched myself with my fingernails and broke into a sweat.

Natasha, lightly batting her very long painted lashes, said she had found a boyfriend named Ilya, who was in the same grade.

Sometimes I thought my grandmother hated me, although I knew she loved me, and she herself often said, "No one else is ever going to love you like we do."

On the day of a parent-teacher conference, I was waiting for Mama in the school lobby when Andrei Yanovsky appeared. I was reading my literature textbook, but because of Yanovsky I couldn't concentrate, turned to the geometry textbook, flipped through it, then put it away, too. Then Yanovsky said, "Have you gone to school here for a while?"

"Since first grade. Why?"

"I haven't seen you before."

"You haven't seen me?"

"Not until this year."

"Well, I haven't seen you, either."

"Are you in eighth grade?"

"No, I'm in seventh. But we don't skip the fourth."

"Us, too."

"What are you doing here?"

"Redoing my physics."

"Oh, we have a parent-teacher conference."

"Oh. We didn't have one. All right, see you later."

Following this exchange I wondered for a long time whether we would say hello to each other when we met, or not.

Yanovsky had a nickname: Cucumber.

Bob posted pictures of my mother wearing lingerie on the internet and wrote that she was a prostitute, providing her email address.

Around this time, knowing nothing about Schleiermacher or hermeneutics, I made the great discovery that every book contains multiple meanings. The five different meanings I identified were the Literal, the Moral, the Origin of the Book in the Experiences of the Author, the Interpretation, and the True Universal Meaning. The Origin of the Book and the True

Universal Meaning were transcendental. So the literal meaning of "The Little Scarlet Flower" was the story of a merchant's daughter and a monster, the moral was that the power of love can turn a hideous beast into a beautiful prince, and the interpretation, which I borrowed from some article in *Komsomolka*, indicated that the beast was Russia, hiding its beautiful, regal essence beneath a hideous visage.

"What is the little scarlet flower, the most beautiful flower in the world?" I wrote in my notebook in thick pen and circled thrice.

"It's the absolute maximum and minimum of Nicholas of Cusa," whispered the voice of philosopher Nikolai (not of Cusa) down the years.

And all my life I will go on telling you what that is.

In those days it still mattered who sat next to me in the subway, whether a salesclerk had smiled at me, if a security guard had sent me a wink.

In that world there were only two cigarettes, hidden in an old satchel, and there was more bliss in those cigarettes than in all the cigarettes that I could smoke in my entire life; there was a single glass of champagne on New Year's Eve and more bliss in that glass than in all the alcohol I could drink in my entire life. There was a dizzying energy compressed into the countless "don'ts." It was a time for knees to go weak for love of people we hadn't even met, a time for hands not to know which one should be extended in greeting, a time for hair to be so long that birds could nest in it, a time when an attempt to introduce yourself, an attempt to kiss, and an attempt to rape were considered roughly equivalent, the way they are for little girls and ancient virgins. That was the way we were: we knew how to live on light alone, with childish dreams in our morning eyes, with bitterness and with hope, with an intolerable thirst for freedom, at midday in summer, at midnight in winter, passing through the gates of the temple on which it is written *NOW IT IS ALLOWED.*

LOVE LIKE NOBODY

Fifteen-year-old Polina dialed her apartment on the intercom. It was ten thirty in the evening, spring.

Five minutes later, deathly pale and stone-faced, her grandmother appeared in the entryway, wearing a light gray coat thrown over a robe, which was itself thrown over a nightgown. Polina was not allowed to pass alone through the entryway or go up in the elevator by herself.

Polina's grandmother responded to her greeting with a nod and demonstratively ignored her while they went up in the elevator. She seemed to be barely holding herself back, and the harsh rigidity of her expression was a sign of struggle, an attempt to postpone the moment when she would no longer be able to control herself and would start screaming at Polina. When Polina tried to catch her eye in order to understand what was happening, her grandmother looked away so as not to explode ahead of time.

When they entered the apartment, Polina's grandfather and mother were standing at the threshold, figures of silent accusation. Her grandmother howled:

"I can't do it anymore! She's driving me out of my mind! Just does whatever she wants! I'm done with it!"

Polina's grandfather said, "You live with us, so you have to consider us, too. Grandma can't have you coming home late. You're only thinking of yourself, you can't do that."

"Come on, you said I was allowed out until ten," Polina tried to defend herself.

"That's when you really begged us. But today you went out and didn't say when you were coming back. So we thought it would be nine. Grandma nearly died!"

"I nearly died because of this brat! Five to nine, nine, nine oh five, nine fifteen, and you're still not back!" Grandma was shouting.

"We had to give her two sedatives," Grandpa continued. "And now you're not going anywhere at night. That's it! You're punished!"

"What do you mean not anywhere? Why not anywhere? What did I even do?!" Polina was losing control of herself.

"You have to spare your grandparents, they don't have long left." Now Mama added fuel to the flames.

"But I have to have some freedom, I can't live like this," Polina was screaming now.

"Freedom is determined by necessity," said Grandpa.

"Bullshit!" Polina yelled.

"Somebody cleverer than you said that," Grandpa retorted.

"Stop mocking me!" Polina squealed.

"Look at what you've raised! A brat! A good-for-nothing!" Grandma screamed. "She's out of control! And who's all this for anyway? Why would a decent girl be out so late? To be with those boys—those worthless hoodlums? Those rotten punks? With your plumber? They're more important to you than we are! Did they teach you to act like this? I've never seen anyone as shameless as you. You're driving us into the grave, you'll be the death of us! And for what? Nobody's ever going to love you like we love you! Who needs you? We'll die and then you'll be sorry!"

At this point Polina's Uncle Andrei popped out of his room and started yelling, too, at Polina's mother. "Lena, just move to the other apartment! How much more of this can we take? One more fight and I'm moving out. Unlike the rest of you, I value my mother's health, I can't watch anymore how your daughter is wearing her out. And you're not going to have an easy time there with just Polina. It's torture for everyone who lives with her! I wish Polina lived somewhere in Moscow, in total isolation from our family!"

"You're killing me! You're killing me, I can't! Enough!" Polina screamed hysterically. "You can all go to hell!" Sobbing, she ran to the bathroom and locked herself in. She turned on the warm water and looked at the mascara running from her lashes in the large mirror specked with dried toothpaste, warming her wrists while her whole body shook from crying. But even over the sound of the water, the noise in the hall was growing louder.

"She's insane," Grandma was screaming. "She needs help!"

They were trying to break into the bathroom. Grandpa shouted, "Open up! Open up this minute!" and was getting more and more worked up. "Open this door immediately or I'm going to break it down!"

"Just let me calm down, then I'll open it," Polina implored.

"Open up this second!" Grandpa cried, flying into a rage.

Frightened for him, Polina opened the door, and he burst into the bathroom with a pill and a glass of water.

"Drink this!" he ordered.

"What is it? I don't want a pill," said Polina, red and wrinkled from crying.

"It's a sedative. Take it!"

"But I don't want it, I'll calm down anyway," Polina said, but Grandpa wasn't listening anymore; he threw himself at Polina, and in spite of her desperate resistance, forcefully opened her mouth and began to jam in the pill.

"I don't want pills for crazy people!" Polina tried to cry out in a breaking voice, began coughing, and swallowed the pill, freezing in horror.

Having calmed down a little, Grandpa said, "You have a terrible character, you don't know how to control your emotions. You're in the wrong, you must apologize to your grandmother."

Polina's grandmother was already in bed, her aching head swaddled in a wool kerchief, tiny and defenseless, smelling of medicine, and seeming weaker somehow after this scene.

"Grandma, please forgive me," said Polina, and kissed her forehead, which her grandmother, with childlike ingenuousness, offered up to be kissed.

Polina curled up in a ball in her room and sobbed quietly. Grandpa came in, hugged and kissed her, and said, "It's all right, it's all right. You know that we love you very much and we worry about you. Don't be angry with us."

His hands were shaking, and afterward he went to the kitchen and took a sedative himself.

Polina began crying again. She felt bad for her grandparents, bad that she was ruining their health and going to be the death of them. She lay there crying and thinking about how much she loved them, and suddenly she felt that coming over her was a wave of really, really huge and totally infinite, tender, soul-rending love, and that love made her want to cry even more. At that moment Mama came in, saw that Polina was crying again, and asked, "What, do you hate your family?"

BEDYA

She was a love child, and they named her Isabella, after her mother. But everyone called her Bedya. My grandmother also called her Gesha. Gesha was a name she had given herself when she was a child, but nobody, except my grandmother, remembered that anymore. Grandma was Bedya's older half-sister through their mother, so Bedya's relationship to me was that she was my great-aunt, as it's usually called, and I was her grand-niece—all in all, not the closest kinship.

She was heavy, with snow-white hair in a bowl cut, stubble on her chin, and a full-body tremor. And she had dentures, she kept them in the bathroom and put them in when she wanted to eat. They said she hadn't always been like that. I saw photographs of her in her youth: a pretty, slightly plump, light-haired fifties girl. I know that when she was young she traveled with her parents throughout the Soviet republics and to some Western European countries, and they brought back souvenirs, dolls in national costumes, all kinds of little mementos that filled her room. Her father, Nikolai Vasilyevich, served as the director of various theaters and palaces of culture, and for a long time he headed the Lensoviet Palace of Culture in the Petrogradskaya district, where there is now a small museum dedicated to him. Bedya grew up in a theatrical milieu; she went to all the premieres, knew the actors. Together with their parents and large, rowdy groups of their parents' friends, she and my grandmother were always vacationing at the seaside in Abkhazia, in Leselidze. The older Isabella, Bedya's mother, was a very vibrant, domineering, and eccentric woman, and it bears mentioning that she launched the sexual revolution in the Soviet Union, having founded Nevsky Dawns, a firm that was one of the first in the Soviet period to offer family planning. She hired the leading specialists in the field—Svyadoshch, Tsyrulnikov, and some others. Isabella fervently loved her younger daughter and shielded her from everything, trying always to keep Bedya by her side. Bedya was a timid, anxious young woman who feared and avoided men, and if anyone anywhere started showing her some attention, her mother-protector would appear on the horizon.

When I was a child, I often heard my grandparents refer to Bedya as an "unfortunate person," sighing sadly. For a while, I didn't understand exactly what made Bedya so unfortunate. In those days, she still lived with her mother, my by-then-ancient great-grandmother, and I knew that Bedya had lived with her for her entire life. Occasionally I was taken to visit the two of them. There was a particular smell in their apartment, more pleasant than not, and lots of antique furniture: a yellow vanity with a mirror, an ottoman on little curved legs next to the bed. I liked to look at the souvenir dolls, the old books, the albums of black-and-white photographs of many happy, unfamiliar people at the seaside, with the faces of my still-young great-grandmother and great-grandfather, or my very young grandmother, flickering by occasionally. Invariably they treated me to tea, layer cake, and kurabiye cookies. I spent these visits largely with my great-grand-mother; Bedya was simply the background, a kind of addendum to my great-grandmother, and more and more she would go to lie down in her room. I loved my great-grandmother, but Bedya . . . There was something the matter with her. She wasn't like other grown-ups, as though she weren't really a grown-up at all but another child, and she would sometimes say confusing and hurtful things. Once, when I was small, I asked her why her hair was so white or something like that, and she was suddenly very offended and in response said something mean to me about my own appearance. I thought it was very strange, this genuine resentment from an adult, and then the nasty reply—as though we were speaking as absolute equals, two small children, and she was all but younger than me. When she was offended by some-thing in a conversation with my grandmother, for example, she would begin trembling, it was terrifying to see. I decided that I should just be polite but try not to spend too much time with her, or she might not like something and take offense and start saying mean things and trembling.

Later on I learned the following about Bedya: when she was nineteen, she went with some other students "for potatoes" and there she suddenly stripped naked and started running around and shouting obscene things. Her parents were called and she was taken away and checked into a psychiatric hospital. Because of her parents' connections, she was treated by the best psychia-trist of the day, someone who "held all of theatrical Petersburg in his hands." He prescribed powerful drugs, saying, "We have to save her mind." As time went on, these attacks continued. Bedya heard voices and was repeatedly institutionalized. The main medications she took throughout her life were haloperidol and lithium salts. Gradually she grew heavier, began to tremble. I was told that her illness had to do with repressed sexual desires—it wasn't for nothing that she undressed and yelled obscenities—and that grounds for the illness were her upbringing and the pressure from her mother. Whether this was true or not, those desires were destined to remain repressed all her life. Not a single stroll, holding hands beneath the moon. Not a single kiss. Things like that never happened for Bedya, and she was viciously, desperately jealous of people for whom they did. Her illness caused her to become even more fearful and avoidant of men. The treatment did help: she remained a member of society, completed her studies at the forestry academy, and spent her working life as an engineer for a small concern. But she was constantly tormented by unrealized sexual desires. Sometimes, she felt that she was starting to think about a man, maybe one of her colleagues, that she was starting to be drawn to him—or someone was just kind to her, flashed her a smile, joked with her, wished her a happy Women's Day—and parallel with these awakening desires her illness grew more acute, the voices built up in her head. I don't know precisely what kind of crude, disgusting things they shouted at her, but inevitably any show of interest in a man exacerbated her illness, and all her sexual feelings were nipped in the bud by haloperidol.

Sometimes I think that in our time Bedya's fate could have worked out differently. Gentler drugs, psychotherapy, psychoanalysis . . . Maybe she was to some extent a victim of Soviet psychiatry, even though she was treated by the best psychiatrists practicing at the time? My grandparents hinted at this. Bedya had received a diagnosis of schizophrenia, specifically some form of it that involves manic and depressive periods, similar to bipolar disorder. Thanks to her treatment she kept her sanity, but she became an invalid. Could this have been avoided? If someone had helped her, if she had been able to figure herself out, to stop repressing natural feelings and stop fearing her mother? If she hadn't immediately been prescribed haloperidol and diagnosed with schizophrenia? If she had started living alone, dating men, seeing an analyst? I don't know. What happened was that she became an invalid early, and then spent the rest of her life under the wing of her watchful mother, without even trying to make a break for freedom. It's possible that she was waiting for a handsome prince to come and fall in love with her, thinking that somehow this would happen all by itself, and her life would be visited by that male love she so needed. But a handsome prince did not appear. We were sitting together once in the kitchen, and Bedya was listening to the radio as she usually did, a song was playing about love coming out of the blue, and Bedya said, with a bitter grin, "It's been coming for sixty years and hasn't come yet."

When my great-grandmother was dying, and in the long period prior to her death that she spent in a state of senile dementia, Bedya harangued her. This always caring, obedient, mother-adoring daughter suddenly began to cruelly remind the dying woman of her old grievances. My great-grandmother had grown weak and helpless, and she didn't understand a thing, but Bedya would remind her of the time she got rid of a kitten that Bedya had taken in as a little girl. All her life, Bedya had been sick at heart about this abandoned kitten, but she was only able to tell her dying mother about it a few days before her death.

Then Bedya was left alone and lived alone for some time, calling my grandmother fifty times a day out of idleness and loneliness, until something happened that Bedya deeply disliked. My mother and I moved in with her. We had always been registered in the apartment she shared with my great-grandmother, and when I turned sixteen, my grandmother couldn't stand living with me anymore, so the decision was made to move me and my mother out. We weren't moving far—just to the next house over. But Bedya was less than pleased, and although officially we were rightful owners of the apartment, just as much as she was, she perceived us as some kind of invasive freeloaders illegally encroaching on her property. Thus began the years of a difficult coexistence. I always tried not to spend much time with her, but sometimes Bedya herself wanted to socialize. Usually, on those occasions, she would come and test my erudition: did I know such and such Soviet actors, such and such artists? I obviously did not. Then she would bring me art books to look at, which she had in vast quantities. Knowing that I wrote poetry, she sometimes brought over and showed me clippings of young women's poems from Soviet magazines. She liked these poems, they resonated with her—at some point she'd clipped them herself. Among the clippings were some poems by Kushner, whom she also liked. Her whole life, she had kept a poem that Alexander Georgievich Kutuzov, a dacha neighbor and a colleague of her mother's, had written for her birthday. In the poem, he calls her "this dark blonde."

For Bedya, anything to do with female sexuality was a vulnerable, sore spot. I didn't spare her: I brought lovers over, walked naked around the apartment. Bedya insulted me constantly, whenever we happened to bump into each other in the kitchen or the hall. Any encounter could lead to an insult tossed off in my direction. I would be coming out of the shower, wrapped in a towel, and upon seeing me, Bedya would tremble and scream, "You think you're pretty? Well, you're deeply mistaken!" She suspected all my boyfriends of wanting to rape her. I remember that she refused to let us call the plumber because she thought he was in love with her and was afraid he'd start coming on to her. She thought our old neighbor, out smoking for hours by the garbage chute, was in love with her—according to Bedya, he was hanging around waiting for her to take out the trash bucket. How nervous she became, how agitated, how she trembled, how her heart pounded when she saw men!

I believe that Bedya was kind in her own way. Touchy, unstable, infantile, but in her own way, kind. She had a lot of love and compassion for cats, and when our cat was sick and dying, she truly suffered, even cried. She was also occasionally kind to me, spoke with me gently, commiserated about things. When something bad happened somewhere, she always had compassion for another's troubles. Once in a while she'd show up with an obvious desire for intimacy, understanding, heart-to-heart conversation, but everything was off-kilter with her, and half an hour later she could become resentful and start saying nasty things.

One day Bedya came to my room with some art books and poetry clippings, and then, without warning, she told me the following story. "I've never told anyone about this. Not once in my life. You won't tell anyone? When I was studying at the forestry academy, I was walking there one morning . . . and a man jumped on me in the park. He was a student there, too. He threw me on the ground and he pawed at me . . . he touched me everywhere . . . then he ran away. I couldn't tell anyone, I kept it all in. I couldn't even tell my mother. I thought about it all the time, for half a year . . . then the voiced started, I got sick." I was shocked by this story, and I didn't tell anyone about it for many years, but I think that now that Bedya and my grandparents are no longer with us, I can share it. After she told me the story, I thought about the man: how he had no idea what he had precipitated, what he might have triggered. He assaulted a girl in the park, scared her, felt her up, and she was ashamed and terrified by what had happened to her, and she became ill, she became an invalid, she has no family, she's alone and she's miserable. While he might be married, might have children, grandchildren . . .

A friend I had when I was young, Lilya, once became afraid that I would suffer the same fate as Bedya. I had told her Bedya's general story (leaving out the episode with the man), and Lilya suddenly sat down on the train tracks and began to cry. It turned out that she was feeling sorry for me, because she thought that something similar could happen to me, too. And honestly, around sixteen or seventeen, I really did look and behave like a person who's about to conclusively lose her mind—that's how wild I was, how entirely fucked in the head. And it's also true that a little later this bad inheritance caught up with me and I finally lost it. I don't know what my life would have been like if I had been treated at the same time, and with the same methods, as Bedya.

There was a particularly scary period when lithium salts disappeared from the market. The lithium supply had run out at that point, likely all used up for car batteries, and Bedya, who had taken lithium salts her entire life, began slowly and agonizingly dying. Lithium becomes part of your metabolism, replacing sodium, and after many years of use, Bedya could no longer live without it. Each day she grew worse. She could barely walk and kept lying down in her room; her face grew dark and unwell, and she became confused; she talked to herself and made frightening sounds that could be heard outside of her room.

"I'm dying," she said to me on one of those difficult days, and she wasn't joking. I understood that we had to get lithium for her by any possible means. With the help of my friend Dima Grigoriev, we found some pure lithium at a factory where his friend worked. My grandfather split the lithium into portions, wrapped them up in little pieces of paper, we started dosing her with it, and Bedya returned to life. For a long time she took this factory lithium that we had found. Eventually her medicine came back on the market.

Still, as time went on, life with Bedya became even more unbearable. She started clashing with Denis, my first husband. Bedya had actually liked Denis for a long time, and even gifted him a hat, but then a period began that was dismal in every respect. Every morning I was woken by Bedya saying nasty things about me in the kitchen. Any little thing could result in a terrible scene. Once I was making soup, and Bedya was very anxious, coming up to me and asking if I would treat her to some when it was ready. I said that I would, and of course I did, but after that Bedya started trying to hand me a hundred-ruble bill as payment for the soup. For a while I turned her down, but she insisted that I take it, trembling with anxiety. Afraid that she would have a fit, I took the money, and Bedya immediately ran to my mother and started telling on me, saying that she was a poor pensioner and I was charging her money for soup. So I went up to Bedya and tore the bill into tiny pieces. Another time, the bathroom door got stuck, and Bedya insisted that Denis and I had purposefully locked her in the bathroom, though we were actually the ones who let her out. A communal hell reigned in the apartment. After Bedya called a friend of hers right in front of us and loudly complained that we were trying to drive her out of her own home, Denis packed his things and left, and I followed. For a while we stayed with friends; I scrounged together money from my family, and then we rented, for three months, a very cheap one-room apartment on the Fontanka River. We didn't have enough money to rent for longer, but soon it would be summer, and I would go to stay at the dacha as usual, while Denis would go home to Krasnoyarsk until the fall. And what we would do later—later we would figure that out.

But the problem of needing to rent a place by fall resolved itself. On that summer day Bedya called my grandfather at the dacha where we were staying. She was watching TV, in good spirits, and about to take a shower. After speaking with my grandfather, she apparently went to wash, while my mother headed back from the dacha into the city. Later my grandfather called Bedya a few times, but she didn't pick up. He began to worry, and when Mama reached the city apartment, my grandfather called her and asked, "How's Bedya doing over there?"

"She's washing," Mama said breezily, "I can hear the sound of water in the bathroom." Then Grandpa understood. "Open the bathroom door," he told my mother. Mama opened the door and saw dead, swollen, terrifying Bedya, drowned and scalded in the boiling water.

At the morgue she lay in a closed casket. Then her disfigured body was consigned to the flames. The urn was large and heavy, and it was buried with her parents, who may have been the only people in the world who loved the dead woman. There, next to her mother and father, her ashes rest. She was a love child, and they named her Isabella, after her mother. But everyone called her Bedya.

AGAINST THE LAW

"Let's fuck someone up," Nastya suggested.

"Let's," Olya agreed.

And they went off in search of someone to fuck up. They were both twenty, studying philosophy at the university, and fond of bringing all kinds of trouble down upon their skinny asses. On that particular night they did not succeed in fucking anyone up. They walked the streets for a long time, looking for trouble, went into Victory Park, and there made the acquaintance of two guys. Nastya and Olya followed the guys into a more distant part of the park to meet their friends, but soon enough some other guys jumped the guys they had met and started beating them up. Nastya wanted to fight, too, but Olya dragged her out of there and to a biker bar called Night Hunters. The girls were so drunk by the time they arrived that they could barely stand upright, and soon enough everyone at the club was watching them: they danced, let the bikers feel them up, and laughed uproariously, and then a biker named Zhenya drove Nastya through the night-time city on his motorcycle and made her promise to marry him.

Then Nastya and Olya went to Nastya's; Olya fell asleep while Nastya spent the night throwing up and crying out of despair and metaphysical nausea.

"Most of the time I can't do anything at all, which makes me feel really awful. I have to lie down somewhere warm and quiet and wait for this difficult state, this inner weakness and nausea, to pass. This makes it very hard for me to attend university, especially to go to class every day and in the mornings. There've been times when I was so exhausted by showering in the morning that I spent the rest of the day lying down without moving. When I was a kid, I saw a psychiatrist and a neuropathologist. I took strong medication," Nastya told her psychiatrist, Mikhail Sergeyevich. Mikhail Sergeyevich listened in silence.

Olya was from Novosibirsk. Until recently she'd been living with a boyfriend, but he tried to strangle her several times in the bathroom, so she left. Olya wrote songs and sang them while playing the guitar; she was interested in everything unusual, extreme, deviant. At the philosophy department she was, accordingly, studying deviant behavior within the framework of social philosophy. Nastya was a well-known young poet; she'd already published a book of her poems that won a literary prize, and she had recently left a man who was twice her age, an adult poet. The breakup was very painful, though it also came as a relief. Having left this man, Nastya felt compelled to live it up. At the philosophy department she was writing a term paper on the philosophy of Nietzsche and the carnival in Bakhtin.

One night, after celebrating her grandparents' golden wedding anniversary, Nastya went to see Vadik. They'd started talking on an S&M website and agreed to meet up. Vadik was a good-looking, sweet guy, a bit of a sad sack and a wimp, and role of the sadist that he was attempting didn't particularly suit him. Nastya and Vadik played with a rack and some light flogging, but Vadik was clearly a little afraid of Nastya throughout, touching her very carefully, as though she were a crystal vase. Finally Nastya had to take charge and perform in a very different role from the one she had imagined for herself—just the opposite, in fact. She did eventually get to meet a real sadist. Through the same website she made plans to meet up with Alexander, who worked as an investigator. He even looked like a real sadist, it was clearly not just a role-playing game for him. He tortured Nastya for a long time and with great pleasure, and then handcuffed her to the radiator for the night, refusing to let her go no matter how much she begged, and laid down to sleep. In the morning he gave her a ride to her intersection, and Nastya went through the court-yard doubled over in pain; her whole body ached and she desperately wanted to sleep.

Nastya experimented mercilessly on her body and her psyche. She considered herself something like a warrior or a soldier, for whom daily transgression—a kind of indirect suicide—was tough and unpleasant work, but also the way to triumph over the kingdom of entropy and death into which she'd been cast, and over that kingdom's laws. She desired an ecstasy of the body that was inseparable from an intoxication of the spirit; she wanted the flesh to become the incarnation of a holy logos, a Dionysian state, that absolute suffering from which all the structures of culture try to lead toward the bearable. Bakhtin's ideas of the carnivalesque and the culture of popular laughter interested Nastya specifically insomuch as they were another form of existence for Dionysus, in the role of a jester with all those comic rites and cults, fools, giants, dwarves and freaks, harlequins, swearing and vows in

God's name. It was as though all that laughter justified the body, brought on an awareness of physiological-bodily limits, and it was that justification that Nadya so desperately lacked.

Olya told Nastya that she had started working at a brothel. Olya thought of this as an experiment, one that came with a decent salary. She was pretty and quickly became one of their "go-to girls." When she wasn't working Olya still spent time with Nastya; they'd get drunk, roll around on the grass, meet guys, get into scrapes and trouble, and finally vomit. At night Nastya often went out alone. She hung out with prostitutes who worked the street and stood all night by the road right beneath Nastya's windows; they chatted and drank terrible cocktails together. Whenever a cop car appeared in the distance, Nastya left so that she wouldn't get caught in a sweep—the prostitutes paid the cops for the right to work that spot, but the cops didn't know Nastya, so there could have been problems. One night, when Nastya was just wandering the streets, a car pulled up to her, a man from the Caucasus behind the wheel. "Young lady, do you need a ride?" he asked. Nastya thought about it, then got in the car. They drove around for a while, and it was really all the same to Nastya where they were going. She sat with her eyes half closed, thinking her own thoughts. The she suddenly asked the driver, "Do you want a blow job?"

"How about anal?" he asked.

"All right." Nastya honestly didn't care. But they couldn't manage anal—it was too painful—so in the end they switched to regular sex. The driver warmed to Nadya. "Do you do this often?" he asked. "You must really like men, huh? You take care of yourself." Nastya went home. She didn't feel anything, she just wanted to sleep.

"My genetic inheritance in terms of mental health is also pretty bad. My grandmother's sister is schizophrenic, and something has been the matter with my grandmother, too, for her entire life, though she never sought medical help. Things aren't easy for my uncle or my mother, either. My grandparents basically raised me. I had a very difficult relationship with my grandmother because of her despotism and the constant psychological pressure she put on me, even though we loved each other. There was always fighting and shouting at home. But despite all of that everyone really loved and spoiled me. I suffer from severe depressive disorder. Often I don't want to live. I think about death, not necessarily my own death, but about the fact that everyone is going to die, and it pains me. During depressive episodes I sometimes think about it day and night, but at other times I forget about it for long periods. I feel bad for everyone, everything makes me cry. When I'm feeling better, I just smile when I think about it. When I was sixteen, I tried to kill myself. I took a huge overdose of medication, lay for several days in something like a coma, then woke up. For a long time after that I felt strange, by the end of the day I couldn't remember what had happened in the beginning or in the middle. My relatives felt bad for me, so they didn't have me institutionalized. Then there was another time I took a huge dose of drugs, though a lot less than the first time. I had a psychotic episode that lasted several days, mostly related to sex. I ran naked around the courtyard, wrapped in a towel—I intended to run away from home. When I was a teenager I'd cut my arms given the slightest pretext. At thirteen, I suffered a psychological trauma related to my first love. For a long period I lived in a state of extreme emotional and spiritual strain. Someone else in my place would probably have gotten off easier, but it affected me to the very depths of my soul. I developed a kind of paranoia to do with the topic, I keep coming back to it again and again," Nastya continued to unburden herself to Mikhail Sergeyevich. She talked and talked, but it seemed like she didn't care much about what she was saying, that she was just fulfilling some onerous obligation, though she was trying to do it as well and as thoroughly as possible. There was likewise no sympathy on Mikhail Sergeyevich's face, and it was unclear whether he was listening to Nastya or had for some time been thinking about something else.

Nastya thought that everyone was looking at her and thinking horrible things about her, as though she were a leper, and that she shouldn't touch other people or even look at them. She wore sunglasses everywhere, even indoors, and almost never took them off. She was anxious, afraid, and full of hate, and she despised herself. She wore the sunglasses to her job as an interpreter. Around that time she had a few assignments through people her mother knew. She interpreted for an American couple from Chicago who wanted to adopt a little girl from a Russian orphanage. Nastya accompanied them to the district office and the orphanage. Another assignment was interpreting at a business meeting about *funduk* transport. The meeting took place in the lobby of the Nevsky Palace hotel, and everything was going well, but Nastya didn't know the English word for *funduk*. *Hazelnut*, goddamn it.

In the meantime, Olya told Nastya about her work at the brothel. Once she called Nastya and said that she couldn't stand to look at herself and that she was coming from church. Nastya said that maybe then she shouldn't do what she was doing. The girls then had a pretty sharp conversation. Olya said to Nastya that she couldn't not do it, citing her poverty and the fact that she couldn't take the last of her mother's money.

"You're being disingenuous," said Nastya. "You could get another job, even as a waitress."

The situation was soon complicated by the fact that Olya met a guy at work, a client, and fell in love with him, but he was a heroin addict, and now they were doing heroin together. Nastya kept trying to convince her to quit the job and stop doing drugs. Olya would describe how she felt on heroin: "When you're high, you like everything you do, you know what I mean? You like how you're smoking, how you're flicking the butt . . ."

"I lack joy. I think I'm just not able to feel it fully. There have been times when the joyless periods lasted for so long that I wanted to see a doctor, to be prescribed medication for it. In the mornings I don't want to wake up, which is because I don't want to live. When I was a kid I couldn't play with my classmates. I was often considered a weirdo. Socializing is very hard for me a lot of the time, though the lack of real, intimate relationships is even harder. A lot of things that have to do with society and other people horrify me. I cry if someone yells at me on public transport or at the dean's office. It's sometimes hard for me to talk even to people who are close to me. Or if I have any reason to believe that someone doesn't think well of me somehow, I can't speak to that person at all. I'm scared of being in public places, I'm even a little scared when I check my email. Sometimes thoughts come into my mind and I get stuck on them; I can't calm down until I do whatever I'm thinking about. Usually it's nothing important, but it can be something really odd, I never know what's going to pop into my head. I'm often in distress, and I put myself in situations where I'll feel that way. And I also get extremely worked up about sex and sexuality . . ." Nastya continued her story. "Melipramin," Mikhail Sergeyevich said quietly, at long last. "Let's try Melipramin."

Then there were the parties, so-called swingers' parties. Nastya went to them regularly. But they weren't really for swingers, people could come without partners, just to fuck. They were really parties where people had group sex. You'd pay for a membership and go. If a woman came with a man, she didn't have to pay at all. The parties happened at saunas in upscale apartments. There were more men than women there, so women were a hot commodity. Since beautiful women were even less frequent, usually all the men would fuck them together. There was a university crowd, there were businessmen. Nastya had never had so many marriage proposals as she did at the swingers' parties. All the guys who came there to fuck women were actually dreaming of love, a wife, their one and only. They were ready to fall in love; they'd try to court you, get your number. But Nastya didn't need any of that. Unlike them, she knew why she was there. There was one guy, a government deputy with a doctorate, the biggest stud at all the parties, who gave Nastya an anthology he had edited, several volumes of Russian thinkers, then fucked her for a long time on a table.

"The path of excess leads to the tower of wisdom." This was gnosis, this was elemental Russian tantra. Nastya heard a voice—it came from beneath the roots, within the lake, underneath the moss, the voice of the elements—and she recognized it as the absolute, primordial desire not to be; it was as though she were falling into a void of nonexistence, unconsciousness, delirium, what happens when you pass beyond all limits in order to belong, it doesn't matter to whom, and you dissolve in it, that cosmic elemental force. Within all this endless fucking there was a dark pleroma-womb, full of newborn stars, the lair of the eternal she-wolf—without gender, without world, above the abyss. There, far from reality, Nastya tumbled into vertigo, oblivion, brushed by something uncreated, not of this world. It was self-destruction and knowledge. It was ceaseless hysteria, suffering, and a complete denial of reality. It was an exploration of the dangerous aspects of the psyche. Nastya didn't care what she did with her body. She wanted to break through to a different life, even if the body had to die for that to happen. It was an endless rejection of the laws of the corporeal realm for the sake of obtaining true freedom from the world.

The Melipramin did not help. It made Nastya start zoning out wherever she happened to be. Once she slid down the wall of the philosophy department bathroom and blacked out. Another time she went to a student party, fell asleep there, and slept for three days, after which everyone decided that she was a drug addict. Nastya stopped taking the Melipramin and decided not to see Mikhail Sergeyevich anymore. She went to a whorehouse instead. That is to say, the brothel where Olya worked. Nastya made up her mind to work a single night at the brothel. It was clear that in order to obtain true, deep insight, in order to bring her heart to life, there was no point in fucking nice boys she liked. She had to give herself to the taxi driver, to spend a night in handcuffs, to work as a prostitute.

The brothel was located inside an ordinary large apartment in a building on Staronevsky. At the apartment were Irina the administrator, a male driver for visits, and five or six young women. Nastya would later remember Jasmine, Vika, and

Amanda—they turned out to be simple and slightly vulgar girls from the provinces. Their names were fake. At the brothel, Olya was called Sophia, as in Wisdom. Nastya was called Maria, as in Magdalene. Sophia and Maria sat on a huge bed at the brothel and chatted, just as they did at a desk at the philosophy department. When a client appeared, all the women came out for a "viewing" in lingerie. Nastya wore her prettiest underwear for this: black-and-white lace. But when she went out for the "viewing" in the pretty underwear, she didn't feel her skinny body to be sexual—it seemed simple and sad to her, as though it had stepped into this scene out of a completely different story. It was a body that should have been doing something else—bathing in the River Jordan in a white robe or riding a bicycle, tanning in the sun or lying on its deathbed—but it definitely should not have been there. The first client, an unattractive guy, looked at all the women, didn't choose any of them, and left. Then two pimply teenagers showed up and both picked Olya-Sophia. Olya refused to take on the two of them, and they left.

That night, anyone could have chosen Sophia or Maria. That night, anyone could have known them. And Sophia said: I have been sent by the Power. And I have come to those who think of me. And Maria said: I am the first and last. I am revered and rejected. I am the harlot and the saint. I am the matron and the maiden. And Sophia said: I am the silence that cannot be parsed and the thought that returns. I am wisdom and ignorance. I am shame and courage. And Maria said: I am shameless, I am modest. I am the despised and the great. Do not be arrogant toward me when I am cast to Earth! And Sophia said: do not look at me, covered in refuse, and do not depart and abandon me when I am cast down. And you will find me in the kingdom. Do not look at me when I am cast among the despised, in the poor places, and do not mock me. And Maria said: in my weakness do not abandon me and do not be afraid of my power. But I am she who is often afraid, and the fortitude in fright. I am the one who is weak, and I am unharmed in a place of pleasure. And Sophia said: take my knowledge that comes from grief. And Maria said: go to your childhood and do not hate it. That night, in that place, Maria and Sophia, Nastya and Olya, were cast down to Earth, and anyone could have touched them or taken them according to his wishes—for an hour, or for the entire night.

In the middle of the night came an untidy, forty-something guy from Chechnya. Nastya was falling asleep and didn't want anything anymore, but unfortunately he chose her, and she had to see the thing through to the end. There was no point feeling sorry for herself, that wasn't what she'd gone there to do. He booked Nastya for two hours, screwed her once, and finished quickly. Then he wanted to continue, to fuck again and again, but Nastya couldn't manage to get his dick, soft after finishing the first time, inside herself. It was painful and gross, and nothing worked. Nastya tried as best she could not to show her disgust, to change it into compassion for this unknown and likewise unhappy person. The situation was made worse by the fact that Nastya hadn't brought any lube, and it was obvious that nothing was going to happen without it. Finally Nastya called in Vika for the second hour, and the administrator split their reward between the two of them.

Nastya spent the rest of the night in a different room, in a big bed on which all the prostitutes slept, unable to fall asleep. "Why did I do this?" she wondered, and could find no answer. It had been a quest for some kind of knowledge, a kind of boundless research project, and awful, unbelievable loneliness and futility. There was no one around to ask about sex and death, pain and desperation, depression, growing up, self-hatred, about this loneliness and longing. Other secrets lay ahead, waiting only to be grasped or remembered: forgiveness and compassion, the tenderness and fragility of everything living, warmth and simple happiness, mercy and acceptance. She had to learn to forgive: to forgive the body that wasn't guilty of anything, to forgive carnal love for containing a seed of evil. To forgive herself—it was unclear for what—and to stop punishing herself over and over. Next to her, Sophia was crying silently. She was sad and ashamed to have brought her friend to this place.

In the morning Nastya left the brothel; it was May 27, City Day. Nastya was supposed to meet two friends from the university, Tanya and Natasha, at Gostiny Dvor, but she got there early. She had to wait and sat down on the steps of the building. A holiday parade was passing by on Nevsky. It was a real carnival, a folk celebration; sounds of laughter and music, balloons hovering above, everyone dressed in bright, multicolored clothes, someone walking on stilts, someone wearing a mask. It was as though the bright colors, the variety, laughter, music, the general folk celebration deafened Nastya. There was something wonderfully plebeian about it, something that spoke of a merry relativity and the world's eternal renewal, its destruction and rebirth. And these joyful, happy people were also living in this becoming world, they were also unfinished and also, through dying, were born and made new, as though in their pure happiness they were ritually mocking a certain ancient deity. In this world, in this city, on this day, on Nevsky Prospekt, there were no masters or slaves, no rich or poor, no virgins or whores—only a single spirit of utterly unabashed life. Nastya sat on the steps and looked for a long time, smiling, at the carnival procession. She suddenly felt emptied out. She felt light, amused, happy, joyful. In her heart there was a knowledge full of pain and love, a light, singing knowledge. And she burst out laughing.

II.

THE MOTOR BAR

RUSSIAN BEAUTY

So I go to the bar. It's daytime.

I go in and I say, "Is your kitchen open?"

"Yeah, it's open."

"Do you have shashlik?"

"Chicken or pork?"

"Pork," I say.

"Decent bar you have here," I say.

This bar's in the woods, at the top of a hill; there's also a big lake out there, an adventure park, and a little resort; there's a lot out there in general—a restaurant on the lakeshore, a hutch with rabbits that sell for five hundred rubles each, there's a beach, of course, there's the Nepalese consul's villa, a stage for parties that's shaped like a UFO, there's a team-building site, I mean, what don't they have out there. And at the very far end of all this recreational bullshit, let's call it, there's a hill in the woods, and on the hill there's the Motor Bar. That's where I went.

So I ask, "What's it like at night here? Does it pick up a little?"

"Depends on the time."

"How about around midnight?"

"Well, sure, it picks up then."

"Good spot," I say. "I like it."

The bar's not too big, it's got a sort of U.S. theme, an imaginary U.S., like a bar in a small town, Twin Peaks or something, that kind of bar. There are license plates from all fifty states, a map of Route 66 from L.A. to Chicago, like in the Bob Dylan song, and on the roof they have car parts. And all around the place are pines and spruces, the deep dark woods, the lake.

"I'll come by at night sometime," I say. "What kind of crowd do you get here? Locals from the resort or kids from the village? Or people coming from the city? Are there hot girls?" The bartender, a little guy, hairy, bearded, in a T-shirt with a tribal-style picture of a wolf, says to me, "We get different kinds, they come from the resort and from the village, and some just come right out of the woods." He winks at me. "Saturdays at midnight we get a Russian beauty. As far as girls go."

"What kind of Russian beauty?" I ask.

"Oh, this kind. Want a beer, by the way?" and he gets out a little bottle of dark craft beer, and the label says Russian Beauty.

So that's the name of the beer. I take the bottle and I see there's a girl on the label, it's not clear whether she's alive or dead, she's gothed up, white face, has a headdress on, her heart's been torn out of her chest and stuck onto her dress, in her hands there's maggots, in her eyes there's fiery rage. And behind her— the woods, tangled branches, skulls, carrion birds, designs that look like demon faces, the hut on chicken legs, Koschei the Deathless's bald head, horrible goosey swans, and all that kind of thing.

"What kind of girl is that?" I ask. "Go ahead and read the text on the back," says the bartender. So I read it, though it's in English and my English isn't great, but I get some of it. Basically there are two artists who live in Petersburg, a married couple, and they draw the labels, and it says that they draw them while in a mystical trance, during which they're transported to the dark Homeland. It's like there are two celestial Homelands: the light one and the dark one. One is like the underwater city of Kitezh, with the white temples, bells, ornate painted houses, and all the rest of holy ancient Rus'. And the other, the dark Homeland, is like a scary fairy tale with all those monsters and unholy filth, Baba Yaga, Koschei, and the forest at night that Alenushka and Ivanushka get lost in. "The dark Russian collective unconscious," the artists call the dark Homeland. And they, these artists, say in their manifesto that they enter the dark Homeland in their mystical trance and draw the different kinds of disembodied things that exist there on the border between the world of the dead and the world of the living. That's where they met the Russian beauty, this lady in the headdress, and showed her the path to our world.

"So yeah, she comes in," says the bartender, "like I said, on Saturdays."

"What do you mean?" I don't get it.

"I mean that guys will be sitting around drinking, and at midnight she comes in, all done up like that, in the headdress, with the heart and the maggots, and she crosses the whole room. She looks at everyone with her terrible eyes, and there's such hatred in her look, there aren't enough words to describe it. Then she looks point-blank at one of the guys, points at him with her finger, and disappears."

"What are you bullshitting me for, buddy?"

"Ask anybody, lots of people have seen her. Vitalik who works the boat rentals . . . Just come by on Saturday, you'll see!"

"You're making it all up. It's a good story, but way too dumb. Here's what I owe you for the shashlik, time for me to go. Thanks for passing the time, though your humor's kind of bleak, you should think up something happier."

"Up to you, man. If you want to, come on back."

So I get up and go to the door. By the door I turn around and ask, "Hey, what happens to the people she points to? Something really bad?"

"I don't really know. Seems like they just go on like they did before. Maybe something changes, but it's hard to talk about . . . She pointed at me once. When I'd just started working here. And I live pretty much the way I did before, but there's something— something strange. Like my life is happening both here and in the dark Homeland. Like there's something I'm seeing but I'm also not, I don't know. Like the deep nighttime forest grows some- where within me. Like that's where I really belong, not in this world. Like there is no world, really—just the forest, this bar, and Her. Like . . ."

I didn't listen to any more of it and opened the door, noticing that in the corner by the door there was a little heap of maggots.

I walked out of the bar, into the deep dark woods.

THE VERY SAME DAY

Today is a beautiful August day, the one day of the year when Nastya's copy *returns to the way she was.* On this day only her childhood returns to her, her past and her future, the way they were before she wound up in the forest. It's a long day, and like all days of this kind, it begins with sunrise, with fog over the lake, with a light chill that changes to a slightly languid August heat. At sunrise, Nastya's copy went out of the Motor Bar and onto the resort grounds, because on this day she was permitted to leave the forest, though she couldn't go farther than the resort. No one was stopping her, she could have tried walking out of the resort and to the village, to the house where she had lived nineteen years ago, and she had tried—over the past nineteen years she'd tried many times to do just that. But then she would just begin to *disappear.* One step, another, away from the woods, from the Motor Bar, beyond the borders of the resort, past the red-and-white road barrier at the entrance—and she'll dissolve. After all, she's only a copy. And copies don't exist outside of the forest.

So Nastya's copy prefers to spend the day strolling by the lake, studying the cars in the resort parking lot, smiling at funny signs nailed to the pines, for example ANTELOPE NEXT 10 MILES, memorizing the forest ranger's phone number on the placard warning about the danger of forest fires, on which there's a blue sphere with a flame burning inside. She sits in the tent by the lake, in the restaurant's wooden banquet hall out on the floating pier, swings on the playground swing set, remembering (though of course they aren't her own memories, she's only a copy, but from the inside they feel like hers) that *in her day*, meaning nineteen years ago, none of this was here, not the resort, not the restaurant, not the Norwegian adventure park, not the Motor Bar; there was only the forest on the lakeshore and an abandoned Young Pioneers camp. Nineteen years ago: the year 1999. That's when it all began. But more about that later. For now, Nastya's copy marvels at the rabbits behind the fence, which you can buy for five hundred rubles each, or for fifty rubles you can get carrots from a special vending machine and feed them. But Nastya's copy doesn't have any money; she walked out of the woods with empty pockets, so all she can do is look plaintively at the vacationers who could easily give her fifty rubles, though she doesn't dare ask. But what a joy it would be to feed the rabbits! Nastya's copy is, after all, only a child. She's always going to be thirteen years old, while the real Nastya is already thirty-two. You may think that wandering around the resort all day is very boring, but Nastya's copy isn't bored at all. After all, it's not a regular day for her. It's the day when she *returns to the way she was*. When her childhood returns to her. When, for a single day, she becomes almost real, and her real life, the life of the girl Nastya, returns to her. It's a happy day. The happiest day of the year. It's a long day, and like all days of this kind, it ends with sunset, with fog over the lake, with a light chill that changes to a crisp night and August twilight, and tomorrow won't be like this, there are supposed to be thunderstorms.

Nastya's copy sits on the pier by the dock. She's dressed the way teenagers dressed back then, nineteen years ago. She's wearing flares and platform boots, and also Mama's light blue sweater. There's no Mama in the forest, but Nastya's copy always wears her sweater. She was wearing it back when she wound up in the forest. On this day, Nastya's copy feels like it's possible to go home, like it's still the summer of 1999. On beautiful August days like these they ate bilberries and wild strawberries at her house. It's Saturday, which means this morning Grandma went to the market and bought milk from the milk drum after waiting in a long line. At the market they sell berries, zucchini, watermelons. Grandpa is probably doing work around the house. In the evening they'll all eat watermelon together. Mama is at the dacha, too, she always comes for the weekend. There's no Mama in the forest; Nastya's copy doesn't know why, but she's never seen her there, though Grandma and Grandpa are there. But they're *different*. Their house is there, too, and even the house is *different*. It keeps moving from place to place. It keeps changing. The house resembles the real dacha where Nastya spent her childhood, but the forest around it is frightening and dark. And the barn looks like the real barn, but it's turned in a different direction, not to the right of the entryway, but behind it. The Grandpa who lives in the forest always says that this forest is much worse. He goes on a lot of walks in it, and the sky is always dark, there's pouring rain. When Grandpa comes home, he sits in the armchair on the veranda and doesn't speak. He and Grandma barely talk to one another. At night they're not in their beds, and Nastya's copy doesn't know where they go. Sometimes Grandma and Grandpa walk around the dacha and their expressions and eyes are completely terrifying and dead; Nastya's copy once found a crack in the wall and peered out: they were walking in circles carrying some sacks and pushing carts that held their things, as though they were trying to go somewhere or thought they were leaving. Both of them were always somehow not right, there was something lacking in them, as though they had lost their souls and only automatic habits remained from the original Grandma and Grandpa, with no life animating them. Nastya's copy once asked the forest Grandpa when the nice Grandpa she loved would be back, and he said never. This set of grandparents often spoke in nonsense, incoherent speech, as though they were half asleep.

Nineteen years ago: the year 1999. That's when it all began. Or rather, that's when it all ended. On a similarly beautiful, long August day, when all was warm, serene, everlasting, and the flowers were blooming. But what exactly happened then, Nastya's copy doesn't remember. She has a few dreams about it, different dreams with different versions of events, but she doesn't remember which one is correct. One of these dreams is about rape. In this dream, Nastya's copy remembers that on that beautiful August day, Nastya was going to the market, where the local kids hung out then. On the way there a Nissan pulled up to her, a thirty-year-old creep with a gold chain around his neck stuck out his mug and said, "Honey, let's go for a ride."

"I'm not your honey," Nastya said, turned up her nose, and kept walking. "Don't be rude," the creep said, got out of the car, approached Nastya, and pulled her into an embrace that made her ribs crack. Nastya tore herself away from him and ran toward the market. The Nissan reversed and drove after her. There were five gangsters in the car—petty criminals from the nearest town—and a gun. The men got out of the car and pressed Nastya up against the wall of Aunt Lyuba's market booth. One of them started pawing at her while another one, the leader, the beast with the gold chain, bought a few packs of condoms at the stand. They explained to Nastya that they would drive her out to the lake, into the forest, and all of them would screw her. There wasn't a single person at the market who could stand up for her. Running away was impossible. The gangsters, in the meantime, were discussing something among themselves and for a few seconds they left Nastya alone. In that time she dove inside Aunt Lyuba's stand, and they locked the door with a latch. Nastya was shaking with fear. "Don't worry, you poor thing," Aunt Lyuba consoled her, "you're like my own little girl. You know my little girl was raped three times. And it was a gang every time. They made her take it in her mouth. She was pretty, my daughter." Meanwhile, the gangsters discovered their loss. They didn't catch on right away that Nastya was hiding inside the stand; they got back in their car and drove around the entire market. But in a minute they were back. They realized Nastya was in there, and the leader started trying to break in. The booth shook, beer bottles started falling. Aunt Lyuba had to open the door before he destroyed the place. He pulled Nastya out, shoved her in the car, and they drove out to the lake. The same lake where the resort is now. As for what happened at the lake, Nastya's copy can't remember exactly, even in her dream. She thinks she got away and ran into the forest, she ran and ran—and then she stayed there. Or they raped and killed her and left her body in the forest. The real Nastya died, or she went home. Or maybe none of this happened at all. That's the first dream Nastya's copy has about the possible past.

But deeper beneath that dream is Nastya's copy's second dream: the one about the mirror. That summer there had been a guy, a grown guy, nineteen years old; he did magic, and the local kids said that he was really out of his mind, and also that he'd cured his mother's cancer, and that he was completely obsessed with fucking and underage virgins. In her dream, Nastya's copy saw him very clearly, and she remembered exactly how they first met. It happened in the second half of July. He was very short, much shorter than Nastya, pale, with dark blond hair and a ruby earring in one ear, wearing work pants and a black down jacket over his bare chest with an upside-down pentagram patch over the elbow, and the pupil of his left eye was shaped like the number eight. He worked in the village as a plumber, and they met by the fire suppression pond; the stone slab next to the pond was one of the places local kids hung out. This guy, Sanya, sang and played guitar and never took his eyes off Nastya; he sang "Phantom," then a song about rain, then "Afghanistan," then a song about vodka, and a lot more after that. Then he said that he was hungry because he hadn't eaten anything in three days, he'd been out drinking in the woods and the swamps, and Nastya went home and brought him some plums from their table. After that Nastya was sick, she was feverish and hallucinated the forest, and when she felt better Sanya said he'd wanted to come and heal her but he didn't want to scare her parents, and he said that he had looked for her. And later they met at Zhenya's house—Zhenya the general's granddaughter who loved Kurt Cobain, whom Sanya happened to closely resemble—and there was a game that involved throwing something at each other, and Sanya sat next to Nastya and caught the thing they were throwing whenever it came near so that it wouldn't hit her. On a day when they were going to Nastya's house to pick raspberries and hang out in the barn, Sanya asked whether Nastya might need a boyfriend. Nastya said she did not. While they were picking raspberries, Sanya told Nastya that he loved her, and then he started saying it all the time. For a while Nastya wouldn't agree to be Sanya's girlfriend, but she spent all her time with him, and eventually she did agree, which is when Sanya promised to marry her as soon as she reached the appropriate age, which, by the way, wouldn't happen for quite a while. When Sanya and Nastya took walks in the forest, or when they sat under a tree somewhere and he laid his head in her lap, he often said some very odd things. Sometimes Sanya clutched his head and said that Jehovah, meaning the god that everyone worshipped, was trying to get into his mind, but there were really many gods, and Jehovah was actually a pretty nasty type, and anyway our planet had initially been given to the one everyone thinks is the Devil. Sanya called him Asmodeus and thought of him as something like a little brother, and as far as the almighty and absolute God, Sanya said that nothing is really known about him, some people think that he exists, others that he doesn't, and out of the gods that were known to Sanya personally, the greatest was Dragon, god of the Rainbow, keeper of the Laws of Worlds. The universe is a living thing, and you should act according to your nature and always listen to your heart, Sanya said.

Nastya started dreaming about the forest all the time. Even when she didn't see the trunks of spruces and pines in her dreams, she felt the forest's presence, watching her closely. Once, in a dream, Nastya saw her and Sanya's wedding in the woods: she was dressed in black, Sanya's eyes shone with an odd, peculiar light, and they were walking between enormously tall, gray trees. The birds and beasts all around were the guests at their wedding, along with other creatures of some kind, monsters, chimeras. Often that August Nastya and Sanya took walks, drank beer and wine, sat in the barn at Nastya's or at Sanya's, and both of those barns were fairly remarkable places. Getting into Sanya's barn required climbing a ladder; inside it always smelled like benzine, tobacco, and beer. Most of the space was taken up by a hay-stuffed fuckerator, as Sanya called it, talking about how, for instance, in the past he'd needed ten fucks a day, preferably with different people, and how he lost his virginity when he was eight years old, and about all of his endless girlfriends and lovers. His friends said that before, as soon as he spotted a virgin he'd approach her with the idea of taking her virginity by any possible means. Men weren't off the table for him, either: Nastya once found him making out passionately with some other guy. Neither did he care about age, and on the night they met Nastya was surprised by the tranquility with which he reacted to the fact that she was only thirteen, saying, "That's fine, I take them from ten to forty." As far as Nastya's barn went, inside it, standing stately over falling-apart bicycles and Grandpa's old tools, there was an enormous vanity looking glass from the nineteenth century, with dark carving on the frame and little drawers with gold-cased handles; ideal, according to Sanya, for scrying and journeys to other dimensions. Sanya began teaching Nastya magic, telling her that in the early stages their lessons would be held in dreams. Once, in Nastya's barn, Sanya asked for a candle, which he lit in front of the antique mirror with the carvings, casting a strange look into the glass and holding his palms to the candle flame. He began to raise his hands and the flame rose with them, rising almost to the ceiling, becoming a thin, glimmering ray. Nastya took note of this and started spending time sitting by the mirror with a candle, too. Once, after she had looked into the mirror for a very long while, her reflection began to change, sometimes fading and being replaced with nothing, and then Nastya saw Sanya, with the forest at his back. Sanya beckoned to her, and Nastya walked into the mirror, into the forest, and stayed there forever. The mirror had mirrored her, copied her. The real Nastya remained in the barn, at home at the dacha, while her copy was lost in the forest forever. Or maybe none of that had happened at all. This is the second dream Nastya's copy has about the possible past. Here, in the forest, she sometimes caught a glimpse of Sanya, but he acted like they didn't know each other. Maybe it wasn't Sanya but his beyond-the-looking-glass copy, or maybe for him she was always only a copy, the shadow of a girl he once loved. There's no way to know. Nastya's copy's second dream is followed by a third, fourth, fifth, sixth, seventh, and so on unto infinity, and each dream tells its own story about how she wound up in the forest. Sometimes Nastya's copy thinks that there's no explanation for it at all and that they're all nothing more than false, deceptive dreams brought on by the forest.

On this long, everlasting, blooming August day, the real Nastya is busy around the house. In the morning she has to feed her husband and her child, then go to the market to pick up the free-range chicken that the child loves, then simultaneously cook the chicken, steam the pumpkin, fry the pork, make a salad, wash the dishes, prepare the child's medicine, and answer emails on her iPad. She's thirty-two, she wears a black-and-white summer dress and a string of garnet beads. Nastya's mother has decided to spend the day weeding their entire plot. Grandma and Grandpa have been dead for several years. There's a new house now. Closer to evening, Nastya leaves the child with her husband and gets on her bike to ride around the village for a while. She gets as far as the resort, leaves the bike on the lakeshore, and sits down on the pier by the dock to look out at the water and relax a little. Right in the spot where Nastya's copy had been sitting just a little while ago. Nastya's copy has already left—she's wandering behind the Motor Bar, through a shallow swamp, over soft growths of horsetail and cold, muddy earth, watching the vacationers from afar, listening to the sounds of their voices—and she's almost still among them, living out the dregs of the day, but already drawing closer to the forest, and things feel darker in her heart, which is taking leave of her childhood and future, filling up with the forest that occupies all eternity. Fragments of her dreams remain on the pier, and the real Nastya hears them like a ghostly whisper from the forest of her own dreams. She begins thinking of these stories, the way that she remembers them. That is to say, differently.

When that gang of five tried to drag her into their car and take her to the lake, a guy she knew, Ivan, showed up out of nowhere, and another guy, Rickshaw, drove up to the market in his kopeika. Ivan whispered a few words to Rickshaw and then called the gang aside like he wanted to chat, but really it was so that Nastya could get into Rickshaw's car. As soon as the men went over to Ivan, turning away from Nastya, Rickshaw signaled to her, and she threw herself into the kopeika. The moment she was inside and shut the door, the leader noticed, swaggered up to the car, stuck his mug in the window and said to Rickshaw, "Hold on, old man." Rickshaw, meanwhile, was trying to start the engine, and—the horror!—it was not starting. One, two, three, four . . . A few torturous seconds and the engine finally rolled over. They drove. Along with Rickshaw there was another guy she knew in the car, Buggy. All three of them thought there would be a chase. But, fortunately, there was none. "That slut's going to come back here anyway," said the leader, and the men sat on the crates drinking and waiting for Nastya. As soon as it became clear that no one was chasing them, Rickshaw and Buggy started yelling at Nastya. "You slut, what were you doing? We could've all been killed because of you!" Nastya said she hadn't been doing anything, they just started bothering her, but the guys said, "People don't just start bothering you for no reason!" When they drove Nastya away from the market, her friend Nadya and a group of other kids arrived, Nastya's Sanya among them. Auntie Lyuba and Ivan immediately told them that Nastya had almost been raped. In the meantime, the gangsters were preparing to leave and getting into their Nissan. Nadya became incensed and kicked their car. The men hopped back out of the car and started shouting at her, "You cow, have you lost your damn mind?"

"You almost raped my friend," said Nadya.

"Who, that slut? OK, now you're fucked."

Nadya said something back, they threatened her, cursed, swore they'd take her to the lake and screw her, too. Then one of them, a little guy, went up to Nadya and hit her in the face so hard that her sunglasses flew into the bushes. But Nadya kept it together and kicked him so hard in the balls that he crouched. While this was happening, the kids who had come with Nadya were standing modestly off to the side—they had seen the gun in the car and decided not to get involved. And all of Sanya's magic was no help, either.

"We're going to take you to the lake instead of that slut," the men were telling Nadya.

"That slut? Do you even know how old she is?"

"How old?"

"Thirteen." The men were somewhat shocked.

"And how old are you?"

"I'm fourteen." They conferred among themselves and left.

Nastya remembers perfectly well the time that she saw Sanya in the mirror. She didn't go to him; she was terribly scared. Right after that she ran to his house, it was raining, her wet plastic raincoat slapped against her legs, Sanya was cold to her for some reason, and she left to walk around the village in the rain and pick early apples from other people's yards, then stopped to visit some girlfriends. After that came the fall, Nadya had to go to school, and it felt very sad to leave; from other people's yards came the sounds of pop songs about separation. Twice in September Nadya came for the weekend and saw Sanya, who because of his plumbing job had to stay in the village and deal with faucets until October, but Sanya somehow seemed as though he wasn't especially happy to see her. Nastya couldn't understand it: he would promise to stop by after dinner but then wouldn't come. She'd go to see him herself, and he'd play guitar and sing her depressing songs about guys who'd fallen out of love with their girlfriends and these miserable, deflowered, abandoned girlfriends. And once, one of those times when Nastya came to visit him in September, Ksyusha was in his barn—a very pretty girl who'd been a friend of Nastya's when they were children, until they had a falling out—and Sanya paid no attention to Nastya at all and only talked to Ksyusha. Nastya went back to the city until the spring, because Grandpa said it was getting cold and he was closing up the dacha, and Sanya promised he'd come in October and call her. In October Sanya did not appear, and when Nastya tried calling him, they told her he hadn't come yet. Leaves were coming down in the parks and courtyards, at night the streets began to fill with slush, and soon Nastya would turn fourteen, but Sanya still did not come. It turned out that he had another girlfriend, or rather two, both of them Nastya's closest friends, and he had long since been in the city and was dating these girls and hiding from Nastya. Apparently that entire summer he had been hitting on her friends, saying, "Give me your virginity, better me than if somebody rapes you later," and even then Nastya's friends had been kissing him behind Nastya's back; someone had seen him kissing Ksyusha then, too. Nadya called him, but he had asked his mother to always tell her that he wasn't home. But Nastya stubbornly kept on calling, and he finally picked up and said, "Forgive me, if you can." In the spring, Sanya and Nastya's group of friends dissolved, everyone broke up with each other and stopped hanging out. Then Sanya disappeared completely. People said that he had married twice and now works as a sales assistant in a hardware store. This is how Nastya remembers it, though who knows what really happened. Sometimes Nastya thinks that none of it happened at all, and that these are all false, deceptive dreams brought on by life.

Today is a beautiful August day. Hydrangeas bloom and smell sweetly in people's yards, and in the woods, on beds of pine needles in shady spots there are the red gleams of foxes. It's a time of berries and the slow approach of fall. In the morning there was a light, brief shower. It rained—and it stopped. It's a happy day. The happiest day of the year. It's a long day, and like all days of this kind, it ends with sunset, with fog over the lake, with a light chill that changes to a crisp night and August twilight. There are two stories about this day in the life of Nastya and Nastya's copy.

According to the first story, that evening Nastya came home to her family, while Nastya's copy returned to the forest, and they never met. Nastya's copy wandered in the forest for eternity, and Nastya never found out about her. But there's also a second story, which resembles a dream that they dreamed together. In the second story, Nastya's copy went into the Motor Bar before returning to the forest, and the real Nastya went into the bar, too, after sitting on the pier, reminiscing about her teenage days. Then, in the Motor Bar, Nastya's copy and the grown-up Nastya looked each other in the eye. They recognized one another. They told one another their stories and their dreams. They had a drink together, and Nastya told Nastya's copy about Grandpa's last words, about Grandma's death, about her own son growing up, about all the things that had happened to her over the past nineteen years, and Nastya's copy told Nastya about the eternal forest, about first love, which has no end, about how she had died in a hundred stories and dreams and found herself in the forest forever, while Nastya never even noticed. Something happened after this encounter. Nastya's copy disappeared. And the grown-up Nastya disappeared. Yet both of them went on living. They became one whole, forever, on that unforgettable August day, which has certainly already happened. Once, many times. As many times as the forest had come between them, with one of them trapped in it forever, while the other one didn't notice. Nastya *returned to the way she was*—her childhood was returned to her for good, her past and her future, the way they were before she wound up in the forest, but the forest stayed with her, too, and sometimes the few people who know *what a forest is* can see it, they see it somewhere at the very depths of her gaze. Nastya left the bar and took the forest path home, wearing Mama's old light-blue sweater from the nineties over her black-and-white dress—it was getting cold.

FAIRY IN THE ROAD

The dacha season was over: the village had fallen into abandonment, neglect. There were neither cars nor people on the highway. The market had petered out, too. On the ground lay heaps of fallen leaves, pine needles, rotten apples; white mushrooms and toadstools grew in the yards. Houses had to be heated each day, but it was still necessary to turn on additional heating panels. The sun was cool and gentle, the sky tired and clear, the gathered apples sweet; in the market square, dogs lounged among the crates, a whole pack; they lay there with their skinny sides in the sun like corpses. There was no one at the Little Borkovsky beach, and the children's toys that lay scattered over the sand in the summer had been picked up by someone and carried away. *I wonder*, thought Willy, taking a solitary beach stroll, *who brings them and who takes them away? Whose are they, and where do they spend the winter?* The black chokeberry growing by the roads was juicy and cold. A silence obtained, no wind blew, there were only the far-off sounds of construction—someone was building a house. They were also building a house on North Street, had dug a huge hole on the lot and piled all the dirt onto the playground where kids played in summer. The main street had been dug up at the intersection with Priozerskaya, and you couldn't pass there anymore. In the lane where Willy lived, all the houses but his were empty; one street over two old men were staying on. At night in the rain Willy saw two guys he knew drinking vodka beneath the overhang by the market stands. One night in the dark there were the sounds of shots and a woman screaming. The air smelled like stove smoke. Dark came earlier and earlier, and there were very few streetlights anywhere. Enormous acorns lay on the roads, the crowns of deciduous trees were touched with more and more yellow and red. They began shutting off the water, and soon it would be turned off completely.

One evening Willy was leaving the Motor Bar. He didn't drink at all, he'd quit many years ago, he just stopped in to have supper, relax, see other people, hear a human voice. But the only other person at the bar was the bartender, Lena. They chatted a bit, and when early dark descended upon the village, Willy headed home, walking along the highway. From the direction of the railroad tracks came the rumble of passing freighters; it was pitch-black out, but Willy, like a nocturnal animal, could see pretty well in the dark. He was humming the song of an old friend, long ago lost to drugs: "You and I are free to fly / I'll ask you and you'll reply / All that happened long ago / La-la-la-la-la-la." The song had another line: "Here in fall I lived and dreamed," and Willy thought that he, too, lived here in the fall and dreamed, worked for himself as an electrician, but there was less and less work to do, and he kept playing the stock market and waiting to make money, but in the meantime had credit drawn from several banks and was hiding from collectors. And his birthday was coming up. Forty-six. It felt like he'd lived a thousand lives in his time.

Willy was walking along the empty highway, whistling a song, when suddenly from the direction of Kalininskaya Street a half-naked woman ran out into the road, crying and screaming, "Help! Help! Those bitches left me! Help!" Willy stopped and let the woman approach him. She was barefoot and bare-legged; on top she wore a short shirt over her naked body, it barely covered her crotch, and Willy wondered with some interest whether she was wearing underwear. It was cold outside, in a little while the first frosts would hit, and Willy wore a thermal camouflage jacket but could still feel how cold and damp the air was. The woman's face was difficult to make out in the darkness, but it looked swollen, the way drinkers' faces can be, and her age was unclear—it could have been anything from twenty-five to forty-five. She smelled like alcohol, male sweat, and her own fear. Crying and cursing, she began begging Willy for help. It was hard to understand from her mixed-up story what had happened to her: she mentioned some "friends" who had brought her here and abandoned her, locked her in a house and left while she was sleeping—*sounds like she passed out drunk after they got done with her*, Willy thought— and when she came to, everyone was already gone, the house was locked, she climbed out through a broken window; she had no clothes, no money, no cell phone, and no idea where she was.

Willy looked up the train schedule on his Chinese smartphone with the amazing camera—that was why he bought it— and saw that there were no more city-bound trains until morning. "If you want, you can come with me," he offered. "You can spend the night and warm up, or you'll be a goner out here. In the morning I'll give you money and you can leave on the first train."

"Is it far to your place?"

"It's not close. But do you have other options?"

The woman and Willy walked along the road—they had to reach the bins, turn left into the alley, go as far as the sand mound, and there turn into the first lane.

"What's your name?" Willy asked when they were already walking.

"Daryana, what's yours?"

"You can call me Vlad. Or Will. Up to you."

Willy lived in one half of a big, old house; the other half was taken up by his mother and uncle. Disorder reigned in Willy's half, there were tools and all kinds of junk strewn around, and it was clear that no human hand had touched anything in there for a long time. All except for one room, specifically the room in which Willy lived. Everything in that room was clean, neat, freshly repaired, the walls newly paneled, the bed made, and by the window there was a desk with a new MacBook on it. Willy turned on the light and the heating panels and went over to his mother's half, to find his guest some old, long-unworn clothes of his mother's, since she had plenty of that kind of thing. He brought Daryana a sweater, wool tights, warm socks, and shoes, none of it in the best condition, but he didn't have much of a choice, and then he finally got a good look at her. She looked pretty worn, to be honest, but there was something appealing about her, maybe her slightly upturned nose or her large eyes, and her legs, as he noticed while she was putting on the tights, were also all right, a little flabby, but straight and long. He also noted as she put on the tights: no underwear. Willy made hot tea for himself and Daryana and asked her to tell him the story of the day's ordeal in more detail. If she didn't mind, of course. At first Daryana tried to say something vague about some friends and a party, but even she tired pretty quickly of calling those assholes friends and confessed that she had been working, had gone with her "friends" to fuck, and they had her and dumped her. It wasn't the first time something like that had happened to her, either. Willy asked if she needed to call somebody—maybe her family was looking for her—but Daryana said she had no family in the city, that she came from somewhere else, nobody was looking for her tonight.

"And who are you?" she asked Willy.

"Me? I'm a retired hit man." Daryana wasn't sure if he was joking or not. Willy laughed: "I'm a man hiding from several banks. A scammer. A simple guy. You're safe with me."

"What kind of goddamn village is this anyway? What an awful place!"

"By tomorrow you'll be one of the local legends," Willy grinned. "You're actually not the first strange woman I've met out here on the road at night. Many years ago, when I was selling vodka illegally, I was driving down the highway at night and I saw a naked young woman with her hair down ahead of me. She was directly in front of my car and watching me without moving, and I didn't have time to brake so I drove right through her. I was horrified, and stopped—but there was nobody on the road. A head trip? Maybe, but that's how it is around here."

There was only one bed, and Willy and Daryana, who was nodding off from exhaustion by then, went to sleep next to each other. Daryana fell asleep immediately and slept like a baby; in the morning Willy reached for her, and she didn't push him away.

Afterward Willy walked Daryana to the highway, gave her money for a ticket, and then she went on alone—to get to the station you had to walk straight without turning off anywhere. They hugged in farewell.

"Good luck to you, retired hit man! May your collectors never find you!"

"Take care of yourself, night fairy!"

She moved farther and farther away in his mother's funny wool tights and her old jacket, and increasingly it seemed to Willy that he had seen her somewhere before—on the highway at night when he was a young man in a cowboy hat, thought God knows what of himself, and transported vodka in the days of the anti-alcohol campaign. Specifically her naked body, flowing hair, and enormous eyes were what he'd seen that night on the road. Only she had been younger and more beautiful then. This morning, when they'd had brief and somewhat awkward sex, he recognized her. She really was a fairy. The night fairy. He thought that if things had gone another way, he could have fallen in love with her.

"Today I fucked a fairy," he said, walking into the Motor Bar that night, after he'd finished some electrical work he had been contracted to do and decided to have supper. This time it was Max working the bar, old Max who'd seen everything. He lifted an eyebrow: "A fairy? There's lots of those around here. Sometimes they come out of the forest, and then they go back in."

"She left on the morning train," said Willy.

"That's what you think," Max chuckled in response. "Don't forget that this bar is at the border of the forest, and in all the years I've worked here, if I've learned anything, it's about fairies. All fairies are prostitutes, I know that for sure. Maybe the opposite is also true: all prostitutes are fairies. They don't need anything from you except to sleep with you and take something from you, from here—" and Max motioned toward his chest. "So tell me, did your fairy take a piece of your heart?"

"Maybe . . ." though Willy himself didn't know the answer to that question. He walked home along the dark road, and it was like he wanted to see a woman's outline in the dark, a naked young woman with her hair down—the one, he thought, he had always loved. *I hope she doesn't get killed, living that kind of life*, he thought sadly about Daryana. "Here in fall I lived and dreamed / I gave half my life for that dream," went the song of his friend who'd been lost to drugs, and Willy thought that he, himself, was the person who had given half his life for a dream. And now there was nothing left for him except living here alone and dreaming. He didn't know anything better, this lonely man with a wolf tattooed on his shoulder. He knew that sometimes at night bats flew in circles above the lake, and foxes ran across the forest path. From the direction of the railroad tracks came the rumble of passing freighters, and Willy thought, *The trains don't go anywhere. There is no city. And there is no world outside. Only this place, and Daryana belongs to it, too. She's here.* And he smiled at the thought. A long fall lay ahead.

WASTED YOUTH PARTY

In the hostel of wasted youth

I spend my vacation

—Alfonso Maria Petrosino

They all received an invitation to the party. An anonymous invitation, sent via email from the strange address party@wastedyouth.ru. The message said: "Dear Mr./Ms. X, your youth has been wasted, and we'd like to invite you to celebrate the occasion at the ultra-mega-hype-party for wasted youth. Hooray! Your entry ticket is attached. Precisely at noon, by Vosstaniya Square, on the last Sunday in June, you will find a person holding a sign, and a bus."

As for how many people got this email—who the hell knows. Probably a lot. Maybe hundreds, maybe thousands, maybe millions. Twelve showed up. They had three things in common: none of them had spam filters in their inbox, they were all still fairly young, mostly around thirty, and they all had had something go terribly wrong in their youth. Just think: what would you do if you got an invitation like that, regardless of whether your youth had been wasted or not? Would you really get up off your ass and go somewhere? Right, exactly. So, in addition to the abovementioned similarities, these twelve people had something else in common, something that allowed them to accept the invitation, get up off the couch, and go to Vosstaniya Square. Maybe it was a kind of youthful openness they'd hung onto, or dumb opportunism and curiosity, or desperation, grasping at every straw, or perhaps it was naïveté, or stupidity, or courage, or they had just grown bored with everything else. In the end, the following people came: alcoholic Aleksey, addict Anton, mentally ill Nikita, mentally ill Anna, Dina who was tyrannized by her parents, Vika who was in love with a married man, Marta who took care of her alcoholic husband, Kirill the cop, Tatiana the former cult member, Evgeniy who was in the closet, lazy Platon, and poet Arseniy.

They were met by a man holding a sign, and a tour bus drove them to a resort called the Pines, to the Motor Bar, where tables had been set for them and an MC had prepared a special program. He was a regular MC, cute and not particularly bright, wearing a bowtie, sort of like the ones who do weddings and other events; his employers, who had chosen to remain anonymous, had hired him and sent detailed instructions by email as to what he ought to do and say, and paid him a good amount of money via bank transfer.

Getting off the bus after several hours on the road, the group found itself on a hill at the edge of the forest, in front of a small, cozy bar. They looked inside: the seating was made of motorcycle seats, and the décor featured race car motors, license plates, and racing photographs. The bartender offered them drinks, recommending a house cocktail called the Motor Oil, or some refreshing cider from Altai, or else they could order limited-edition bitter beer from a private brewery, or dry wine, whiskey, or rum.

The MC, who called himself Ivan, congratulated the partygoers on their wasted youth and immediately asked for their tickets. He said that the party would be held outside, in the nearby covered gazebo with a panoramic view of the pine forest, where the tables had already been laid with appetizers, and that the guests could later order shashlik, or juicy beef burgers, or even soups, or hot dogs, or whatever else they wanted—everything was paid for.

In the middle of the gazebo stood a microphone; the bow-tied MC hovered by it, wished the guests a pleasant meal, and then relayed that the only thing required of them was that they come to the microphone and talk about their lives and the specific way each of their youths had been wasted. After that they could drink, hang out, enjoy themselves, dance, and then there was even more entertainment planned for them, the party would last all night, and in the morning the bus would bring them back into the city, though if anyone wanted to sleep, there was a room reserved for each of them at the resort hotel.

The first to speak was alcoholic Aleksey. He stepped up and said, like at an Alcoholics Anonymous meeting, "My name is Aleksey, and I'm an alcoholic. I drink because my father drank. Or maybe that isn't the reason. Maybe I drink because of my arrogance, because I despise everything, or maybe it's because of love. I was born in a small town in Karelia, I went to Petersburg to study and started drinking, I dropped out and drank, I lived with a woman but then she threw me out, then I worked and didn't drink, then I drank again, had a procedure to stop drinking, worked, drank again, went to a special work camp for alcoholics—my mother sent me—ran away from there and drank, and today I'm going to get drunk, too, and when my mother dies, that's the end of me." Alcoholic Aleksey stood there, already a little buzzed and red in the face, but it was clear that once he had been haughty and beautiful. He said nothing about how he wanted to be a writer and had written enough stories for a whole book, but there was no one to read it, and not a single publisher had accepted it.

"I take all kinds of drugs," said Anton, "I'm almost always on something." Anton had shoulder-length hair, a little beard, a mean face, and skinny elbows. "I had a life before drugs," said Anton, "I worked in IT and I wrote music for myself, but that wasn't really a life. Drugs are life. I was afraid at first, but then I decided to go for it; I couldn't get high the first time, but the fourth time it worked. Other people got high earlier, I thought they were stoned assholes. And then I got it. I turned on. You love everything that you do. Bliss spreads through your entire body. It's indescribable. It was psychedelic. I saw Beauty, flowers. People get annoyed that other things in life, everything other than drugs, don't interest me anymore. But that's their problem. I came here looking for a high, too. I brought something with me," and Anton returned to his seat.

Mentally ill Nikita was very tall and bloated, likely from his medications, a man with the look of a four-eyed nerd. He stood by the microphone as though he were at an oral exam but couldn't remember the question and was having difficulty stringing words together. "I . . . uh . . . was studying the philosophy of mathematics, writing my dissertation." Here he grew silent and obviously forgot what he was saying. "You were writing your dissertation," the MC offered helpfully. "Electroshock therapy, I can't get back to the diss . . . I want to be an academic, but I work in the coat check at the theater, my mother found me the job. I'm going to go back to my studies, I'm doing better already."

Anna's hair was cut short, a buzz cut, and she looked like a pretty bird with huge red-brown eyes, dressed in an enormous, oversize smock. "Recently I read about a twenty-nine-year-old woman from Holland who got permission to be euthanized because of her mental disorder. I can't get this story out of my head," Anna began. "I keep wondering, would I want to be euthanized if I had the option? I guess not, though I'm not opposed to dying. After death I'll be grass and stone, forest and swamp, soil and moss. I'll be with the earth and the water. I'll be part of the Spring. One summer at the dacha, when I was four years old, I lost my mind. I looked at the curtains and the ceiling and I saw strange images. There was a green ballerina dancing on one leg, and animals of some kind following her. Then I became terrified that my mother had died. She slept in the bed next to mine, and I started waking her every second and asking her if she was alive. When I was a university student, I went to see a psychiatrist because I wasn't feeling well, I always had a sense of 'nausea and fog' in my head, my symptoms were that most of the time I couldn't do anything and it was really hard for me to go to class. There were times when I was so exhausted by showering in the morning that I spent the rest of the day lying down without moving. I felt worse during the colder times of year than during warmer times. I would usually sleep for a long while, go to bed by morning and wake up around evening. They tried to expel me from the university for absences. When I was sixteen I tried to kill myself. I took a huge overdose of medication, lay for several days in something like a coma, then woke up. Then there was another time I took a huge dose of drugs, though it was a lot less than the first time. I ran naked around the courtyard, wrapped in a towel—I wanted to run away from home. When I was a teenager I'd cut my arms given the slightest pretext.

In the summer after I graduated from university, after a totally trivial incident in my love life cast a shadow on my relationship with a person I loved, I gradually fell into a state that was completely incompatible with living. I was sick for over half a year, I thought I was decomposing from AIDS while still alive, I couldn't move my arms and legs, they would go numb and have these strange stabbing sensations, pins and needles, and I had strange, frightening sensations in my head and body, cenesthopathy, sores formed on my skin, I got neuritis in my eye, the muscles in my legs hurt so badly I wanted to scream, I had a constant fever that wouldn't even go down with Aminazin. I was prescribed one kind of medication, then another. They made everything blurry, gave me akathisia, I lost my appetite and all interest in living; I remember the period spent finding the right prescription as the hardest, worst time. By the end of it I was in a state that resembled a panic attack in every way, and was completely unbearable, except that it differed from a panic attack in that it just wouldn't end. You could maybe call it extremely intense general anxiety, but it would be more accurate to refer to it as 'all the torments of hell experienced in life.' It was a state of incurable biological breakdown, you just can't live like that. If they hadn't gotten me out of it with drugs, I would be dead. After half a year and change they found a medication that brought me back to life, and they told me I would probably have to take it forever. It's been ten years now that I've been on neuroleptics and antidepressants. Really, I have no complaints. It's all fine, not like it is for healthy people, but fine. So no euthanasia. Bye."

Dina who was tyrannized by her parents was a black-browed beauty who dreamed of a reciprocal love and a family of her own, but that hadn't worked out so far because she always had to be with her mama and papa, and they didn't like any of her suitors.

"They're not worthy of me, they say that about all of them." Dina was nearly in tears. "There was one guy I really liked, I had such a good time with him, we laughed, it felt like he was family or something. We were out together all day, we had ice cream, and then at night Mama started calling my phone every ten minutes, and I can't not pick up or she'll have a heart attack. When we got to my building, she was outside by the door, hands on her hips, all pale and in her nightgown, and she started screaming at me like I'm a little kid, she didn't even let me say goodbye to the guy properly. He didn't call me after that. And I've never liked anyone else the way I liked him. I keep thinking, what if he was the one?"

"I don't know why I got this invitation," said Vika, a young woman with the face of some exotic fish: bow lips, large, slightly protuberant eyes with deep blue shadows underneath, and bright makeup. "I'm doing just fine, and I'm still young. I mean, I'm thirty-three, but I feel completely young, you can be young until you're sixty these days, or even after, my mother is young, too. It's true that my friends think I'm completely screwed, but I don't think so. I've just been waiting. For eleven years. I fell in love with him then, and he promised to get a divorce. But his wife isn't well, he can't just leave her, she's sick all the time; he's waiting for her to get better and then he'll leave, and in all this time she's had two kids with him while I'm still waiting, and I've never been with anyone else, I want kids, too."

Marta looked deeply exhausted and worn out. Once she had been a student in the university's history department, but now she was a cashier at a store and used her tiny salary to support her alcoholic husband, an ex-actor, who was always quitting drinking and starting up again, getting help and going through withdrawal, all while Marta took care of him, bailed him out of trouble, called all the hospitals and morgues at night, spent all her money and all her free time on him and tried to save him, leading him by the hand to visit doctors and psychologists. The husband had by now suffered irreversible alterations in mental status and never called Marta anything but "bitch" and "hag," sometimes he beat her, and she was deathly tired of him, but she didn't know how to live any other way. "I can't just leave him," she said, "he'll die without me. And I do love him, after all. I'm going to have his kid."

"I work for the police," said Kirill, who had an athletic build, a short haircut, and expressionless eyes that looked nowhere. "And I think I have professional burnout. It's like something wrong is going on, but I don't really know what it is. I wanted to help people, to fight crime, I wanted to be good, you know, but all the time now there's something wrong happening, everything around me is wrong, but anyway, I don't know what it is. For example, all right, I get an assignment: find some people who deal drugs, we need to make a report, so my partner and I start stopping people, young people; we stop them, we take them to the station basement and we question them, we questioned them really hard, they told us to do that, we read through their phones and tablets, we threatened them, we stripped them, but we didn't plant anything on them; anyway, it was really tough for me at first to hit people, I wanted to be good, and now I don't want anything at all, now I'm a robot, but really I'm just a normal guy, I watch *Game of Thrones*."

Tatiana was a sturdy, stocky woman with the severe mien of a Motherland monument, apparently a little older than the rest of the people there. "There is no God," she began. She paused, looked around at everyone. "There is no God, but I looked for him all through my youth. I joined different sects and cults, the Baptists, the Neo-Charismatic-Pentecostalists, the Jehovah's Witnesses; I sold my apartment, I traveled around, I felt God, I prayed, and I felt joy when my brothers and sisters joined hands and prayed in the forest, and I had mystic visions, I had all of that. I started going around the cults when I was thirteen. The country was wrecked, people were degenerating, there had to be something to counter all of that. There were only lies everywhere. I could have killed people. I thought about becoming a killer, but instead I joined a cult. We wanted to save the whole world; we spoke to God. I saw God in my heart as clearly as I see all of you now in this gazebo. And then I got up one morning and I knew: there is no God. Nothing precipitated it, it just suddenly became obvious to me. I understood why people join these cults. For psychological reasons. But my psychology had died, all the psychological reasons no longer mattered. I saw why I needed God, and then I didn't need him anymore. I had needed him because I wanted to be part of a community, a family, I wanted some alternative, and also because I was afraid that there would be nothing after death, and I wanted there to be someone above all these criminals who rule us, someone who was the most important, more powerful and greater than all of them, who'd put them all in their place, and I wanted there to be a book that held all the answers, so you could live accordingly and not suffer. And suddenly I didn't need any of that. So I asked myself: do I want God for himself, without the rest of it? And I understood that the rest of it was what I'd needed, that God himself was neither here nor here. What are you supposed to do with him, with God? And so, if I don't need him, it means he doesn't exist."

Brawny, extremely muscular Evgeniy went up and said, in a moderately quiet voice, that he had been hiding his homosexuality his entire life, and so it was like he'd been living someone else's life, not his own, and he was miserable. For a long time he couldn't even admit it to himself, and his parents were very strict, old-school people, they wouldn't have survived it. Now they were no longer living, but Evgeniy was married, he had children, his friends thought he was a macho womanizer. In secret from his wife and children he met other men in hidden corners and spots, in general he led a double life. "And it will probably go on like this forever," Evgeniy concluded.

"I haven't achieved anything," said red-cheeked, chubby Platon, "because I'm lazy. A weak-willed person. Not much else to say about it. Lie by the hearth, eat all your worth. My mother supports me. I'm afraid of life."

Curly-haired Arseniy, wearing a blazer torn at the shoulder, took the mic and said, in a deep, low voice, "I'm a poet. This tells you everything. Like Marina Tsvetaeva said, the poet inevitably fails on all other paths toward self-realization. I have failed. But I'm a poet. And a poet in Russia is more than a poet."

When all the attendees had given their short speeches, each of which was followed by applause initiated by the MC, the MC said, "Attention, please! Hip-hip-hooray! For coming here and for your honesty, you've all been awarded a second chance! It's a gift from an unknown benefactor. Take it and enjoy! Let the dead bury the dead! You can begin your lives with a clean slate, and may all your dreams come true!"

"A second chance? I don't need any second chance," Anton raged immediately. "Is that so I can stop doing drugs and go back to so-called normal life? No, no thank you. I've tried your normal life. I'm better off with the drugs."

"I don't need a second chance, either," Vika agreed. "If I start my life over again, the man I love will never marry me, and I have to wait for him."

"And I can't leave my husband, so what do I need a second chance for," Marta said tiredly.

Poet Arseniy said, "Your proposition is absurd. I'm a great poet, and there isn't and cannot be anything better than that."

"Second chances don't exist," said Tatiana. "I don't need one, therefore it doesn't exist."

Aleksey said, "I've had a shit-ton of second chances, I screwed up each one, and I'll fuck this one up, too. You're really getting on my case with these second chances, just let a man live without hope in peace."

Black-browed Dina thought it over, and then said, a bit guiltily, "I'm so sorry, but I think my mama and papa wouldn't like it if I took the second chance."

Mentally ill Nikita mumbled, "Uh . . . uh . . . no, thank you, I don't need it, I'm doing better already, or why else would I have had shock therapy all those times, it couldn't have been for nothing. I'm scared to change things, it's all going to work out for me anyway . . . uh . . . soon . . . I'm going to be an important scholar . . ."

Lazy Platon was in solidarity with Nikita. "Right, exactly, I'm also afraid of change. I don't want to stress. It wouldn't work out in any case. We're all going to die anyway."

Anna thought for a long time and then also declined, saying, "It's my life, it may be hard, but I've learned to live with my illness, and in many ways it's thanks to the illness that I am who I am. And I'm suspicious of anonymous benefactors. But I'm still happy to be here. I saw a sign in the bar that they're looking for a girl to bartend and live at the resort, the pay is decent. I'm actually looking for a job outside of the city, in the fresh air, one that comes with a place to live. I'll try my luck. Maybe that'll be my second chance. I think you always have one anyway, until you're in your death throes, and no one has to specifically give it to you. You have chances for as long as you're alive. Another day is another chance. That's how I live, and I don't mourn what's lost and can't be brought back again. So I'll manage on my own somehow."

Evgeniy got angry: "What does that mean, a second chance? A chance to not be gay? To be gay and not hide it? I'm telling you, I have a wife, kids, a reputation, I'm bound hand and foot."

Kirill, looking at everyone present with his expressionless eyes, said in a way that was somehow both indifferent and pitiful at once, "I don't need anything from anybody. Everything is wrong somehow. I don't really get what's going on at all."

The bartender, old Max, was passing by; he heard the guests' responses and smirked into his beard. "All the same as last year," he winked at the MC, "same as always."

"Of course, you're free to decline your second chance," the MC said to the guests, "it's voluntary. Please help yourself to the food and drinks, go ahead and mingle, soon there's going to be dancing."

After that there was a regular party. Everyone ate, drank, mingled. Alcoholic Aleksey rolled up to Marta and proposed that she exchange her alcoholic husband for him, she'd keep doing all the same things, but he would treat her better. Anna went to scope out the resort and to chat with the management about a possible job. Anton took out a substance that had to be ingested through a dropper, dropped it into his own nose, and offered some to Dina, whom he liked, but she kept fending him off, saying that her mama and papa wouldn't approve. Nikita went looking for Anna, to compare their experiences of overcoming mental illness. Poet Arseniy asked Vika, who had waited for a married man for many years, whether she would be his muse. Letting loose among people he didn't know, Evgeniy flexed his muscles and hinted to Platon at a possible hookup in the bushes, while Platon lazily and warily resisted his advances. Kirill drank alone, gazing nowhere, and Tatiana left to pray in the forest; although she no longer believed in God, from old habit she liked to pray in the woods—it was relaxing and good for your health, God had nothing to do with it. In order for it not to look like she was praying to the God she didn't believe in, she found an old stump in the forest and prayed to that.

A NEW YEAR'S WITHOUT
MAMA: FIVE LETTERS

On December 30, Alexander and his nine-year-old son took a double room at a countryside resort called the Pines. Their plan was to celebrate New Year's there the following day and to stay at the Pines until January 2. This pleasure didn't come cheap, but Alexander simply didn't know how to celebrate New Year's alone with his son, and he was afraid that at home they'd be bored and sad: this would be their first New Year's without Anna, Timofey's mother. Seven months ago she had left them to start another family. Anna called Timofey once a week and asked how he was doing, and once a month she came to visit him, bearing gifts and a guilty expression; she was already pregnant by her new husband. She couldn't take Timofey to live with her; there was no room, she and the new husband lived together in a small studio apartment, and Timofey wouldn't have gone anyway. So Alexander thought that he had to entertain his son at New Year's somehow, and at the Pines there would be a banquet with a holiday program, contests, prizes, dancing. The Pines were next to a forest and a lake, far from the city, and for Alexander there would be a banya, billiards, and the Motor Bar, where you could sit and have a drink in the evening. And they could cross-country ski in the forest, both he and Timofey liked that.

Father and son took an unhurried stroll over the grounds; there was so much snow that even the cars in the parking lot and the wooden security booth at the entrance were nearly buried in it. A Victorian streetlight on a wooden pole protruded from a snowbank. The Lakeside Restaurant glowed with orange and gold lights, and through the glass wall you could see neat little tables. The blindingly white beach flowed uninterruptedly into the enormous, snowy lake. On the playground, which had been cleared of snow, some kids played on the swings and the merry-go-round with happy shouts. Nearby, behind a fence draped with artificial ivy, there was the unexpected residence of the honorary consul of Nepal. On the hammered-metal gates there were pictures of huts, geese and swans, a mill, trees, a peasant and an ox, and the sun. Timofey grinned, examining their surroundings, while Alexander thought about how to answer the letter.

In the evening, after supper, Timofey went to their room to play computer games, while Alexander headed to the Motor Bar to throw back a glass or two and finally write a response. The letter was from Timofey to Father Frost. Timofey wrote Father Frost a letter every year, detailing what he'd accomplished that year and what he wanted; he dropped it into the mailbox, and his parents fished it out and bought him the presents he'd asked for. This year, Timofey had written a strange letter.

Hi Father Frost. I know you dont exist. Im very disapointed.
You lied to me for so many years, pretending you were reel
when your not. I dont want any thing from you any more.

This year school was boring and life was sad. If Mama came home, I would be a good student again, but I know you cant make that happen. A preest came to our school and told us every thing. Now I know there is no Father Frost, but there is God. So I understand that you dont exist as Father Frost but you do exist as God. Your called YHWH, Jehovah, and Sabaoth. Grown ups dont beleive in Father Frost, but they beleive in God. But you cant do any thing any way, because Grandma died and Mama left. And even if you could, I dont care any more. Im just writing you this letter so you know that I dont want any thing from you and now I know who you reelly are.

Alexander approached the Motor Bar, tucked away on a snowy hill at the very edge of the forest. Parked by the bar was a beat-up black Jeep plastered with stickers, and on the roof of the building an old kopeika could vaguely be seen through the snow. Inside, Alexander immediately noted the "Run Forest Run" graffiti in the bathroom, the many stickers on the walls, the holiday lighting. There was a TV in the corner, and on the wall, among car photos and license plates, hung a red banner with a picture of a tiger. Alexander sat down at a little round table next to a stove with a very long pipe and a small firebox, diagonal from the door. He ordered a strong beer, began to write a reply, and downed a few more mugs of beer as he worked, since he was, to put it mildly, not a very gifted writer. His reply turned out as follows.

Hello, Timofey! You're right, there is no Father Frost. And I'm glad you're grown up enough now to understand that. All these years, I, the nonexistent Father Frost, have celebrated your accomplishments and believed in you, and I'll always believe in you. As for God, YHWH, Sabaoth, or whoever—don't listen to priests, you can decide for yourself whether there's a God or not when you're older. I'm very sorry that Grandma died and Mama left. You're right that I can't bring them back. I would really like to, too, but I can't. Please don't be sad and work hard in school. Everything in your life will certainly turn out well. And I'll always help you. Fight on and never surrender! I'm proud of you. Happy New Year!

Here he was supposed to sign, but Alexander couldn't figure out how to sign such a letter—as Father Frost, as God, or maybe as someone else entirely?—and in the end he didn't sign at all.

In the process of writing he had gotten fairly drunk, so he decided to continue this epistolary exercise and try writing a letter to God himself. He took up the next sheet of paper and began.

Hello, God. I know you don't exist. I'm very disappointed.

It was unclear what should come next. Alexander sensed that he didn't have anything to discuss with God, there was no point. He wanted to write to someone close to him, his kin, a loved one, someone who would understand him, to whom he could pour out his soul, someone he could talk to about everything. That was definitely not God. There was only one person like that—his dearly departed mother. Alexander crumpled up his letter to God and threw it in the trash and, sipping his beer, began a letter to his dead mother.

Mama! Mamochka! I miss you so much—if only you knew. I feel like a child, I need you so badly. Anya left, that bitch, she left me. Timofey keeps to himself now. I'm alone. I'm not doing well. I'm scared. I feel like crying, and I want you to come. I'm so sorry I neglected you. Forgive me for everything, for leaving you, for paying you so little attention. It scares me to think that you're dead and underground. Get out of there, Mama, wake up from being dead and come out! It's your son calling you. Under the snow, at the cemetery, let your heart beat again! Arise! I order you to rise! I can smell the oat por- ridge from your chest.

By now Alexander was extremely drunk, and he knew that he had to send the letter to his mother right away. "Where do you get in touch with the dead around here?" he asked the bartender, bearded Max.

"Best place is the forest," said Max, and winked. "That's our best spot for getting in touch with dead people."

"And how am I supposed to send a letter to someone who's dead?"

"You should bury it in the snow," Max said.

"Then it will definitely get there?"

"It certainly will," Max reassured him, "you just have to bury it real deep."

So Alexander went off into the woods.

He went down the hill, put on a headlamp brought along specifically for evening walks, passed beyond the red-and-white road barrier, and found himself in the forest. At first there was a cleared path, but then the path split into two in the snow; he turned onto one of the two new paths, and this path soon also split into two barely visible tracks; then finally Alexander was walking along no path at all, and by a very thick pine he buried his letter. His hands nearly froze while he dug; then he pissed in the snow, sat down beneath the pine and cried—for the first time in many years. And then he sobered up a bit and realized that he didn't know how to get back. He had intended to follow his own tracks, but the tracks had disappeared somewhere, the snow lay flat and undisturbed around the pine beneath which he stood. There were no tracks, and that was that. A strange light began to glow in the sky. Alexander became afraid. It suddenly occurred to him that drunken stupidity had led him into the forest at night, and that there was something wrong in this forest, there was something weird going on. Meanwhile, Timofey had probably gone to bed alone in their room, and he had no idea that his father was going to freeze here, or . . . Or what? Obviously nothing good was going to happen to him. Even the light was somehow hostile, and he no longer needed the headlamp. It must still have been night, but the forest had gone white. Not just the snow, but the tree trunks, and everything else around. Alexander sensed that he was somewhere he shouldn't have been, a place it would've been better not to go, but there he was, and now a white fox ran past—a polar fox, was it? There was a rustling up in the tree, and snow fell from a branch. Alexander looked up and saw a strange white bird. And what's more: it was like the forest had begun to move, he'd look at a tree and find that it wasn't in the place it had been a moment ago, like the entire forest was burning in a wandering white fire, inside an icy flame, and there, inside, it altered as the flame altered. And in the sky there was that strange light, and its rays dove down like wild ducks from above, and even the down jacket Alexander was wearing had turned from black to white.

And his boots, too, and his pants. Someone behind the branches was watching him. Nearby stood a bare old tree, no snow on it at all. It was smirking. Then suddenly its trunk came undone like the zipper of a jacket, as though it were inviting him to come in. From inside the dark opening in the snow-white bark came a horrible screech. Obviously someone was being noisily devoured in there. Music sounded from under the earth. Suddenly a huge, well-fed swan walked up to Alexander. Trumpets played in the bird's throat. The swan said something, Alexander knew that the swan had said something to him, it wasn't clear what it was, but probably "Welcome," Alexander decided it must have been "Welcome." Goddamn, why were there swans in here? Alexander broke into a run, not knowing where he was going in this shifting forest that changed with every second. Huge white flowers grew on the pines. The wolf's mother howled. Alexander somehow knew that it was the wolf's mother. He saw dancing monsters, boars with insolent, nearly human faces; he saw eyes without pupils, heard downed trees crying, heard stones screaming as they bled. A long-haired shield flew across the sky. In a forest meadow Alexander saw a female deer with her fawns; they had stopped stock-still in the moonlight and were listening attentively to someone's creeping footsteps—the tread of someone neither dead nor living.

Then, suddenly, from a place beyond the branches, Alexander heard a familiar childish voice. "Papa!"

"Timofey!" Papa darted toward the sound. Dear God, Timofey had gone looking for him and also ended up in here! Timofey was standing some distance away. "Papa, follow me, I know the way," and he was off. Alexander bolted after him. A shaggy figure astride a moose passed him, and in the snowfall a wolf's muzzle took shape and faded away again. Creatures with long, streaming bodies and round, burning eyes chased after them. Arboreal eyes gazed from the tree trunks, and in the darkness of the sky gigantic, round, rotating planets shone. Lower than low, by the very tops of the pines, a comet passed, and it had a tail like a magpie's tail. Heads with snowy hair protruded from the tree stumps and stared furiously after them. Chunks of ice started falling from above. Timofey dodged them nimbly, while Alexander barely avoided them and ran on, trying not to lose sight of Timofey. He ran, still drunk, and shouted to Timofey through the snow and the wind, ducking the ice: "Son, forgive me, son! You're right, there is no Father Frost, and no God! There's nobody! The priests are lying, the president lies, everybody lies! There's just these things in the forest, with the burning eyes! There's just the goddamn swan! That's all there is! There's the wolf's mother! There are eyes in trees, heads on stumps! That's what's real, that's the truth! Forgive me! Mama left because of me, because I drank so much! I won't do it anymore! Forgive me, son, it's my fault! Your mother left, your grandmother died! There's no one left! Just the swan! Just you and me, there for each other! We won't surrender! They won't catch us! We won't surrender, son! We'll get them! The fucking swan! They won't take us without a fight! Remember, son, Russians never surrender! You're everything to me! I always believed in you and I always will! Study hard, cheer up! You'll be all right! Fight on and never surrender! I love you! Forgive me!" Then they ran out of the woods and found themselves by the resort.

The strange light in the sky disappeared, and things looked pretty normal, but a savage, knock-you-off-your feet blizzard had started up. Alexander and Timofey walked side by side, almost without seeing each other, silently making their way through the storm. They passed the empty playground and the restaurant, the banya and the gazebo, and arrived at the hotel. His hand barely obeying, Alexander felt in his pocket for his key and unlocked the door. He turned to let his son go ahead of him, but Timofey wasn't there any longer. Something flashed oddly in the sky, as if one of those rays of light was taking a final, farewell dive right next to him, into the neighboring snowbank, and something glinted there, like a patch of particularly white snow, snow shimmering with its own whiteness.

Alexander came closer and saw a tree ornament of mysterious provenance—maybe someone had dropped it there. But how familiar this ornament seemed! It was a dove, an all-white dove, as though sugar-spun, nearly indistinguishable from the snow, and in its beak it held an equally white envelope. It was identical to one of his mother's favorite ornaments, he remembered it from childhood. Mama had really loved New Year's and trimming the tree; she always did it herself, she had a box of antique ornaments left to her by her own parents. And in that box there had been an identical carrier dove. Slowly, with pleasure, she would open the box and take out the ornaments one by one, lifting them from the old, yellowed cotton, and she'd hang them on the tree, carefully selecting each spot, and at the very end she would hang some of her favorites, including the carrier dove. She did this all her life, and when Alexander didn't live with her anymore, that ill-fated year when he and Anna and Timofey had come to visit her for Christmas, and he and Anna got into an argument in front of his mother and their son over the fact that he had once again had too much to drink, Alexander had stood up angrily, abruptly, to go smoke on the balcony and bumped into the tree in such an unfortunate way that the dove fell and shattered. Mama hadn't said anything, hadn't blamed him, and it was only a few years later, when she wasn't thinking clearly anymore, that she kept looking for the dove before New Year's, unable to understand why it wasn't in the box and complaining to Alexander that she couldn't find it. And that had been her last New Year's. Now an identical dove, a whole one, lay in the snow. Alexander picked it up with care and went into his room.

Timofey was sleeping in his bed; he had fallen asleep waiting for his father to come back. Alexander sat down on the couch. He undressed, shook off the snow. The letter to his son fell out of his pocket—the letter that had a recipient but no sender. Alexander reread the letter carefully and signed at the bottom—"Papa"—after which he slipped it neatly under Timofey's pillow. Then he took out the present he had hidden away, a Canon camera, and put it on the nightstand by his son's bed.

III.

IVAN THE BOAR'S KNEE

LORD OF THE HURRICANE

We don't know what goes on in the apartment upstairs. We've never known. How could we? There's a ceiling between us—I mean a floor—I mean a ceiling—well, you know what I mean.

As a matter of fact, I don't want to know. It's like they say, the more you know, the older you grow. I think that an old man lives up there. All of us think so.

An old fart, totally out of his mind. He's always lived there, probably even before the building was built. At least, when we moved in fifteen years ago, he was already there. According to indirect evidence. There's no other kind of evidence for this guy. Just indirect.

We haven't seen the old man. We've never seen him. Or maybe we've seen him somewhere by the front door or in the courtyard, and we just didn't know that it was *the old man*.

It's the music. The indirect evidence of his existence has always been music. How would you like to be someone about whom people say, *wherever you are, there's always music*? It's easy enough to say you would, but an intelligent person might say that it depends on the music. Because anything could happen, like for example wherever you go they could play Philipp Kirkorov. If that were the case, I would definitely not want to be anywhere you are, but somewhere else, maybe even just somewhere where they're playing, like, Mozart or the Rolling Stones. But honestly, hearing the same music all the time, beautiful as it may be, gets old. It starts to bug you. Even Mozart. And here, for fifteen years, we've had Soviet songs. I generally like them, Soviet songs, particularly ones from kids' movies, but only if I happen to turn them on myself, if I'm in the right high-minded mood; I'll lie down on the couch, cry my crocodile tears, and think: *What a country we fucked up, what an anthropological project we ruined, what a childhood is lost now, lost forever.* The upstairs neighbor is apparently always in this mood, and from the room above us, for years, we've heard Soviet songs at maximum volume, the same compilation: "The Door Creaks as in a Tale," "Maryusya Silent and Weeping," "Forest Deer," "Bear Song," and so on. The soundproofing here is poor, and you can hear the music like it's playing in your own apartment. He's been listening to these songs practically every day for the last fifteen years.

We've long since made our peace with it. What hasn't happened to us over the years, to the tune of these songs? We all lost our minds a little bit, lives were ruined, families fell apart and came together, the older generation drowned in the bathtub, boiled to death in hot water. On the worst days I've thought that there isn't even anyone there above us, just a psy-ops machine slowly destroying us, playing Soviet songs as it goes along. An enormous, mysterious machine with all kinds of buttons and lights, emitting a destructive psycho-field. Maybe the old man is the machine's operator. I shared this idea with my family, and at a family meeting it was decided that we would make little tin-foil hats and wear them, just in case. Not that we're serious, it's really just in case, we definitely don't believe in that stuff, but there's so much harmful radiation around anyway, a little tinfoil hat can't hurt. These days you should probably wear a tinfoil hat even if you don't have the kind of neighbor we have, and we do have that kind of neighbor, so I think you can't blame us too much for wanting to protect ourselves, somehow.

Recently the neighbor made himself known. Twice. Showed a new side of himself, so to speak. Produced some new indirect evidence.

Two days ago the baby was crying, and the neighbor started banging furiously. For fifteen years we've been listening to his music and saying nothing, but the moment a baby starts crying in our apartment, the neighbor starts banging furiously on the ceil-ing—I mean the floor—I mean the ceiling—well, you know what I mean. Probably he was banging with his old man's cane. I could feel all his outrage and indignation in this really very expressive knocking.

And then, yesterday afternoon, something really strange happened: instead of Soviet songs, from above us came the sounds of a hurricane, a noise of unknown origin, howling wind, a racket of trees being pulled up with their roots, a roar. You could hear it all very clearly and it went on for several hours. We all gathered in a room and listened. "It's not like he's got a hurricane up there," we said, "there can't be a storm in his apartment," "that surely isn't a whirlwind wreaking havoc," "it's certainly not a tornado . . ." These were precisely the sounds of a hur-ricane, a storm, a whirlwind, and a tornado. In the evening we found out that during that time there had in fact been a tornado in Moscow, and that people had died.

The apartment is empty. There is no furniture. There are no people. And inside are the sounds of a thunderstorm, a gathering roar, the ringing of glass shattered by the wind, the creaking of tree trunks, the rustling of their leaves, the smell of bird cherry quivering in the gale, the cries of people dying, a clangor of cars whipped up into the air.

And maybe there's a single old man, older than old, sitting on the floor in the center of the room, cross-legged. There's wind in his eyes. Wind in place of his face. Wind blows from the fingers of his upraised hands. Hints of blooming lilac, lead-gray streaks of sky.

We don't know what goes on in the apartment upstairs. We've never known. We walk around our apartment in little tin-foil hats. There's a tornado in Moscow. Our neighbor is a bastard.

TREASURES IN HEAVEN: A TALE OF GOD AND THE BILLIONAIRE

All the world's billionaires know: sometimes God drops by and asks for a loan. God is poor, man is rich; God is reckless, man is reasonable; God spends, man sighs but gives. Who says that God isn't just a guy in the sky? There's that guy in the sky and everything else is the devil's work. Once upon a time there was, and so on and so forth, over land over sea, God came to ask for money from our billionaire. He needed money because he'd lost everything to the devil again, though there's no sin in that—worldly money is fine to lose, though not to win, there's something not quite decent about that. It went the usual way: God came by, asked for money, saying, you know, I'll pay you back later.

The billionaire replied, "You don't have to pay me back, I know you're broke, but I heard a rumor that money isn't worth anything in heaven. So repay the loan with whatever they treasure in heaven." This billionaire is basically swimming in money, but it doesn't spark joy.

God said to him, "Maybe you'd like something that you lack? Palaces, yachts, lovers?"

The billionaire said, "No, I have everything, I'm sick of it all. Just repay the loan with whatever they treasure in heaven."

"All right," God said, "I have a couple of things for you, they don't cost much, but you'll like them. You'll see them soon and think of me. In the meantime, pass along the cash."

The billionaire gave God the money, and then his wife berated him at length for helping that penniless rascal God; if it were up to her she wouldn't let God on her doorstep. For three days she bawled him out, but he didn't mind, he was used to it, and they went on living.

A tale is told but a deed is done, and the billionaire met a bum. The bum was wearing the same torn jacket that the billionaire had worn when he was still poor. He got the jacket when he was twelve years old, a gift from an American, Bob, who bought it from a Native American. It was a cowboy jacket with a fringe. The jacket went through thick and thin with the billionaire when he was poor, it was with him through fire, flood, and fortune. The jacket saved him and preserved him. He wore it all through his youth, slept with it under his head in attics and in cellars when he had nowhere else to sleep, hitchhiked in that jacket when he was a young hippie, rode a motorcycle in that jacket, hid in that jacket from the cops. The jacket got older, frayed, but the billionaire refused to trade it in for a new one. The jacket was a symbol of his youth and his freedom, and a memento of those things. The billionaire's elderly mother, when she was still alive, patched the jacket up. Then the billionaire became a billionaire, he got married, and the jacket displeased his wife. He started wearing it less frequently, just on special occasions, and then came a time when he looked for it and couldn't find it. His wife had thrown it away in secret, and when he asked her why she had done it, she said, "It was so shabby." Now the billionaire saw a bum in that very jacket, he'd found it at the dump and was wearing it around. The billionaire's heart brightened, he remembered what God had said, approached the bum, and got the jacket from him in exchange for a new apartment, expensive clothes, and a monthly pension.

A song is sung but a wagon is wheeled. First one thing, then another. Our billionaire was a pretty decent person and donated to orphanages, funding purchases of clothes, toys, and medical care for sick kids. One day he paid a charitable visit to an orphanage and there he saw his kitty-bear. The kitty-bear was a round, stuffed, sunlight-yellow half-cat, half-bear. It had been his favorite childhood toy, and he recognized all of its particulars: a spot of iodine he'd spilled on the tip of the kitty-bear's tail; its torn left ear. When the billionaire was a child, he was the son of a poor man and owned very few toys, and his favorite toy was the kitty-bear. He slept with it in his little bed until he grew up, and then his toys were stored in his elderly mother's apartment. When his mother died, the billionaire's wife threw out all of her things, including the billionaire's childhood toys. The billionaire found out about this and was very upset, but his wife said to him: "It's not like you need those things anymore. You own expensive luxury items, you don't need cheap, nasty, low-grade toys." And now the billionaire saw his kitty-bear at the orphanage, his heart brightened, and he remembered what God had said. Once some kindhearted person brought toys from the dump to the orphanage, where they washed the kitty-bear and kept it. The billionaire asked for permission to take the kitty-bear and bought all the children new, expensive stuffed animals.

A story unfolds, often retold. Thunder roars, grass shakes, and the robins sing after, come morning. More time passed, and the billionaire traveled to the village where his grandfather and then his elderly mother had lived—in a poor, tumbledown little house with a garden. Only there was neither house nor garden there any longer; his wife had had them torn down and in their place built an expensive cottage. When the workers were tearing everything down, they followed the billionaire's wife's order to chop down the cedar pine, because it was "in the way." The billionaire had planted this tree in his youth, while he was still poor, together with his first girlfriend, whom he had loved. They planted a sprouted pine nut and every year they checked to see how it was growing. But things didn't work out with that girlfriend, and his wife had the cedar pine chopped down. But now, the billionaire arrived, walked along his land to the cottage, and suddenly saw that in the grass, in the same spot where the cedar pine had been, a new cedar pine was coming up. The old one had dropped its seeds, and a young one had taken root. The billionaire's heart brightened, and he remembered what God had said. He had a fence built around the tree, and ordered it to be watered and cared for, and he himself stood next to it for a long time, reminiscing and crying.

When God came to the billionaire again to ask for money, the billionaire asked him, "How did you manage to return my jacket, my kitty-bear, and the cedar pine?" God said, "Like this: I let them come down from heaven. I had them up there and I really treasured them, but you asked me to give you what they treasure in heaven, so I did." The billionaire was confused: "But how did they get there?" God said, "In a person's heart there's a needle that's always hurting, it has an eye, and through that eye pass caravans of camels taking up to heaven all the things that people have loved with all their hearts." God left, and the billionaire's wife started berating him for giving God money again. The billionaire said to her, "God paid back the loan with what they treasure in heaven." And he told her about the jacket, the kitty-bear, and the cedar pine. His wife scoffed and scoffed, and then she said: "I threw your jacket out thinking it would rot at the dump, and I threw out the kitty-bear thinking nobody would pick it up, and the cedar pine was cut down on my orders, and the garden paved over with concrete—so how did God manage to return these things to you? Do things really go to heaven from the dump? How is that possible?"

"Like this," said the billionaire, "in my heart there is a needle, it has an eye, in the eye is the gate to heaven." As soon as the billionaire's wife heard this, she decided that she wanted to live in heaven, thinking that everything is expensive there, they have all kinds of things, and she climbed into the billionaire's heart, found the needle, and tried to pass through, but she couldn't. She tried this way and that way, she was pretty thin after all, she did all sorts of workouts, she took care of herself, but she couldn't pass through the eye of the needle. But she saw caravans of loaded camels passing through, carrying everything that the billionaire loved with all his heart. The puppy they just bought went through, their British Shorthair kitten went through, the little mouse that the billionaire had found recently in the cottage basement, all of these passed through, but she couldn't. Then the billionaire said to her, "Get out of my heart, it looks like I don't love you." And he sent her away and lived happily ever after, helping children and the poor, planting trees, and always giving God a loan.

IVAN THE BOAR'S KNEE:
A PRAGUE STORY

Better if Ivan himself tells you the story of what happened to him.
And anyway, he likes to tell the story whenever he gets drunk,
and sometimes he tells it a dozen times over, going on about how
he took a trip to Prague, who he met there, how it all went down.
We've all heard it time and again, but you're new around here,
you can't even imagine what it's all about. So hurry up, come and
sit at our table, Ivan's already begun:

". . . that year the heat in Prague was phenomenal, over
thirty degrees Celsius in the shade, over forty in the sun, the
whole week was like that. Someone told me it was the hottest
week on record in the Czech Republic in the last sixty years. I
was staying on the right bank, pretty close to the center, about a
ten-minute ride on the trolley. I walked around every day, sometimes on the high, hilly left bank, sometimes in the Old Town
among crowds of tourists. What were my favorite parts? I mean,
there were a lot of things: Saint Vitus Cathedral, the Jewish
Quarter, but there were so many tourists in the street that you
could hardly see Prague, just tour groups from China with little

flags. Though I was a tourist, too; my parents paid for this trip to Prague in the summer after my third year of university, and like a good tourist I went on a series of tours. On the first day there was a walking tour of the Old Town and the remains of the Jewish Quarter, and in the evening a very funny old guy straight out of a 1930s clown show took us on a "Mystical Prague" tour, where he talked about various city legends and all that mystical stuff. I took trips to the town of Český Krumlov and the castle in Hluboká nad Vltavou. I even bought a map of the Czech Republic that had all the castles marked. You can't take a step in that country, it's just castles on castles. And poppy fields everywhere. The castle in Český Krumlov, the Žleby castle, and the Loket castle reminded me of the castles in the Barrandov Studios Czech fairy tale movies from the 1970s. They were shot in those same castles. There were always these young, pale, blonde princesses. I even watched *Zlatovláska* again on my computer. But my story isn't about all that, it's about how on my last day in Prague I got drunk and encountered the boar's knee.

I was drinking in a little hipster bar, and I remember that a student from some Western European country sat down next to me, but he spoke Russian, however badly. We got into a teleological argument, though I don't remember what it was about. I just remember that in the course of our conversation I mentioned that I'd like to try some boar's knee. The student said that he knew a good spot for boar's knee, a restaurant called Peklo, and that we should go to that place specifically, because there they make it with real boar, not out of ham hock, and there's a big difference.

When they brought out the boar's knee, I kid you not, it was like a roar rang out in the distance. The knee was enormous, it barely fit on the plate, and I don't think I've ever had anything more disgusting in my entire life. Didn't matter where you poked it with your fork, there was no way to get to the meat. Finding the meat was physical exercise, and when you did, that meat was fatty and gross. I tried choking it down and couldn't eat even a bit of it. I decided I'd just finish at home and got it to go, but then I thought that there was no way I could ever eat it, and I put the whole thing in a trash can. As I was tossing it in the trash, again from the distance came the roar of a boar. But when I got rid of it, I felt much lighter. While I had it with me, I felt oppressed and vaguely afraid. That's actually why I threw it out. As soon as they'd brought it, this huge thing on a plate, I started feeling oppressed like that, afraid, like something very powerful, deeply ancient, red-bristled and roaming the oak forests, had come for me, and I had to eat it. And so we parted ways, me and the student, both of us pretty drunk, and I went to my hotel, because I was supposed to go to the airport the next morning. I slept badly, the way you do when you're drunk, and again I was seized by a feeling of oppression and anxiety, like something very bad would happen any minute, and just as I began to drift off, there was a knock at my door. It was the knee knocking. I heard roaring and stomping hooves, grunting, clattering; I saw fangs, tusks, snouts, brown bristle with a reddish tint—and then I blacked out. When I came to, the sun was rising outside the window, and I had this—" Saying this, Ivan rolled up his pant leg, and all of us saw a bristly boar's knee.

"What's it like having it?" someone asked incredulously, and gingerly felt the knee.

"It's mostly OK, I just don't sleep well," Ivan said. "As soon as I fall asleep it keeps wanting to run somewhere, you know, restless leg syndrome, so at night I tie it to the bed with a belt. And it needs regular mud baths. Otherwise it really doesn't bother me. If it's there, it's there. Anyway, if you go to Prague," Ivan continued, "and stop by the Peklo restaurant and order boar's knee—think of me."

When he said this, simultaneously from the direction of his knee and from somewhere far, far away, where the oak forests grow, came a roar.

"Settle down now, settle down," said Ivan, and rolled down his pantleg.

ANXIETY

There's nothing more anxiety-inducing than a butterfly beating against the glass. nothing as tense as the silence before a storm, its barely audible, plucked-string, electric ringing. tiny invisible ants scatter through the grass, and the world falls into the bottomless well of an instant blackout. ripples run along the glass, and it becomes clear that the glass is liquid, that it flows like a brook or a lake, only very slowly. its tinkling is barely audible, like string music, it's blazing hot when you press your forehead against it. from afar, through the fog of sleep, comes the sound of an accordion, sharp and muffled.

he remembered that day, that overflowing world, the festive and majestic city. how, nearly beside himself, he got the highest possible score on his final exam, which meant definitively that he got in. mitka serkov got in, too. they drank beer together, then wine on vasilyevsky island. mitka laughed, then left to catch the commuter train, and he went to wander the streets, squares, parks, gardens. he met some girls—olya and katya. he got their numbers, walked around with them, then left them somewhere around the kazan cathedral. on a bench in the summer garden some thoughts came into his head. or not thoughts, rather, but youthful romantic nonsense, but he got some paper out of his bag, he'd been carrying it for the exam, and he wrote it down:

the world is like a mirror reflecting a happiness incomprehensible to man. i don't believe in evil, but i believe that when goodness arises, evil fades like shadows. but sometimes when i think about evil i feel strange, as though i were thinking about an unimaginably beautiful catastrophe. if any rules exist in this world, i'm going to break them anyway. it's likely that i'll pay an enormous price. it's likely that all my life i will walk through mud but not even the soles of my shoes will get dirty.

he'd have kept writing in this vein for a while but suddenly jumped up and ran along through the city, until he finally found himself at the train station. he had to go home, to snegirevka. the commuter train, then the bus, then a walk, and then in the late white dusk of a summer night he reached the porch of their old house. there were lights in the windows: his grandparents hadn't gone to bed yet, they were waiting for him, and he felt ashamed that he stayed out for so long instead of going home right away to tell them that he got in. he had never had a father, and for many years now his mother had lived abroad, where she had other children. it smelled of jasmine and the wooden, slightly stale and familiar smell of home. sensing his footsteps, the goats bleated, the chickens clucked in their coop. his granddad was sitting in the room watching tv and drinking a bottle of strong hunt-brand beer. "grandma! granddad!" he called, "i'm in, i got in."

his grandmother threw up her hands, and, having scolded him for coming home so late, started asking about the exam, and his granddad even turned off the tv. "i'm going to live in the city, in a dorm," he explained, "mitka serkov got in, too. call mama and tell her how i did." they ate, had tea and gingerbread cookies on the veranda, and his grandmother went to bed. granddad first walked around their yard in the light dusk, slowly mulling over the fact that his grandson was going to be a university student. then he came back, grunted, and went to bed, too.

their grandson couldn't sleep. he sat on the stiff child's bed in his book-filled room—he'd been a bookish boy, nobody knew where he got it from, but even when he was very young he loved books more than toys. his happiness that he got in today and that now he'd be studying at the university, would have new friends and probably a girlfriend, was mixed with something strange, a feeling previously almost unknown to him, of sadness and anxiety. or, rather, he had known it but it hadn't been inside of him— sadness dwelled in thunderstorms and sunsets, in the white steam that rises above the lake while you sit on the shore at night, or in the way leaves glide downward in the fall. now it seemed to him that it lived within him, as in nature, this anxious sadness somewhere at the very bottom of joy, like a quiet, imperceptible song. he sat at the writing desk by the window, turned on the desk lamp, and decided to record his thoughts once more:

> two stories sound throughout the world: the spring story and the fall story.
> one is the story of hope, the other the story of catastrophe.
> in one of them, the strings of your soul ring quietly,

responding to the snowdrops, the birds, and the wind. in the other there's rain, leaves falling, the dark sky, and the strings of your soul are torn. the way back is wiped out.

the window's small upper pane was open, and the scent of ozone entered the room: a thunderstorm had started. pouring rain hit abruptly via hundreds of night streams let loose in an ocean of white and green, and there was the cavalry gallop of water and the groans of the earth as it was struck by sudden electric flashes. the window glass streamed and blazed, and a cherry-brown mourning cloak butterfly flew through the open pane toward the light of the desk lamp. he put out the lamp, put his notes into the desk drawer only to forget them there and never return to them again as long as he lived, and lay down to sleep. all night, waking periodically from a slumber made restless by overexcitement, he heard the butterfly beating against the glass and the pouring rain.

TENEVIL

Once upon a time there lived a writer who was one of the Luoravetlan, otherwise known as the Chukchi. He belonged to the Maritime Chukchi, hunting Baikal and harbor seals, walruses, and whales. The writer lived in a traditional yaranga home; there was a typewriter on his sled, and on this typewriter he typed up his novels. The writer usually walked around the yaranga naked, drinking coffee, smoking Dunhills, making notes in leather Moleskine notebooks, and then typing up the chapters of his novels on the typewriter. The novels were full of myths, fairy tales, folk histories, and stories of daily life. He wrote about the raven Ku'urkil, about the lords of water and fire, about the moon, the sun, and the stars, about evil spirits and wintertime sacrifices to the star Altair. Then the spirits spoke to the writer about changing gender, and the writer began to wear the clothes and lead the life of a woman. The writer had a lover, a young shaman, who visited the yaranga in the evenings, and after sex the writer would read the shaman chapters from a new dystopian novel, *Dirty Snow*. The writer's entire life boiled down to hunting, fucking, and art. The writer wrote in Russian but never read anything. Still, the novels of Tenevil (this was the writer's pseudonym, in honor of the reindeer herder who had worked to create Chukchi literacy) were extremely popular and translated into many languages. Dressed in Chukchi robes with an opening at the chest and wide sleeves, with hair dyed green, Tenevil was a fixture at bookfairs and international festivals. And although Tenevil never read, the novels seemed to be written by someone who'd read everyone in the world and subtly alluded to them all. The work was compared to Kafka, Kharms, Platonov, Yerofeyev, Petrushevskaya, Zoshchenko, Dombrovsky, Babel, Ionesco, Brecht, Elfriede Jelinek, Thomas Bernhard, Pelevin, Mamleyev, Rimbaud, Baudelaire, Turgenev . . . Must it be said that Tenevil had never heard of half of these people? Tenevil's seal-fat-rubbed body was still unused to the fine cloth of context, but there was no other way for the writer to write, when, after periods of deep contemplation, during which Tenevil could neither eat nor sleep, at the brink of death, came inspiration. It was for this inspiration that the writer became beloved around the world, the seer who spoke with the bear and the raven, simple and sophisticated, sublime and mocking, ingenious and ingenuous Tenevil.

A QUIRK

After marrying her husband and moving in with him, Inna Leopoldovna discovered that he had a particular quirk. At first she thought that he never put things back where he'd found them, instead leaving them scattered throughout the apartment in the most chaotic and whimsical way. But then she understood that it wasn't even right to say that he scattered things: the things just turned up, all by themselves, in utterly unpredictable places, no matter where Inna Leopoldovna or her husband had put them, and the difference between Inna Leopoldovna and her husband lay in the fact that this made her feel totally lost, while her husband inevitably found what he needed thanks to his astonishing intuition. He would walk through the apartment as though he were following a scent or playing hot and cold, like he was led by an invisible compass, and he'd find the bicycle pump in the refrigerator, the book that Inna Leopoldovna had left on her nightstand in the grain box, a pill pack in the corner of the shoe rack, a winter hat in the cupboard, and a packet of spices in the washing machine. "How do they end up there?" Inna

Leopoldovna implored. Her husband could not say. "How do you find them?" the poor woman would inquire. "I just know," her husband would shrug, "I think about something and I start getting a sense of where it might be." In principle there was no need for him to maintain any order or to return things to their proper places—with his astonishing intuition, he could find anything anywhere, so he didn't find it necessary to assign permanent, designated spots. The things themselves were aware of this and moved freely about the apartment, as they are wont to do when no one is in charge of them and they direct their own movements. The same object could be on the windowsill today, behind the wardrobe tomorrow, and under the bed the day after that. Their movements had no limits and no logic. But Inna Leopoldovna's husband always knew where they were, existing as he did in a state of symbiosis with things. "You can never find anything," he grumbled at Inna Leopoldovna, taking her handbag out of the oven.

THE SAILOR'S WIFE

"Darling, you're a whore, and I'm shipping out." Thus sailor Yasnov began his conversation with his wife. "Darling, what are we going to do about it?" asked sailor Yasnov's wife drunkenly, pulling on her cigarette. "I have an idea. You'll see," said sailor Yasnov, and went to pack his things for departure. His wife went on boozing on the sofa, crossing her long legs in their fishnet stockings. That night, when sailor Yasnov's wife had drunk so much she passed out, sailor Yasnov tied her up, got a needle and thread, and sewed her cunt shut. His wife tried to scream, but sailor Yasnov put a gag in her mouth and finished the job. Then he took his things and left on his voyage, and their neighbor in the communal apartment found his wife in the morning, half dead and with her cunt sewn shut. The neighbor lady called an ambulance; they took out the stitches sailor Yasnov had put in and treated her wounds. Some time passed, and sailor Yasnov's wife was back to normal and returned to fucking around, so much so that her neighbor in the communal apartment said, "Vanya was right when he sewed up your cunt. We should have left it

that way. Now you're just bringing them back here day after day."
And some time after that, sailor Yasnov returned from his voyage, came back to the apartment, saw his drunk wife in her fishnet stockings, and from the look on her face realized everything. "Well, Natasha, have you been fucking around without me?" he asked reproachfully. His wife embraced him, and after that they lived long and happily for many years, even to this day.

THE RHINO WIFE

There were obsessions for sale, and people were coming in to pick some up. Ivan Kuzmich stopped in, too—he's no worse than the next guy, why shouldn't he also have an obsession. With an obsession, you're all set; without one, you stick out like a sore thumb and don't know what to do with yourself. Becoming obsessed is like buying a goat: it's a struggle at first, but you're in the clover once it gets going.

"Get the pedo one," it was suggested to him.

"What do you mean, the pedo one?" asked Ivan Kuzmich, spooked.

"Like when you don't know if you're a pedophile or not."

"No, no thank you, that's too scary!"

"OK, then get the one about psycho killers."

"But I want one that's original, not something everyone else has. All my friends got that one already, they keep calling me and asking, 'Ivan, what do you think, I'm not a psycho killer, am I?' I want a unique obsession for myself, an obsession no one else has!"

"All right, then get the one with the rhino wife."

"What the heck is that?"

"It's a cool designer obsession, you should take that one, you won't regret it."

So Ivan Kuzmich bought that one, and he began to think that his wife was growing a horn from her forehead. He couldn't shake the thought; he kept studying her forehead, parting her bangs while she slept, feeling her head with his fingers—was there a bump? He was so scared, it was just awful. He tormented his wife with questions: "Nadya, are you growing a horn? Tell me honestly, are you? You're definitely not, right? What if you are, though?" He lost weight, made himself sick, spent days on the internet looking up "what to do if wife growing horn," "horn on person's forehead," "how to know if growing horn or not," "horn on forehead cure." And then it stopped. What's a horn anyway, he began to think, it's no big deal. He sighed with relief. He felt light, lifted, given wings. This is happiness, he thought, that was a good obsession, a strong one, unusual, I should get something else from that brand. Then his wife came in. Growing from her forehead was a pretty noticeable horn, no doubt about it now, but this did not concern Ivan Kuzmich in the slightest.

HERE TODAY

A young woman sat at a bus stop, lost in thought. An old lady came up and tore into her right away: "Excuse me, young lady, give me your seat, I'm old."

"Oh, of course!" The young woman roused herself and readily gave up her seat for the old lady. The old lady sat down but kept going: "Young people are so rude these days! They see an elderly person coming and just keep on sitting there!" Nearby old ladies, who'd already been sitting and waiting at the bus stop with the young woman when this new old lady arrived, joined in. "That's what manners are like these days, all of them are like that!" the old ladies complained. "What do you mean 'these days'? Manners are manners, they either have them or they don't," complained the new old lady. The young woman stood by them, smiling dreamily, as though none of this had anything to do with her. She was many thousands of years old, she remembered Egypt and Mesopotamia, she remembered when the first primitive, wild tribes had come to populate these lands. Now these here-today ladies are complaining, she thought, but just yesterday they were children, and I was exactly the same as I am now—ancient and eternally young. Eighty years ago I rocked them in my arms, just like I once rocked their mothers, and now they're old women yelling at me. Everything takes its course. Tomorrow they'll be gone, but that little girl in the stroller is going to be just the same sort of old lady cursing the youth. Ah, people! The bus came. The young woman let all the old ladies board first, watching to make sure they got on, then took a seat that had remained empty and gazed out the window with eyes that were young, shining, in love with the world.

WE LOVE YOU, DARK FOREST

A SONG HUMAN CHILDREN SING
ABOUT OLD OKKA, AS SHE WALKS HOME
THROUGH THE DARK FOREST

Human offspring, foolish human children, hide behind the branches in the winter woods, spying on old Okka. Old Okka walks along a trail to her house; beyond the trail is a lake and falling snow. The children watch Okka and sing without singing:

we love you, dark forest
we love you, o forest troll
we love you, dark forest,
we love you, o forest man

BOYS DRESSED IN COTTON
SHAKE DOWN APPLES ON THE RIVERBANK

Boys dressed in cotton shake down apples on the riverbank. In the river lives a dead pike with a wide-open mouth. With its sharp teeth, the pike gnaws through fishermen's boats and sings about the enormous Sun that rises above the stars, the foam, and the bulrush thickets.

THREE HOUSES

In a house blanketed with snow and moss an old mother tearfully begs something of her son. In another house lives a naked woman with a guitar; in this house are many handwritten poems, artists' pictures, flowers, and carpets. The third house stands directly beneath the Moon: inside it, men with mean faces drink vodka and wine, and someone without name or face rises above them toward the smoking old Moon.

A LITTLE BOY IN A FIELD
WATCHES A CROW PECKING AT SEEDS

A fair-haired little boy in linen pants in a field watches a crow pecking at seeds. There's a freshness in the air; wafting over from the village there's a smell of smoke.

"Crow, do you know the river?" the boy asks.

"Do you know the rriver in winterr?" asks the crow.

"What do you eat?" the boy asks. "I like kasha."

"Smarrt cookie," says the crow, "wherreas I wouldn't turrn down a chicken egg."

NAKED OLD TREES

Naked old trees have a particular rough, gnarled beauty. Sometimes a tree of this kind grows right by the highway and keeps watch over the road. Those who know how can open up such a tree just like they're unzipping a jacket, and then step inside. Inside is a movie theater where they show long, slow films that are like dreams and spring.

BEYOND THE HIGHWAY

After the rain the highway is wet and resembles a lake; on its smooth surface lie occasional petals and rainworms. Beyond the road there are red lava fields traversed by the shadows of disintegrating clouds. And beyond that there's nothing, only music from under the earth, heard by monsters.

SONG OF THE THREE BEGGARS
STOPPED TO REST AT THE EDGE OF THE FOREST

When you fall in love with a beautiful woman, you can never really be sure whether she's a monster or not, particularly if such a thing is indicated by the ravens on an old, burnt tree, or three beggars who have stopped to rest at the edge of the forest.

earth and forest, these are the monster's body
stars in the sky, these are the monster's eyes
we love you, o forest monsters
we love you, o forest wonders

A LOG CABIN WITH THE SUN LIVING ON ITS ROOF

Gaga Goose laid her eggs on the cliffs at the edge of the sea. A forest grew on the cliffs, the beach was strewn with enormous boulders, and the outlines of ships could be seen upon the water. Not far from the shore stood a log cabin with the Sun living on its roof. Inside the cabin lived an old man with a hatchet; in the evenings a bear would come to visit, and the two of them would drink currant tea.

CROWS GOSSIP IN THE EARLY MORNING

At the tops of three pines sit three crows; they're telling one another the latest news.

"The Sun has come out above the sea, the starr is no longer visible, the Moon has gone pale, but the old boulderrs that prrotrrude from the waterr arre a little warrmer now—they moaned so pitifully all night thrrough," says the first crow.

"In the lake therre's a swan called Jan Hus, he's strretching his neck towarrd the rrising Sun, and it's like trrumpets are playing in his thrroat," discloses the second.

"A prretty big boulderr, elongated, like a duck's egg, is lying therre in the grrass and is completely indifferrent towarrd everryone," complains the third.

HUGE WHITE FLOWER
AT THE HEART OF THE STORM
IS IT FOR GOOD OR ILL THAT YOU'VE BLOOMED AT SEA?

A storm has begun, lightning flashes in the sky, the boats creak, the birds vanish, and a huge white flower bursts into bloom right in the sea.

"Who are you?"

"I'm the child of two empty boats and two wild birds. I'm the child of a big, old tree on the shore. I'm the lightning's son. I'm the cliff's son-in-law. I'm the water's grandson. I'm the loon's cousin. I'm the wolf's mother."

"What are you for?"

"I've come to destroy everything."

SOMETIMES THE SUN EATS A PIECE OF THE WALL...

Sometimes the Sun eats a piece of the wall or the roof of a house. Sometimes a woman with white hair to her ankles and a red beak walks across a meadow. On those days the faces of the pigs in the pens look especially impudent.

GRANDMOTHER LOOKS FOR LITTLE MIKKO
IN A FOREST FULL OF MONSTERS

In the evenings boys build a bonfire in the forest and watch the monsters dancing on the shore of the forest lake. Little Mikko's grandmother looks for him, walking through the woods, calling, "Hello-o," but her grandson has long since turned into a fir branch.

SONG OF THE WEREWOLF'S WIFE,
WAITING UP FOR HIM ON A SLEEPLESS NIGHT

Beyond the bare trees there's a bright round yellow moon that looks like the werewolf's pupilless eye. The wolf-man's wife tosses and turns on the bed, waits for her husband to return, and mumbles:

my husband is a forest wolf
he's running back to me
along the roots of the old pines
along the fluffy snow

THE LOG WEEPS

A crow and a log sit on the shore of the lake. The ruins of clouds swirl and dissolve ceaselessly above them, while the Moon rises, covered in a delicate fuzz, like a pink peach.

"You'rre a wooden frreak!" the crow mocks the log suddenly, for no reason at all.

The offended log weeps, and from beneath the bark of its eyelids pitch seeps out in steady drops.

WOMEN IN A SWAMPY MEADOW
EAT POISONOUS WATER HEMLOCK

There are nights when all young women are stalked by crones in black who whisper into their ears that they should slit their husbands' throats, strangle their children, and go to the place where the eagle-owl hoots above the forest flowers, the wandering-place of the dark beast with the enormous white horns in which butterflies and fireflies make their homes. There, in the swampy meadow, the women should eat their fill of water hemlock.

CLEVER EDLA
FOUND IN THE MORNING
THAT BOOKS HAD GROWN ON HER HEAD

Through their pages, translucent as though cut from green verglas, through all of their shimmering veins, sunlight shines. Morning is underway, and Clever Edla, who read all night, has grown books on her head in place of hair. And now please be so kind as to tell me, just how is she supposed to leave the house? How can she show herself to her fiancé? Now everyone will know what's on Edla's mind: the books contain all of the poor girl's thoughts. There's one consolation: Edla's fiancé is illiterate, he won't read about how day and night Edla worries over his stupidity and wonders if he's going to give her stupid children.

GRANDPA DEKHOR KNOCKS DOWN THE MUSHROOMS ON THE FALLEN TREES

Grandpa Dekhor walks through the forest knocking down all the mushrooms that grow on fallen trees. One of the fallen trees is his granddaughter. Once she went into the forest to sing runes and became a tree. Though she could have become a waterfall or a footpath.

AYNIKKA'S SONG ABOUT THE WHITE FOREST

The white forest is on the other side.
Grandma said not to go to the white forest.
The trees there have white leaves even in summer, and the grass is
white as clouds.
In the white forest all the animals and birds are white,
the fire has a rushing face,
as though it's in a hurry or just ran away from somewhere,

and the rays of light diving down look like wild ducks.
The dwellers of the white forest
lend their glow to the sky,
their glow which they got from the seagulls.
But I'm going to put on a white dress and go into the white forest.
Go ahead: try and stop me.

WOUNDED STONE

The stone cries out as it lies bleeding. Gleams of the setting Sun alight on the handle of the sword stuck into it. The stone lies beneath an oak, in a thicket of ferns. The sword has passed clean through it, like through a loaf of bread. Stone lips have swallowed the sword, and it has entered the beating of the stone's stilled heart, the sheath of its dried-up, dead heart. The night puts its sensitive horselike ear to the stone and hears: the stone is dead, it's no longer breathing, but its mossy bones are whispering, and music sounds in its marrow. Lodged in the scales of an ancient lizard, encrusted with ice, the stone lies, protecting the lizard's belly. The sword protrudes from the stone's back, and it would be quite happy to get out, but it's stuck, can't go this way or that. Just try going where you're not wanted next time, thinks the sword.

DEER SKULL

Old fools occasionally grow deer antlers, as do old wise men. But the young shaman loves a dead deer. He wanders the forest naked to the waist, holding the deer's skull in his hand. In a meadow he uses deer skulls to lay out bone flowers.

RAVEN, OWL, AND WOLF

A gutted raven lies in the snow. Flap-flap, lop-lop—from a branch, an owl looks down at it with round, orange eyes. A wolf hides behind the trees. He's only a wolf, nothing more, but nothing less than that.

HAND OF A WITCH

Sometimes, in some dry branches, you'll come across a woman's muddied hand. Once its owner smeared her hands with clay and menstrual blood, stewed serpents in a cauldron, wore wreaths of autumn leaves and berries on her head. She lit candles, muttered spells from a thick book, and spoke with a deer's skull. Indeed, she had beautiful hands, but her heart was probably eaten by a white wolf.

SUMMER'S END

The silhouette of a butterfly flits against the backdrop of the setting Sun. The summer is ending, and the silhouette of a wolf runs against the backdrop of the Sun's huge round disk, already touching the surface of the earth.

"Goodbye, Sun," says the spruce tree on the hill, "Goodbye, summer," says the world.

ON A WARM FALL DAY
A BUTTERFLY DRINKS NECTAR

Near a weak bonfire lit by Edla, a butterfly flits. Today is a warm day, and it drinks the nectar of fall flowers. The nectar is sweet, but ahead there's maybe hibernation, or, possibly, death.

LIGHT IN THE NOVEMBER FOREST

The one who hides his face behind yellow fall leaves loves to watch the light in the bare November forest.

NIGHT TREAD

A long-haired shield flies through the starry sky. An old volcano smokes. A deer and her fawns freeze in the moonlight and listen to someone's creeping footsteps—the tread of someone neither dead nor living.

LITTLE SPIDERWEB AT DAWN

In the blue moonlit fields the chamomile flowers droop their white petals. Far beyond the meadow there are purplish smoke and the dark, low prongs of the forest. Tiny dewdrops dot the lengths of fuzzy shoots of grass. It's a spring night, and the grassy meadow runs to the horizon. Smoke at dawn, dew, flowers gathered into buds. So far nothing is trapped in the spiderweb in the flowers, dew, and sunlight, and it seems like even the spider has gone, and that it made the web with no ill intentions, just for the beauty of it.

INSECTS HIDE FROM THE RAIN
BENEATH MUSHROOM CAPS

The toadstools have been strung with lights, now their caps and skirts glow in the dark. All mushrooms now have light bulbs inside them, and beneath their caps night insects hide from the rain. Two fireflies embrace each other, ducking beneath the cap of a giant birch bolete. They watch the rain, kiss, and dream.

ON A MOONLIT NIGHT
IN A ROCKY FIELD
ELVES PLAY PUNK ROCK

When the Moon rises over the grove, the little stones near the grass become a stage for a punk band of little elves. They have mohawks on their heads and little green boots on their feet, and their leather jackets sparkle with glimmering pollen. Elf punk has a harsh sound, and anyway these are toadstool elves, but each time a filthy little elf with a guitar rips a primitive chord, a million bellflowers ring all around, and glitter scatters as though from the flick of a magic wand. Then the elf roars, hammers his guitar against an old tree stump, and destroys it, pulling the remains onto his head. Climbing the toadstool, he pulls down his pants, and, in a blur of bellflowers and glitter, pisses right into the audience. Well, what can you do, punk is punk, elves are elves.

A WOLF WHOSE MUZZLE
BLENDS WITH THE SNOWSTORM

The young woman who liked to ride through the forest on a moose, the house with a mossy roof that stood in the dense thicket, the Sun that the deer carried in its antlers, the orange leaf the color of an owl's eyes that hung by a thin filament in the transparent wood, the forest spirits with burning eyes who hid behind the trees—where have they gone? Only the wolf whose muzzle blends with the snowstorm knows. But just try finding him, especially now that the storm has ended and not a trace of his muzzle remains.

DEAD MAN'S BOAT

In the boat a cross stands and a dead man lies. For a long time now the boat has been washed ashore by the foot of the cliffs. At the top of the cliffs, the Sun is lodged like a bronze coin. The creator of this world lies in the boat and rests. Once in a while a peasant sits down on his field and sighs over him. The god of death, with a horned skull for a head, also sighs. The dead creator of this world doesn't come to the god of death. He just lies in the boat and rests. And why not, honestly?

AFTER THE NIGHT WATCH
THE GUARDIANS OF THE MOUNTAIN
MELT INTO THIN AIR

At night the guardians of the mountain patrol the stone run. They have long, streaming bodies that you can see clear through; round, burning eyes; and a glow around their heads (if you can call those things heads). After the night watch the guardians of the mountain melt into thin air, as though they never existed.

ON A WINTER NIGHT THE FOREST IS BLACK AND WHITE . . .

On a winter night the forest is black and white, some tree trunks gape with arboreal eyes, and planets hang in the sky. The pines list, thickly swept with snow. A comet passes, and the crow-woman, with snow in the hem of her dress and a tambourine in her claws, looks after the comet's tail for a long time and caws.

THE BEAUTIFUL ZMROK

The trees reach out their branches in the dark. In the spring, flowers will grow from the mouth of the young lady Zmrok, they'll grow from her eyes and her ears, and in place of the hair on her head, too. The head of the young lady Zmrok itself grows from the middle of the stump of a downed tree, her hair is covered in snow, and her face is full of malice.

IN A LITTLE HOUSE AT THE EDGE OF THE FOREST

In a little house at the edge of the forest the rug is snowed under; pine cones lie on the fleecy blanket. Candles burn in the candle-holders, logs burn in the fireplace, lights burn on the tree. In the kitchen there's cinnamon and lemon zest, and soon Joulupukki with horns on his forehead and a bag over his shoulder and a necklace of bones will pay a visit. Naughty children live in this house, and he's going to boil them alive in a cauldron. He doesn't have a team of deer—he ate all of them. The naughty children are hiding in the wardrobe; they know that it's their turn soon.

RED DRESS

A woman in a red dress wanders the snowy cliffs. In the distance and snow her house looks tiny and dark—there, where the mountains covered in pine forests descend to the smooth, icy lake. The woman's dress is red as the breast of the robin who lives in the pine forest by the river valley, the same robin whose breast was once wounded by the thorns of the Savior's crown. Her dress is as red as the rowanberries in the snow, pecked by the bullfinch who eats the seeds and leaves the flesh behind. It's as red as the bloodstained hands, shorn of their bodies, that hug the trunks of the trees.

THE OWL AND THE DRAGON

The owl is covered with snow. It sits on a branch and daydreams: it sees the outline of a castle where there are ruins of cliffs, a gigantic statue of the warrior who slew the dragon at the tops of them. This warrior, in his horned helmet and animal hides, once climbed these cliffs with his sword in order to fight their master. And so he remained there forever in the form of a stone statue, when the dragon's black blood spilled on the snow. The owl misses the dragon a little; there was a time when they got on pretty well, and you had to give the dragon his due—he was brighter than the rest in this forest.

THREE DEAD WITCHES

Once upon a time there lived three dead witches. One had a red pointed hat and a noose around her neck, another had a rag for a face and long, hardened fingernails, and the third, dressed in a long woman's dress, had a swollen body, and for a face she had something baffling, flat and rotating around its axis. What else can I tell you about them? One liked to work at her spinning wheel and light candles, another liked wooden spoons, little rusty locks, and clay dolls wrapped up in scarves, and the third liked men's cut-off heads, particularly bearded ones.

THE ICE CRACKED, AND IT TURNED OUT THAT . . .

The ice cracked, and it turned out that in the lake, beneath the ice, a tree was growing. A black wolf circles the tree and howls: black heart, red blood, ooo-oo, skull on a stick, toadstools on a stump, ooo-oo, moon underwater, moss with birchbark, ooo-oo, horned bird, bear's beak, ooo-oo, and so on and so forth, ooo-oo.

CAST TO EARTH

The man who had the berth above mine on the train from Siberia to the Caucasus fell off about ten times—though mostly not from the berth itself but in the attempt to climb up or down. He fell about as many times just standing on the floor of the train car. In this way he became the hero of the entire train. In the morning young women came up to his berth and said, solicitously, "Hello from our hangover!" All the other men in the car became his friends, and at one stop I heard a guy say, "Misha, I have more respect for you than anyone." Misha, meanwhile, had fallen for our fellow traveler Lera—there were three of us in the couchette coupé car, starting in Krasnoyarsk. From the very beginning, as soon as I saw twenty-five-year-old Lera and thirty-seven-year-old Misha, I knew that he was going to start hitting on her, based on some very simple logic: a single guy (he told us almost immediately that he was divorced) riding in a coupé compartment with two women was naturally going to start coming on to one of them, and it wasn't going to be me. It was also perfectly clear to me that I wouldn't socialize much, mostly sitting there reading my book, lost in my own thoughts, and that Misha and Lera would conclude that I was aloof and not like them, and they'd start chatting because they had nothing else to do on the train but talk, and then he'd start coming on to her. And that's exactly what happened: I sat there engrossed in my book, because the most boring thing about train travel for me is the presence of strangers and the obligation to talk to them, though I feel a general sense of camaraderie with all people; meanwhile, they struck up a conversation, started drinking, and by the evening of the second day he was hitting on her.

Lera—small, tan, plain, with greenish bulging eyes, a minuscule nose, dark hair, and an oddly-shaped faced that broadened toward the bottom—did not appeal to me particularly: in a categorical tone of voice she said things that attested to her ironclad narrow-mindedness and had a short, artificial laugh. Though around the second of four days the annoyance I felt at the unbreachable borders of her consciousness, revealed in the first ten minutes of our acquaintance, abated through the power of habit, and her short, artificial laugh was replaced by more genuine, drunken laughter. There was also the fact that Misha's drunken flirting awakened in her a simultaneously angry and adoring wife and mother; she manifested instincts that from time immemorial have been engendered in women by the drunken morons who are their husbands and sons: reproach and abuse alongside the desire to protect this large, howling creature, which, in turn, when drunk is drawn to the soft and the feminine, tries to climb onto her berth, and gives her his bloodied arm to bandage. "You want me to do it," Lera guessed from the mute gesticulations of the drunk man assailing her with his blood and his bandage obtained from the neighboring compartment. She screams at him, curses, and he can hardly stay upright, maybe even falling on purpose, so that she'll yell at him some more with that air of caring, motherly reproach. She shouts, "Stop bothering me! What did you get so drunk for? You're on that berth, go there!" But he keeps trying, knowing that it'll set her shouting, because for him she has now become that age-old, thousand-year-old wife and mother of the Russian man, and the schoolgirl whose braid a boy pulls so she'll turn around and hit him over the head with her textbook. And Lera turns and hits him over the head with her textbook, and the boy, his heart skipping a beat, pulls her braid again. "I can see why your wife left you," Lera hits him where it hurts. "Have some pity on me, there's nobody in this world who cares for me except my mother," Misha begs straightforwardly.

Misha was going to Sochi to visit his father, whom he hadn't seen for eleven years and who had stage four cancer; Misha was going to say goodbye to him and start a new life in Sochi. His twenty-three-year-old ex-wife remained in Krasnoyarsk; she'd left him and kept him from seeing their daughter, Sonechka. His first wife and their children lived in Germany. Misha had visited them in Germany, remembered the trip well, and talked about it a lot on the train—how they did this in Germany, how they did that. He himself had once worked at the Krasnoyarsk Aluminum Plant; the factory closed during perestroika and he went into business of some kind. Lera was from Achinsk, had studied to be a computer operator, spent time as a salesgirl in Krasnoyarsk, and now worked in residential management and was traveling from her parents, whom she had been visiting, back to her husband in Krasnodar. Lera was used to the harsh cruelty of life; she reminisced: "After college I moved to Krasnoyarsk and worked at a gas station. There was one really little chick there, shorter than me, everyone called her Button. One time we did a shift together and she says, 'Let's go get a beer.' So we went. We had a drink, and you know, there are people who drink and really lose it, they go crazy and can't control themselves—so she says to me, 'Here I am, I'm studying, I have a husband and all that, but you, you're always gonna work at the gas station.' So I say to her, 'You don't know what you're talking about. How do you know what's gonna happen to us tomorrow?' So we move on, but she keeps saying it, I can tell she's trying to pick a fight. So anyway at some point she hit me, I didn't even notice. We started fighting, the cops came, they took us to the station, and she made a statement that I beat her up. So I made a counterstatement. But they never summoned us anywhere, nothing happened, the cops don't give a fuck. And the next day I go to work and my boss says, 'You so-and-so, you beat her up'—anyway, he fired me. She came to work first and told him her version. And another time in Achinsk three guys beat me up at night . . .''

"They just beat you up?" Misha asked the pressing male question.

"They just beat me. It's dangerous on our streets at night. Anyway I knew them, one of them . . . I yelled at them, saying, 'Fuckers, I'm gonna have you put in jail!' So they let me go. But they didn't beat me up that bad."

The whole train car grew fond of Lera after the incident with the Kazakhs. When we were passing through Kazakhstan, three Kazakhs came into the car: two men and a woman. They sat down in a side compartment next to ours and started talking about something. Not very loudly, but not quietly, either, and in Kazakh. It was daytime, but Lera, worn out by the boredom of travel, which oppressed her particularly in my silent presence, was trying to fall asleep and dream sweet, vivid dreams about a happy and exciting life. The Kazakh conversation bothered her, and she started shouting at the Kazakhs like a rowdy bazaar lady: "What are you sitting there and talking for? Have some respect for Russians!"

"What does who's Russian have to do with anything?" asked the stunned Kazakh.

"It's got lots to do with it," Lera replied.

Fortunately the Kazakhs got off at the next station, but the train car took note of Lera and was struck by her patriotic valor. Misha was drinking with the men from the neighboring compartment, and they saw that he had a thing for Lera and began to hold her in high regard as the object of his affections, the way teenagers fall in love with the girl their leader chooses; they'd heard how she shouted at him, like any decent woman should, and they'd heard how she shouted at the Kazakhs, and they came to her to express their admiration. "Good job, girlie!" said an old ambulance driver. "I liked you straightaway. They should show some respect for Russians!"

"What are you, not Russian?" Lera asked Misha every time that he, in her view, failed to understand something obvious, such as the fact that she had told him not to touch her and to climb on up to the upper berth, but he wasn't budging. Lera would say this in a way that implied "not Russians" were made-up fairy-tale monsters, which was amusing considering that Lera herself was half Russian at most and half from the Caucasus, and was married to an Armenian.

Crushes are contagious, and together with Misha, the old ambulance driver also fell in love with Lera, as well as another drunk, Sergei. Sergei came up to Lera and asked to see her hand, held it for a long time rapturously in his palms, then said to her, "I know who you are. I noticed you right away and I understood. You're the greatest beauty. I can see it—you're extraordinary." While saying this he held her hand with such concentration that you could have thought he saw all this precisely through her hand, and Zhanna, a thirty-year-old former history teacher who was sitting with us then, a woman whose hobbies included fantasy and sewing old-fashioned dresses, plump, with bristles on her face, someone you could have taken for fifty, asked him, "What are you, a psychic?"

"I'm just a guy," said Sergei. The men's feelings for Lera grew with each day of the trip; they fell in love with her as we passed through Kazakhstan and she yelled at the Kazakhs, they were fully devoted in the Urals and the Volga Region, and their passion became all the more ardent and agonizing as we approached the Caucasus. At each stop of the train, when we all got off to walk a bit along the platform, they paid Lera more and more attention, hugging her more and more possessively, taking her by the hand and whispering things in her ear with their drunk tobacco lips, smiling blissfully. The female conductors, sensing the situation, joined this chain reaction of love and also became particularly pleasant and friendly with Lera, joking around with her and calling her by her first name.

The culmination of these events came on the last day of the trip, toward evening.

On that last day, Lera, who until then had not been drinking much, went to drink in the neighboring compartment with Misha, the old ambulance driver, Sergei, and Zhanna, also joined there by some woman from the other end of the train car. I didn't feel like joining because I had no desire to partake in drunk intimacy. In the neighboring compartment they were taking Lera apart; I could hear guffawing and meaningless conversation. The old ambulance driver was saying that he drives the psychiatric orderlies and has seen some things, and for a long time he tried to talk Lera into going with him as far as Adler, but Lera told him he should meet her mother, meaning that as a woman she was a better match for him than young Lera. The ambulance driver didn't want to give in and asked, "How old is she?"

"Fifty-two."

"That's old. Even my lovers are twenty-seven," said the old man.

Sergei also asked Lera to get off the train with him; Misha promised her a hundred roses and asked her to go with him, or at least to give him her number. They kept reminiscing about Misha's drunken falls of the day before and Lera yelling at the Kazakhs. The overall conviviality grew with the number of empty bottles. Coming to share in the men's love for Lera, Zhanna and the other woman also became besotted with her and started trying to talk her into going with them. "You people are tearing me apart," yelped Lera in dim drunk joy. Five pairs of greedy hands stretched toward her in order to take her with them, and Lera— little, shallow, unintelligent, unpretty Lera—was the object of men's and women's yearning and desire, that sweetest thing in which people imagine the fulfilment of all their hopes and dreams, the realization of a happiness not found on this earth, a living godhead; it was as though Lera, like Süskind's perfumer, had doused herself with the finest scent in the world, which granted her the love of all people, their adoration and their lust, a perfume to turn a public execution into an orgy of love, driving those who smell the scent to tear apart with their own hands the too greatly desired being. And the culmination of the journey was this orgy of delight without good reason or basis, a senseless delight, groundless and gratifying, bestowed for nothing, nothing at all—not for beauty, nor brains, nor talent—upon the most unremarkable creature in the world.

Drunk Lera was upset with Misha for some reason and alternated between shouting, "I'm being honest with him, and he's being like that!" and occasionally warming to him and yelling, "We're countrymen! He's my countryman! We're Siberians, only Siberians are open like this!" (In response to Lera's shouts of "We're countrymen!" Misha, who'd spent time in the army, at one point said, "In the army they say, 'Your countrymen are the ones in the trench eating the horse.'") Over the past few days, in response to Misha's flirtations, Lera had repeatedly brought up her husband, emphasizing that she was married—but now, sitting in Misha's lap, when someone mentioned her husband she announced, laughing loudly, "Husband! Husband doesn't do much!" Misha wrote Lera a note: "Lerochka, I really like you, and I'm always going to be bored without you if you don't give me your number." Lera gave him her number, saying, "Looks like he likes crazies, he's crazy himself."

Meanwhile the party on the other side of the partition was growing more and more crazed, and seemed to take over all of reality; the revelers were joined by another young couple—a man and a woman, who, forgetting each other, immediately partook in the group sentiment about "our Lerochka," as they called her. Then they were joined by a few more people, and a few more, and after some time everyone in the entire train car, in a sort of delusion, had massed by the compartment next to mine, where Lera was, and all of them were asking her to go with them and trying to get her for themselves. Some sort of shared madness or magic had altered the reality of time and space, and it was as though our train car, together with all of its enchanted passengers and conductors, had been transported to another dimension, an invisible switch was flipped—and human logic is unable to describe what followed. Laying my head on the book I'd been reading, I fell headlong beneath the building, deafening noise and Lera's frenzied, drunkenly joyful laughter, fell into a bittersweet titillating dream that was full of Lera, the golden, heart-shaped keychains on her trendy purse, her bulging, long-lashed green eyes, now grown gigantic, in which I suddenly saw a light that I had never seen before in my whole life but at the same time had always seen, even before I was born, and I understood that Lera was the only vessel in the world for this light, a single touch of which would grant eternal bliss, but without slaking your thirst for it once and for all, instead driving you to crave and desire more and more, and granting more and more in return. I dreamed that people from all over the world had come to see Lera and stretched their arms out toward her, and in my half delirium I thought I was saying to her, "Come with me and we'll always be together, after all I love you more than anything in the world," and it seemed to me that from among this crowd of humanity from ages past and hence, all come to worship her, she who had walked the earth unrecognized from the time of its creation but had suddenly been revealed in the guise of a random, common young woman from Achinsk, she had chosen me and responded to me with a look. I begged her, I called out that I had never seen anything more beautiful than she was, I exulted in her, and I knew that she was the first and the last, worshipped and despised, whore and saint, matron and maiden, mother and daughter. And all these people of ages past and ages hence, and Misha, and Zhanna, and the old ambulance driver, and Sergei, and the conductors, and me along with them, we all stretched our arms toward her to take her with us or to tear her to pieces, to possess at least a part of her.

When I woke I was frightened by the silence that reigned inside the train car. All the people were back in their original spots, sitting quietly in some sort of strange stupor. Misha, black-out drunk, lay in his spot on the upper berth. Perhaps because he had bumped into something again, his hands were covered in blood. The old ambulance driver sat with a joyful smile frozen on his face, like a corpse. An elderly woman in glasses, who had worked on crosswords throughout the entire trip, looked puzzled and spooked. Zhanna had blood on her lips and tears in her eyes. Lera was nowhere to be found. There was an hour and a half left to Krasnodar, but Lera was nowhere. No one was trying to look for her, nobody moved, in the hungover silence only the wheels rattled and cried mechanically: you who awaited me, take me for yourselves, do not be arrogant when I've been cast to Earth, cast to Earth, ta-dah, ta-dah, cast to Earth.

THE SECT

Gunya and Kipa were unskilled laborers at a factory. The factory was near the port, there was always a cold wind blowing, and in November the sky came low to the ground and clung to the factory buildings. The factory produced ships, tankers, floating cranes, docks, and the like. Gunya was the gas, Kipa the breaks. One day they were loading boxes, and then Kipa sat down, lost in thought.

"What are you thinking about, Kipa?" Gunya asked.

"It's hard to explain."

"Hell, I'm not an idiot, I'll understand, I understand everything. Tell me, Kipa."

"So, in my head there's a sect of either devil worshippers, or adherents of the primordial abyss, or acolytes of the resurrected dead, or they believe in vampires and mermaids, or it's something even worse than that. It's the worst sect in the world, Gunya. It has a really bad reputation."

"Kipa, where exactly does it have a, uh, bad reputation?"

"In my head, Gunya. But to counteract the sect there's a kind of—what should I call it—a special police. But even still, they, the sect members, occasionally make their way into my dreams, and they always say the same thing: 'We can't live without love. We're dying. We can't live without love.' Just imagine, Gunya, that's what they say, and then it's like I recognize them, the sect members, like I've always known them, before I knew my own mother, and I understand exactly what they mean, and it really hurts me. And then order gets restored in my head, they disappear like momentary glitches, and I stop feeling like they're dying because they can't live without love. But they are dying, Gunya, they're dying because they can't live without love, I know it deep down in my heart."

"You're a motherfucker, Kipa, for telling me this. But you know what, Kipa, that really is the worst sect, don't listen to them. Or you're gonna lose your mind."

"You're a motherfucker, Gunya, I'm telling you—they're dying. Without love. That's how it is. And that's a motherfucking horrible disaster-catastrophe."

"You should see a shrink, Kipa. A good shrink. Maybe there's not enough love in your own life? And your, uh, psyche, is letting you know that you don't have enough love, that's if we follow what's-his-name, Freud, here?"

"I have so much love in my life, Gunya, it's coming out of my ass. I live on it, love. I love my family, I love my cat, I love you, Gunya, I love everyone I meet, I love this factory and these boxes. I love everything, Gunya, but that's not enough for them. I get it. You see, it's not specifically my problem. It's a general problem that exists—a problem of matter, of substance, of the place where we are, basically it's a problem of everything. There's not enough love, everything dies because of that. That's still the case even if you're Mother Teresa."

"Kipa, is there a place where there's enough love to live? For them to live?"

"I don't know, Gunya."

"Kipa, you know what, I can live without love. I can live just fine. I just don't have this problem at all. I can't live without money or without food. And it's pretty hard to live without fucking. But your sect members—they're just spoiled. A real man can live without love, I'll tell you that for sure."

"No, Gunya, one day you'll die, too, because you can't live without love. You just won't know what you're dying of. I think that everyone dies of that, matter doesn't just wear out for no reason." Gunya walked away from Kipa and started carrying boxes again. Kipa should get taken out, he thought, Kipa has completely lost it. He dragged and carried the boxes until lightning flashed before his eyes, and for an instant he saw a figure with a hood drawn over its face, and somewhere from the very depths of the abyss came a voice, wounding, severe, and full of grief, unmistakably familiar and heartrending: "We can't live without love. We're dying, Gunya. What are you doing, Gunya. We can't live without love."

"Who are you, what are you," Gunya's heart beat wildly, "you you you."

"You bitch!" Gunya shouted, "bitch!"

And it passed.

THE AMATEUR PORN STUDIO OF TRISHKA STRYUTSKY

> Yea, a sword shall pierce through thy own soul also,
> that the thoughts of many hearts may be revealed.
> —Prophecy of Saint Simeon the God-Receiver

> Trishka is going to be someone astounding . . .
> —Ivan Turgenev, "Bezhin Meadow"

TRISHKA STRYUTSKY IN THE FLESH

Trifon Iogannovich Stryutsky—generally considered a complete nonentity, an absolute zero, but in reality an underground pornographer—is looking out the window. His assistant, Vavila the idiot, an ex-boxer, is having tea with a bublik. In the room designated as the porn studio there's only one window, and nothing to be seen through it but clouds. In those clouds the sun shines in the night and the moon thrice in the day; woods grow in those clouds, and blood drops out of the wood, and the birds take their flight away together; the clouds cast out fish, and make a noise in the night which many have not known, and women bring forth monsters.

There's only one window, but the apartment itself is on the Obvodny Canal—an old apartment, filthy, with high ceilings. The room is spacious, by the wall there's an imposingly large bed made up with satin sheets, and above the bed, in a massive frame like the frame of an old portrait, there's a photograph of a pale woman in black against a background of clouds. There are seven swords stuck into her heart: three on the left and three on the right, and one from below. A rusty crossbar protrudes from the wall, with handcuffs hanging from it; on a rusty hook hangs an equally rusty collar; on a shelf there's a rubber mask; in a wardrobe there are leather belts and whips. The walls are bare, there are rolls of electrical tape, a spotlight, desk drawers full of rope . . .

The porn made by Trishka (that's what we'll call our hero) isn't regular porn—it's special. Trishka shoots on a camera with a tripod, all in one take, no angle changes, and lights the scene, while Vavila the idiot rapes and murders. Trishka has a client base: politicians, businessmen, show-business people, and other aesthetes. Trishka's videos are expensive; they're distributed through a special service, passed along hand to hand.

Trishka himself looks like this: his right eye is like a morning star rising, his left is like a lion's eye; his right hand is iron, his left is copper. He's balding, his eyes are tiny, there's a leprous rash on his forehead. With the raw blood of murder he waters the earth.

FIRST SWORD

Vavila is playing with the breasts of a plain but heavily made-up woman, teasing her. She's teasing him, too, treating him like a big dumb puppy: she goes about it mechanically, but honestly, working to earn out the sum, an unexpectedly large one for her, that

Trishka paid for the shoot. She doesn't hear the sounds of the trumpet announcing murder and death, and the voices of a multitude, like a very strong wind, like a whirlwind of an unreal flame coming across the desert.

She called herself Amanda online, where Trishka found her photo and her number. As for her real name, Trishka didn't ask. Katenka, Katenka was her real name. She liked him right away: at the Coffee House on Vosstaniya Square he ordered her a huge coffee cocktail with cream and syrup and asked her about her life. He had come to her in sheep's clothing, but was inwardly a ravening wolf.

Amanda had lived in Petersburg for two years; she was from Omsk but she had nobody left there but her penniless mother, her father had drunk himself to death a long time ago, when the factory where he worked had closed. Amanda came to study at the University of Service and Economics, which was hard for her; she worked nights as a waitress, failed her exams, and left after the first year. She found an ad in the paper offering "work for young women" and started working on the side as a prostitute to make enough to rent a room and pay her tuition at the university. Then she decided not to get involved with any agencies but instead to find clients herself, on the internet, and rented a room with another woman also who worked as a prostitute. They occasionally went out to clubs, and Amanda fell in love with the keyboard player in a little-known band, because he had long hair and sad eyes and his band played vulgar songs about love that Amanda liked. But she couldn't bring herself to approach him—she was fundamentally a shy, quiet girl. And far from beautiful, though she tried to look fashionable and up-to-date and went regularly to a salon to tan her face the color of brick. But Trishka understood everything about her right away—most importantly, he saw that nobody would miss her, she'd drop of out sight, and God help her.

That's how Amanda-Katenka was lost. Here she is now, in the light of the lamp: her face the color of brick, cheap foundation, small breasts, dyed hair, rusty collar around her skinny neck. The poor woman is thinking about how she'll spend the money she got from Trishka: she'll see a cosmetologist, buy herself a purse, and she needs a new jacket, too, what kind of jacket does she want, she wonders . . .

Trishka indicates to Vavila with a look: it's time. Vavila pulls a sword from the heart of the lady in black and stabs it into Katenka's heart. From the spot on the photograph where the sword had been runs a thin stream of blood. Katenka's head falls back and to the side in surprise, her eyes are looking out the window, at the clouds—like when she was a child, when she'd fall on the ground and her mother would scream, "Get up, bitch!" while Katenka looked up at the sky, and it spun around her, and it was like nothing else—no houses, no stores—existed, and then Katenka would be helped to her feet and all those things would reappear, and Katenka would smile.

SECOND SWORD

Vavila ties up a girl who may be about thirteen and whips her. On a table, swaddled, sleeps the baby she brought with her, evil Trishka has pressed a chloroformed cloth to its temples so it'll sleep more deeply. "You're not a virgin?" Trishka asks the girl suddenly.

"What do you mean," she says, "that's my baby over there!"

"Right, of course," says Trishka through his teeth, continuing to film.

Vavila smirks: he knows that Trishka likes virgins most of all. His dream is that all of their victims should be virgins, but for technical reasons this is usually impossible: "Not many virgins in the world these days, they're all whores starting at twelve," Trishka likes to say. "And if someone's a virgin you can't get through to her, she's got parents, a happy family—we need girls that won't be missed," Trishka likes to say.

Trishka feels a particular piety and esteem for virgins. And for mothers, too. The figure of the mother is sacred to him. "The goddamn liberals ruined everything," Trishka says. "Before all the girls were virgins, all the women were mothers, now they're all childless whores." Vavila has the vague idea that Trishka killed his own mother. Sometimes Trishka gets drunk and laments, "Woe to me, mother-killer, goddamn Nero . . ." Or he'll stand for a long time, tears in his eyes, in front of the photo of the lady in black. Vavila asked him once, "Who is that? Did you kill her or not?"

"That's her, the Beloved, my mother," said Trishka brokenly. Then Vavila decided that he definitely killed her.

The thirteen-year-old girl's name is Nezhdana, meaning "unexpected," that's the name her father gave her because he didn't expect that he'd get that teenage slut, her mother, pregnant. All her childhood Nezhdana's mother beat her, saying, "You're gonna get knocked up." And Nezhdana did get knocked up—by her stepfather. After that Nezhdana ran away from her mother and stepfather and lived in an abandoned apartment with some addicts. She started shooting up, too, and working as a prostitute in order to feed herself and her child and make enough for a fix. She met Trishka in the street, pulling at his sleeve: "Would you like to relax a little?" Trishka looked at her: bruises under her eyes, swollen lips, straw-colored hair falling onto her forehead, and said, "Why don't you come with me, Cinderella, how would you like to be in a movie?"

And the sheep became wolves, and love became hatred. And Vavila took as a nest the riches of her: and as one gathers the eggs that are left, gathered he all her earth; and there was none that moved a wing, or opened a mouth, or peeped. And Trishka left the camera and went toward the baby, and said to her, "Watch!" and began to squeeze the life from the babe right in front of her. Nezhdana tried to break free, to scream, to spit the black gag from her mouth. When he was finished, Trishka returned to the camera and gave Vavila a sign, and Vavila pulled a sword from the heart of the woman in black and stuck it into Nezhdana's heart.

Nezhdana looks out of the window, into the clouds, and sees an angel standing in the sun, holding her baby in his arms; and he cries with a loud voice, saying to all the fowl that fly in the midst of heaven, come and gather yourselves together unto the great supper; that you may eat the flesh of kings, the flesh of captains, the flesh of mighty men, the flesh of horses and their riders, and the flesh of all men, both free and slave, both small and great. On the film shot by Trishka there are reflections created by the window in the room, and, as during a fortune-telling session, Nezhdana's image disappearing into the depths along the reflective surface of the glass.

THIRD SWORD

Aunt Lyuba sucks Vavila's dick; tears stream from her violet, vodka-soused eyes from the effort. Vavila is smiling happily. He found Aunt Lyuba for Trishka all by himself—you could say he fell for her.

Aunt Lyuba is about fifty, she works as a janitor and aide at a school, lives alone, and is halfway to being a real bum. At first Vavila saw her ass on the school's porch, which she was sweeping, bent over, and then she turned around with her alcoholic mug and violet eyes, and Vavila was thunderstruck. Smiling widely and even drooling a little with excitement, he went up to her and invited her to visit him and Trishka and make a movie. He said, "Come see us, darling. I'll introduce you to Trishka. You know what he's like? He's like Cain, Lamech, Nimrod, Chedorlaomer, Pharaoh, Abimelech, Saul, Goliath, Absalom, Balaam, Antiochus Epiphanes—that's our Trishka."

Aunt Lyuba comes, they give her cognac, she gets talkative with these two respectable gentlemen paying attention to her, gentlemen who can afford such decent liquor. "I can do anything," she says. "I can get naked and dance on the table. I can suck dicks. So."

"I can do anything, too," Trishka says to her, and pats her hand, "a word from me and the sun will rise in the middle of the night, and the moon will appear at the sixth hour of day; I can do anything in this world that I desire, and I do and speak as the Beloved . . ."

"You are the Beloved, Trishka," Aunt Lyuba exclaims, "who are you if not the Beloved! You're my Beloved! You're my heart's desire, Trishka!"

"All I do in this life is fulfill people's heart's desires, Lyuba. What do you desire?"

"I'd like to dance and sing, Trishka, and you can make a movie about me, the Queen of Heaven!"

"You're the Queen of Heaven, Lyuba, go ahead, sing and dance, Beloved!"

Aunt Lyuba gets naked and dances while Vavila claps along. She dances and she remembers herself as a young woman, a member of the Komsomol. And her hard, mixed-up life seems funny and bright to her—her husband leaving her, bringing up her daughter alone on the money she made as an illegal peddler at the market, a seamstress at a factory, now a school janitor. And her daughter grew up, moved far away, married a rich guy, an American, and doesn't even write. A beautiful daughter, with violet eyes—looks just like her mother. "Want me to bring you some girls? Schoolgirls?" Aunt Lyuba asks. "They need money, too, the little jerks, they can dance for you and make a movie . . ."

Vavila takes Lyuba by her hair and throws her onto the bed, and she laughs. He pulls a sword from the photo of the strange lady against a background of clouds, aims it at Lyuba's heart, and blood runs from the wound in the portrait, and Lyuba sees clouds like milk kissel, and they fill with a red dawn and unroll like scrolls, and in them is the village where Lyuba's Grandma Mavra used to live, and she'll warm up the samovar, and there will be pies waiting for her, and Lyuba thinks, "I was out for so long," but where she went and what she saw—she can't remember a thing.

FOURTH SWORD

"How low you've fallen, Verochka. Come with me, and ascend into heaven. I will exalt my throne above the stars of God and we will sit also upon the mount of the congregation, in the sides of the north, we will ascend above the heights of the clouds." In this way Trishka talked Verochka, a homeless woman, into coming with him to be in a movie. Verochka didn't want to come at first because she thought that Trishka was a social worker making a film about homeless people, but Trishka calmed her down, saying that the movie wasn't about homeless people but about love and death.

Verochka smells, so Trishka and Vavila run her a warm bath. They dress her in a long black lace camisole. "That's the color of the world," says Trishka. They give her blood-red lace stockings. "That's the color of the world dying in fire," says Trishka. They give her a snow-white garter belt to go with the stockings. "That's the color of the world to come," says Trishka, "the future world," and he winces. Verochka nearly purrs with pleasure. Here she is, in the light of the lamp, her mouth taped shut with electrical tape, in handcuffs. Trishka is filming, Vavila is giving her the wine of the wrath of fornication.

Verochka has been homeless for a long time. At one point she was married, and she and her husband had an apartment on Bucharest Street. Her husband drank and in a bad moment made a deal, and their apartment was taken away. Verochka tried to sort out what had happened; she mentioned some black-market realtors, there was a court case, but the judge confirmed it—everything was over, they'd lost the apartment. Verochka made a fuss, shouting that it wasn't fair, that the judge was a bought-and-paid-for whore, that her husband was an alcoholic and a moron, that she had nowhere to go, in her little hometown in Central Russia she had nothing and no one left . . . Her husband disappeared along with the remainder of their possessions. Verochka got a job as a janitor, and they let her live illegally in an attic apartment without doors or furniture, where some teenage fascists held meetings and a whole wall was covered in swastikas. Verochka stayed there for two years, working as a janitor, started drinking,

and then couldn't work anymore; then she started living anywhere she could, sleeping in subway crossing tunnels. At first she
tried to get back on her feet, find another job, but no place would
hire her if she didn't have an address, and she didn't look pre-
sentable; for a while she found work as a walking billboard, but
then Verochka abandoned these attempts.

And so Trishka and Vavila lead Verochka in by her white
hands. Walking toward them in the stairwell are orderlies from
the insane asylum; they're taking away the resident of the neighboring apartment. The man tries to break free, screaming that
he'll waste them all and that in Trishka's apartment there's a psy-
ops machine being used against him, and that he thinks Trishka
is invisibly violating him, anally. In the apartment above this man
lived a woman with her intellectually disabled son, and Trishka
sometimes considered her but preferred to abide by the maxim
of not shitting where you eat. By the garbage there's a blooming pepper plant without a pot. "Can we take it?" Verochka asks.
She loves plants and animals. Trishka and Vavila obediently pick
up the plant.

Vavila pulls a sword from the heart of the lady in black, Vera
screams like a struck gazelle. And she sees clouds in the window—or are they the clouds in the photograph, behind the lady's
back? She sees in the clouds a multitude of feathery eagles who
fly to her, screeching, from the direction of the sunset. And there
before them she feels pity for something small, childish, maybe
that plant or the homeless kitten that she loved and fed when she
was a janitor. As though there had been nothing else in her life,
just this kitten.

FIFTH SWORD

A naked five-year-old girl sits on Vavila's knee. She has huge eyes, shining like gold among coals, black curly hair, and tan skin. She's remarkably beautiful. Her name is Lailo, but at the orphanage from which Trishka took her, paying the orphanage director a bribe, everyone just called her Lyalya. She got used to it.

At the orphanage everyone disliked her being darker-skinned, and they beat her for it, and she cried every day. Then the director and Trishka came to look at the little girls. Lyalya was drawing, and Trishka asked, "What's that?" The drawing was of an animal a bit like a snow leopard, with legs like a bear's legs, and a mouth like a lion's mouth. "It's a animal," said Lyalya. "Want to come with me?" Trishka asked. "No," said Lyalya, so Trishka chose her specifically. "They filled up all the orphanages, the damn dirty migrants," commented the director.

Five years ago Lyalya was born to a Tajik woman named Sitora, meaning "star." Sitora came to Petersburg to earn money, worked as a janitor, then as a waitress. One elderly gentleman seduced Sitora, and she became pregnant. The elderly gentleman then wanted nothing to do with her, and Sitora had no place to live and no registration stamp in her passport. She called an ambulance and waited for the medics on a bench by the nearest apartment building. She gave birth, but she and the child had nowhere to go. She was terrified, and the next day would be even more terrifying, and she signed a document giving up her daughter. "Maybe in the city of Petersburg there will be people with money and a home, and they'll take care of you, little Lailo," she said to her daughter in farewell.

These people turned out to be Trishka. He has friends

among the directors of orphanages, sanctuaries, shelters, among the police, the functionaries, the city officials, among businessmen and politicians. While Vavila abuses Lailo, in the city council they're discussing a bill to outlaw kissing in the street. "Kisses in the street offend the sensibilities of law-abiding citizens," screams a representative from the Just Russia Party. The representatives whisper to one another about something, pass something along to one another surreptitiously—the latest, exclusive porno from "our Trishka," as they call him.

Vavila pulls a sword from the lady's heart and stabs it into little Lailo. The clouds part, and the snow leopard—symbol of the 2014 Sochi Olympics—meets the little girl and leads her to the orchard in the Tajikistan in the sky, full of fruits unfamiliar to her—cherries, peaches, pomegranates—and a woman in white with black braids walking among the trees and glowing brightly, like a sitora-star.

SIXTH SWORD

Gayana is screaming loudly, her tangled dark-blond hair, with some gray locks mixed in, falling in her face. "You're a tsar! You're a dragon! You're an eagle!" she shouts, standing on all fours, looking at Trishka and his camera and rocking with each move Vavila makes. Trishka is delighted—Gayana has turned out to be a virgin. She has huge pupils, a thin body, sharp facial features, deep shadows under her eyes. "Our land has been devasted by the wicked," Gayana screams.

Trishka took her from the psychiatric institution where she'd spent the last fifteen years. The director of this institution was another friend of his and gave him Gayana for a bribe.

Trishka wandered through the wards for a long time, choosing a woman, but he liked Gayana best of all. "Have you come for me, Beloved?" she asked as soon as she saw him.

Gayana's mother hadn't allowed her to date, had controlled her every move, and said that "All men are traitors. You'll trust him, you little fool, and he'll have his way with you and leave you with a belly." This was exactly what had happened to Gayana's mother once, and she put all of her efforts toward ensuring that her daughter wouldn't suffer the same sad fate. But all Gayana had wanted to do since she was fourteen was go out with boys. She wanted to so badly, she bit her lips until they bled and cut her arms with a razor blade. But although Gayana was a pretty girl, she grew up so stifled and repressed that there was no chance of any men. Gayana was afraid of them and believed her mother when she said they were all traitors.

She lived quietly with her mother, studying at the forestry academy, and there was one young man there, quiet and repressed like her, a lousy student who barely spoke to anyone; the other students all disliked him and treated him like an outcast, but Gayana liked him. Sometimes she looked at him, and he looked back at her, and she dreamed about him. Once, on a dark winter morning, as she passed through the park on her way to the academy, he caught up to her, threw her to the ground and started touching her, put his hands under her clothes, touched her breasts and between her legs, and then ran away. Gayana never told anyone about it, but she knew that she must be guilty of something terrible if something like that could happen to her. My mother will kill me if she finds out, she'll say that I'm a prostitute, Gayana thought. My sin is probably having thought about this boy, he decided to give me what I wanted and what I deserved, this happened because I'm so corrupt.

Gayana decided to ask God for forgiveness and went to church, and then she started going to church all the time, praying constantly and sticking needles into her arms. After a while she began hearing voices calling her various bad names. The voices mocked her, and once, when she was in class at the academy, they ordered her to undress, and she took off her clothes and ran naked through the school, shouting. An ambulance was called, and Gayana was taken to the hospital. After some time there they brought her back to normal, and for a few years Gayana lived quietly with her mother and suffered only infrequent episodes. But her mother died, and her only living relative, her mother's sister, wanted their apartment for herself; she used her connections, paid some bribes, and when Gayana had another episode her aunt had her committed to an institution, which is where Trishka found her.

Trishka indicates to Vavila with a look. Vavila pulls a sword from the photograph and stabs it into Gayana's chest. Gayana sees clouds in the window, and her departed mother, and she remembers how they would take walks when Gayana was little. Gayana wanted to ride the Ferris wheel, but her mother said no, said it was too scary, and here in the clouds there was a giant Ferris wheel, and her mother was smiling and calling Gayana, and it wasn't scary at all.

SEVENTH SWORD

Ninel Vladlenovna lies beneath Vavila like an old, petrified log. Occasionally she calls out: "Materialism is the best philosophy! Consciousness is an aspect of matter! Quantity becomes quality! Development is achieved through the struggle of opposites!

Knowledge is the reflection of objective reality! Practice is the criterion of truth! The mode of production in material life determines the processes of life! The state is an instrument of class rule! The masses are the makers of history! From each according to his ability, to each according to his need! Friendship of the peoples!"

"That's right, that's exactly right, Ninel Vladlenovna," says Trishka, filming the events.

He'd found ninety-year-old Ninel Vladlenovna in a home for the elderly, where her children and grandchildren had deposited her because they were sick of caring for her at home. How much more can we take, they thought, she's unbearable, she's had dementia for ages and shits herself and still takes up a whole room while the kids have nowhere to live, and they're going to have children themselves at some point. And all she does is shout her slogans all day long! The slogans were particularly problematic—they couldn't have anyone over, lest this ex-Party worker and professor of Marxism-Leninism start shouting from her room, things like "Democracy for the workers! The working class is the liberator of laboring humanity!"

How embarrassing! said her children and grandchildren. How embarrassing! You're not supposed to think that these days, but in the depths of her dementia she's putting all her insides on display, and we know what she's like on the inside, it's just all Marxism-Leninism. A person is like a toilet bowl, what you shit into it is what you'll find. That's how Ninel Vladlenovna wound up in a home for the elderly, from which Trishka took her up, for a bribe, while the director of the home filled out the documents saying she'd died of old age.

Ninel Vladlenovna pisses herself. "Will capitalism ever be rid of economic crises?" she asks in a tremulous but still firm voice, looking Vavila in the eyes. "Enough already? Enough? Can I be done?" Vavila can't take it and turns to Trishka. Trishka nods. Vavila pulls a sword from the photograph of the lady in black and stabs it into the old woman's heart. The clouds are waiting for her, and in them she sees, for some reason, the maternity ward, and the ward is full of clouds. Ninel has a bundle in her arms—her firstborn son—and she feels happy and proud that she's brought another person into the world, and he'll live for socialism and the brotherhood of all people and won't let the strong oppress the weak.

TRISHKA AND THE LADY IN BLACK

Trifon Iogannovich Stryutsky—generally considered a complete nonentity, an absolute zero, but in reality an underground pornographer—is looking out the window. His assistant, Vavila the idiot, an ex-boxer, is having tea with a bublik. In the window there are clouds. "She's coming! Vavila, she's coming!" Trishka suddenly shouts. "Who's coming?" Vavila doesn't understand. "She is! The Beloved!" Trishka whispers.

The doorbell rings, Vavila goes to open the door; Trishka freezes, unable to move. Vavila and the lady in black from the portrait come into the room. The lady looks very young, she's wearing sunglasses, in her arms there's a swaddled dead infant. "Mama," Trishka says to her. "You've come! I've always dreamed about you, my whole life!"

"Film this! It'll be a video the likes of which the world has never seen," Trishka calls to Vavila and starts tearing off his clothes. The lady stands there without moving. Vavila hops to the tripod and begins to film. When Trishka is undressed, Vavila sees a wound opposite his heart, as though from a sword. Trishka goes up to the lady in black, takes the infant from her arms and puts it on the table, then throws the lady in black on the bed, lies on top of her, and prepares to enter her in one swift movement, but as soon as he makes that movement, ice and fire, horror and light run through his body, and at that very moment he dies. In that moment Vavila looks out the window and sees a gathering in the clouds: Katenka-Amanda with the brick-colored face and cheap foundation, thirteen-year-old Nezhdana with straw-colored hair, Aunt Lyuba with her violet eyes, homeless Verochka in blood-red stockings with a white garter belt, tan five-year-old Lailo, insane Gayana, ancient Ninel Vladlenovna with her stern scowl. They are all looking into the room, pointing at Trishka, and singing poignantly and sweetly, triumphantly and bitterly.

The lady in black rises up from the bed, removes her glasses, gives Vavila a long look that he'll always remember, leaves the room, descends the stairs, and disappears forever, and Vavila hears her low heels clicking on the steps. The infant cries out; Vavila unwraps him and sees that he is alive, though opposite his heart is a wound, as though from a sword. The infant looks at Vavila with a long and intelligent look full of light and majesty, similar to the look of the lady in black. In his eyes is the clarity of someone who has woken from death as from a long illness, and in his gaze the world is cleansed, as though it were being consumed by flames and being born again for a new, different life. Vavila looks at the infant for a long time, then picks him up, saying, "Now you'll be with me. I'll bring you up. I'll call you . . . Trishka. You're Trishka, you're the Beloved."

FAREWELL TO VAVILA AND TRISHKA

Vavila took little Trishka in his arms and headed to the train station to get out of this city once and for all. Birds were chirping all around, countless couples were kissing. Vavila and little Trishka passed through it all as though through layers of cloud. In these clouds Katenka-Amanda spun with her arms out, smiling, and Nezhdana with her baby in her arms stood on the sun together with the angel. Vavila carried Trishka past the village in the clouds where Lyuba and her Grandma Mavra were drinking tea from the samovar and eating pies; eagles screeched, and in the clouds Verochka played with a kitten; Lailo walked in the cloud orchard in the Tajikistan in the sky among cherry trees, peaches, and pomegranates, Gayana rode an enormous Ferris wheel, its top lost in the clouds, and Ninel Vladlenovna walked out of the hospital with her son, and her face was shining.

We greet You, Beloved!

EPILOGUE

"Let's watch this video, I found it online yesterday. You know, it's pretty weird, but there's something about it. There's a chick, she's really hot, she's wearing black, and there's this guy trying to fuck her. He gets naked and throws her down on the bed, but as soon as he starts fucking her—he dies. Just out of nowhere: he starts giving it to her and just drops dead. That's cool, huh? Anyway, fuck . . . It's like he wanted her so bad, I don't know, his heart couldn't take it. But it looks kind of mystical, even. Anyway, you can jerk off to it, for sure."

SEVEN EDELWEISS FLOWERS FOR MY BETROTHED (A SHAMANIC JOURNEY)

A priest had come to hold a service in a mountain chapel. Roe deer roared in the forests, vipers crawled across the road, stone obelisks in prickly grass made sounds resembling throat singing. Two lovers got lost in the wild currant bushes, while a young poacher in a cowboy hat dug up golden root. I was picking edelweiss flowers in the valley for my betrothed, and when I plucked the seventh flower I fainted and woke up in the iron castle of Erlik Khan. There was a pretty decent bunch gathered there: dark shamans who'd burned on the cursed mountain (yes, that too happened once upon a time); old village ladies; an agronomist and a veterinarian, Klara and Tamara, who performed shamanic rituals at night; a young shaman who'd recently gotten out of prison; even that one powerful shaman from the Bely Anuy village; and a few others who had nothing to do with shamanism: a redheaded guy with a rifle who had been afraid of mountains for a long time after Chechnya, a girl from Moscow named Emma, a strange dark-complexioned guy who looked like he was either Roma or a roadside bandit, said nothing about himself, and gave such contradictory answers to questions that everyone suspected he was lying. There were others, too, people I didn't know. After the end of the service the priest appeared. We were seated at a table in a fissure in the earth, everything was made of iron, our faces began to lose their shapes, blood flowed across the table, shadows hovered and joined us in raising goblets full of bloody iron. Lizards darted, subterranean waters rose, something was tearing our bodies, smashing the atoms, hissing, rattling. A bear and a wolverine entered. From the castle I saw mountains and valleys, and water flowing over fields of golden root, and riders stopping to rest. We had become very drunk, and Erlik was with us, he had long black hair, he looked like a death metal fan. He tucked his mustache behind his ears and quoted Nietzsche. He called himself a nihilist, wore seven bearskins, and carried a sword of green iron. The sun of the lower world glowed dully. Erlik told us, "I love the color black, because I love sorrow and dirt. That's the color of sorrow and dirt. The color of the cosmos and of earth." When he said this, it was like I drowned in sorrow and dirt, dissolved in the cosmos and in the earth, and I went to cry on the shore of the River Toybodim, and I saw the dyutpa. And Adam Erlik taught us to enter other worlds and took us to the swamp to huff benzine, and then to the lake of the suicides. Adam Erlik told us that it was he who had breathed life into people. Once, in his cup, a flower had bloomed—the flower of the creator. He created the mountains, the wild beasts and the reptiles, he created misfortune, diseases, bears, badgers, moles, camels, cows. When someone dies, the soul returns to him, the creator. He led us to great halls encircled by streams and into rocky screes. He saw us to the black stump, to the cauldron of boiling water, and we emerged from beneath the earth. We were no longer people;

we were flowers in a blinding alpine bitterness. Emma became a burnet, the redheaded guy was a tansy, and I was a mountain cornflower. It was fall, and I saw that I could kill with a look. And then we became birds, then rain in a burning garden, then sudden rays, river fog, blueberries. And the priest said, "We must have died and become Kermes demons, Erlik's servants." But I said, "No, we're alive, we're alive! I can hear my heart beating." After that we became music. I was the sound of an ocarina, a whistle that the village children played with. We were weapons: bows, arrows, knives, spears; we were the newest weaponry: lasers, railguns, coilguns, intercontinental ballistic missiles; we were called Sotka, Voevoda, Topol, Rubezh, Sarmat. We were drones moving faster than the speed of sound, we destroyed the world, destroyed humanity, and there, in the infinite space we moved through, I remembered who we were: the thirty-eight antiatoms once caught in a Penning trap, we were returning to our antiworld, reverse space-time, and here came the stars—not stars but antistars, and I saw that between them the edelweiss flowers were spinning, the seven edelweiss flowers I had once picked for my betrothed . . .

A SCARY STORY

Lying in her grave, a dead woman asks: "oh, feet, my poor feet, what did you ever do for me?"

"all your life we walked for you, went door to door, rushed around, took care of things, served you loyally. now we're tired, let us rest."

"isn't that the truth. rest in peace, you've served me well." the feet fall asleep.

then the dead woman asks: "oh, hands, my poor hands, what did you ever do for me?"

"all your life we worked for you, labored at the factory, cooked at home, cleaned, rocked the children, served you loyally. now we're tired, let us rest."

"isn't that the truth. rest in peace, you've served me well." the hands fall asleep.

then the dead woman asks: "and you, cunt, what did you ever do for me?"

"all your life i served you, lived with your husband, birthed your children. now i'm tired, let me rest."

"isn't that the truth. rest in peace, you've served me well."
the cunt falls asleep.

then the dead woman asks: "and you, ass, what did you ever
do for me?"

"all your life i served you, cleaned you out every day, sat on
hard things and didn't complain. now i'm tired, let me rest."

"isn't that the truth. rest in peace, you've served me well."
the ass falls asleep.

then the dead woman asks: "oh, stomach, my poor stomach,
what did you ever do for me?"

"all your life i served you, digested your food, carried your
children. now i'm tired, let me rest."

"isn't that the truth. rest in peace, you've served me well."
the stomach falls asleep.

then the dead woman asks: "oh, back, my poor back, what
did you ever do for me?"

"all your life i served you, stooped and toiled. now i'm tired,
let me rest."

"isn't that the truth. rest in peace, you've served me well."
the back falls asleep.

then the dead woman asks: "oh, breasts, my poor breasts,
what did you ever do for me?"

"we fed your children, raised up three of them. now we're
tired, let us rest."

"isn't that the truth. rest in peace, you've served me well."
the breasts fall asleep.

then the dead woman asks: "oh, neck, my poor neck, what
did you ever do for me?"

"all your life i served you, held your unruly head up, bent

down before the powerful, but didn't break. now i'm tired, let me rest."

"isn't that the truth. rest in peace, you've served me well." the neck falls asleep.

then the dead woman asks: "oh my wretched head, what did you ever do for me?"

"you know what i did. i ruined your whole life, poisoned it, thought black thoughts, suffered and ached."

"isn't that the truth. be gone from here, damn you! there's not going to be any rest for you!" the head breaks through the lid of the coffin, tears through layers of earth, and rolls away.

the head goes rolling through the cemetery and it meets a crow. "hey, head, i'm going to peck out your eyes!"

"what do i care, i'm dead!" and the head rolls on.

the head goes rolling down the path and it meets a cat. "hey, head, i'm going to scratch up your face!"

"more the fool you, you mangy cat!" and the head rolls on.

the head goes rolling through the grass and it meets a dog. "hey, head, i'm going to bite you right in the—in the—head!"

"oh yeah? i'm going to bite you instead!" and the head gnashes its teeth. whimpering, the dog runs off, and the head rolls on.

at the edge of the cemetery, by the woods, the head finds an abandoned trailer, rolls underneath, and settles in. it lies there, teeth chattering, thinking its black thoughts, not at rest. sometimes it snows, sometimes flowers bloom, but the head stays there. it hasn't got anywhere else to go. it's there even now.

THREE MURDERERS

The face of the Other [signifies]: You shall not kill me.
—Emmanuel Levinas

Three terrifying murderers ran into one another and got to talking. The conversation revolved around what, precisely, had made them into murderers.

"I'm not actually a bad person by nature," said one, "but the environment I've been in since childhood has sent everything good inside of me into hiding and gave succor to everything that was bad. I grew up surrounded by criminals, amid brutality and crime, and my very first steps took me down the wrong path. Eventually, not right away, I became a murderer, too."

"That makes sense," said the second murderer, "I'm not so bad, either. But when I was a child, I was subjected to horrific violence. My mind is occasionally clouded by bursts of rage, and then I lose control of myself and kill anyone within reach. I even killed my beloved wife."

"And what about you?" they asked the third man, a skinny guy who was looking at the ground; it was unclear whether or not he'd been listening to their stories. He had the reputation of being the cruelest and most terrifying murderer of all, there was no one who compared to him. "What about me?" he looked up.

"What about you, why do you kill people?"

"Oh, that's what you're talking about. OK, listen." And he began his tale.

"The way that some people are born without an arm or a leg, I was born without a particular sense that most people possess—it seems like even you have it. I was born without the ability to feel that other people are alive, that they're just like me. No matter how much I looked at people and at the world around me, everything lacked life, as though I were surrounded by soulless machines. Living was nauseating and boring, since I was the only one in the world who really existed, and everyone else was just a moving image. But everything changed when I saw death and agony, saw another person suffering and dying. In those moments, as this person was suffering and dying, I could suddenly feel that he was alive. That he was just like me. So in those moments, an infinite world was revealed to me, and everything became real. For the first time in my life, I felt reality around me. As though the canvas on which all those moving images had been drawn was torn to pieces, revealing the huge, infinite reality it had concealed. But my only access to this reality was by way of agony and death. Having opened this door once, I wanted to open it again and again. I wanted to feel that other people were alive, too. In order for that to happen, I had to kill them. That's why I became a murderer, torturing my victims ingeniously and at length."

"Uh-huh," said the first murderer.

"Well now, isn't that something," said the second murderer.

"Isn't there another way to, uh, feel that other people are alive?" asked the first murderer.

"Nope," said the guy.

"Why do you think you were born that way, without that sense?" asked the second murder.

"I don't know," said the guy, "I just was. I mean, it happens that people lack something, like a genetic defect. That's how it is with me, too." The murderers parted ways.

"I'm not so terrible, it turns out," thought the first murderer. "Sure, I kill people, but my environment made me that way, I'm a victim, too. This guy, on the other hand, is a moral monster, barely a human being."

"There's some folks out there worse than me," thought the second murderer. "I killed my wife, but I did love her, and I respected her as a person. And my mother, but I loved her, too. I regretted it. But this guy's scum, a total psychopath, a degenerate."

The third murder walked on and on, not thinking about anything at all. The world he walked through was somehow colorless, plastic, unreal. The sun shone like a drawing of the sun. People walked toward him like moving mannequins. Only a cry of pain at the brink of death could strike, like lightning, through all this falseness, this emptiness and loneliness, could rend the curtain, return reality to things, throw him into a live eternity, in which the Face of the Other looks upon him: others like him, writhing, screaming "No, no, don't," real, living people, his brothers and sisters.

THE GRAY MAN

A friend of mine turned into a total zombie. He stopped being
interested in anything, would hardly speak, and really became
a living machine. Looking at my friend carefully with the true
sight, I saw that he was not exactly himself—that his personality had been driven inward, and there was now a gray headless
man living inside of him, making him be like that, like a zombie.
This gray headless creature served the warlock who had cursed
my friend. The creature lacked a head precisely because anyone
cursed in this manner is no longer able to think or have a personality. The gray man's purpose was to obey the warlock and also to
bring everything evil upon himself. Up until yesterday, I had no
idea how to break the curse that had been placed on my friend,
but a twist of fate led me to the Gold of the Inca exhibition at
the Museum of Ethnography, where I noticed an ancient musical instrument. On the instrument was the depiction of a man
and a gray headless creature that was withdrawing from him,
targeted by flying darts. I recognized the gray creature immediately—it was the same one that now lived inside my friend. It

occurred to me that the scene on the instrument showed the creature's exorcism, the breaking of the curse. It was a song played on this particular ancient instrument that would drive the gray creature from its host—that's what the instrument was made to do. I brought my friend to the museum right before it closed, made us invisible to the guards, took the instrument from its glass case, and began to play. As soon as the instrument sounded its first note, my friend brightened, a smile appeared on his face, and I saw that the gray headless creature was leaving him. In this way, I freed my friend from the headless gray man and solved the riddle of the Inca.

WRITERS

1

Once upon a time there lived a New Age psychologist. But he
didn't just exist—he excelled at every single thing he did. So he
decided to write a novel. The novel would reflect his key ideas,
which he believed in with his whole heart and soul. There were
three of them:

    I. Thoughts create reality.
    II. You are responsible for everything that happens to you.
    III. The true causes of all your problems are internal.

But once a dove shat on his head in the street, and the Spirit came
upon him. And everything in his novel came out backward, not
the way he'd wanted. He had tried to describe a world in which
there was room enough for everyone's potential to be realized,
but instead he described a world in which everything was somehow wrong. It was difficult to say what was wrong, exactly. It
wasn't even that the structure of society was somehow not right,

but that the structure of eternity wasn't right, and the characters who lived in this world just had no good options at all. They were all deeply decent, sensitive, thoughtful, and honorable people who wanted to realize their high-minded dreams. But in the end they either died, or went insane, or just grew sick of themselves and their dreams and gave up. No matter how the New Age psychologist tried to revise his text and steer it in the right direction, he wound up with a kind of objective reality wherein eternity itself was riven in half, and there were different ways to dress up the destruction of a person's soul, but the point was always the same: ruin, madness, exhaustion.

2

The New Age psychologist had a neighbor who was a handyman-philosopher. This man was a total loser, but other than that, he was a pure, beautiful, high-minded person. He didn't make much money, and what he made he spent on heroin. He was also working on a novel and wanted it to reflect his three main ideas:

I. Life is shit.
II. Life has no meaning.
III. Everyone's gonna die, and good riddance.

But a dove shat on his head, and the Spirit came upon him. And regardless of his intentions, his novel became full of people who succeeded at everything. Their thoughts shaped reality and became true; their willpower allowed them to change the world. They created, and birds and beasts obeyed them; they created and did not tire of their work, because they saw that it was good. By the end of their days they were old, wise, and enlightened;

they regretted nothing and accepted the world completely as it was. Through their creations they achieved immortality and eternal happiness.

3

Neither the New Age psychologist nor the handyman-philosopher finished his novel. The New Age psychologist abandoned his because it was distracting him from his private practice and making money, plus he was stressed out by the fact that he was producing some kind of depressing, incomprehensible bullshit. The handyman-philosopher didn't finish his because, first of all, he didn't believe in what he was writing, and, second of all, because he died of a heroin overdose.

The dove continues to shit on whomsoever it can.

So, basically, it works all kinds of ways.

MY FIRST
PSYCHOTIC BREAK

At the insane asylum, a group of patients at an art therapy session were asked to write an essay on the topic of "My First Psychotic Break."

Patient Demidov wrote about the time when, as a child, he was riding the subway with his mother, and on the seat in front of them lay a sleeping vagrant with his hand pillowing his cheek. The vagrant had a beard that looked like a yellow bath sponge, and an old, wrinkled face. He smelled. Demidov pointed to him and said to his mother, "Yuck, poopy!" His mother said, "And yet this man was once someone's beloved son, their favorite person in the world, just like you are mine. And yet someone fell in love with him once and dreamed about him." And that's when in the mind of Patient Demidov two and two did not make four for the first time.

Incidentally, Patient Demidov was brought to the asylum after a long period of vagrancy.

Patient Smirnov wrote about walking down the street with his adored grandmother and seeing some blue-gray pigeons.

"Birdie-birds," said Smirnov. Smirnov's grandmother said to him, "Pigeons are nice birds. You shouldn't be mean to them." The pigeons were cooing noisily, like meowing cats, strolling about in the spring sunshine. Little Smirnov smiled, clapped, said "Birdie-birds." The following day, right in front of Smirnov, the neighbor boy Nikita murdered a pigeon: bashed in its head with a rock, then wrung its neck for good measure. And that's when in the mind of Patient Smirnov two and two did not make four for the first time.

Incidentally, Patient Smirnov is a hardcore sadist, and his neighbors at the communal apartment had him committed after he skinned their cat.

Patient Konyukhov was an unimaginative person with no tendency toward introspection. It was hard for him to come up with an essay about his First Psychotic Break. So when Patient Konyukhov's elderly mother came to see him and bring him some gingerbread cookies and cigarettes, he asked her to go online when she got home and find him an essay about My First Psychotic Break. His elderly, obedient mother, whom Konyukhov had been beating for years, went home and started searching online for such an essay, but instead she found a poem by Yaroslav Mogutin, "My First Fist," which went like this:

I wanted to fuck him but I couldn't get hard I can never get hard on cocaine so I just let go and fell into a state of complete mindlessness and slavish submission and he started feeling around in me with his fingers eventually getting all five inside me folded up I thought that was the limit but he knew what he was doing and after a brief effort there was a whole fist inside of me the first fist of my life and I even thought I heard to mark the occasion a kind of earsplitting universal chord.

This poem, not a word of which she understood, Konyukhov's mother copied out by hand for her son. She didn't know what a "psychotic break" was in any case, but she remembered her son's heavy fist very well and decided that this would work. Patient Konyukhov turned in the poem as his essay.

Listless and yawning from time to time, Psychotherapist Lifshitz read through the patients' essays, but when he came to Konyukhov's he perked up. The following day he called Patient Konyukhov into his office and considered with great interest his coarse, feeble-minded face and enormous fists. And that's when in the mind of Psychotherapist Lifshitz two and two did not make four for the first time.

PATIENT Y

Patient Y sees both a psychiatrist and a psychoanalyst. He visits
the psychoanalyst twice a week and the psychiatrist twice a year,
for his prescriptions. He really loves going to the psychoanalyst,
but not so much the psychiatrist. This is because he's forced to
use two different modes of discourse with the two of them.

Let's say the psychoanalyst asks him, "What's changed for
you over the last ten years?" Patient Y describes in detail how he
came to lead the life he does, and what he's become, and what it's
all moving toward. He says he's a finished man, he has no future,
he's a pathetic nonentity, everything he held sacred a decade
ago has been betrayed and defiled. He says he lost everything—
family, love, career—and now sleeps with anyone at all, and his
only joy is shooting up. He says that he's developing apathy-
abulia syndrome, that he can't get anything done, lacks willpower, and nothing matters to him; he just lies prostrate at home,
he can't read or write or work, and his pensioner mother supports
him, meanwhile he thinks about suicide all the time but can't
bring himself to do it. The psychoanalyst is empathetic, and for

Patient Y it's pure joy that someone accepts him the way he is. Particularly because the psychoanalyst has no concept of normality, so he doesn't think that Y is a total psycho, no matter what he says about himself.

But then all the medication he has stocked up runs out, and Patient Y has to visit his psychiatrist to get the prescriptions refilled. Before writing out the prescriptions, the psychiatrist talks to Y and asks about things, for instance, that same "What's changed for you over the last ten years?" Patient Y knows that the psychiatrist is asking him this question in order to gauge just how low Y has sunk and decide whether to prescribe him something stronger, haloperidol, for example. Patient Y would prefer not to take haloperidol because for ten years he has remembered all too well what that's like. So Patient Y switches to a different discourse: "I think I'm doing much better," he says. "I'm a much calmer person now, more mature. I understand life better, I've gained some valuable experience. I got divorced, but that's for the best, and I lost my job, but it's better that way, too. Now I can start on something new and good. Life is interesting, I'm meeting a lot of new people, I read a lot, I write, I've written such and such pieces. And I have some thoughts about a job coming up, one that pays well." Y says all of this and sees profound skepticism in the eyes of his psychiatrist. Then the psychiatrist, shaking his head, writes out the prescriptions Y needs, and Y leaves, happy. The psychiatrist lights a cigarette and thinks, What a deeply disturbed psycho is this Y.

SPONSORED CONTENT

Allow me to introduce myself: I'm the angel of pure consciousness, an interior auditor, or, simply put, the proofreader of all your work. But not a regular proofreader. I work for an agency that reviews all the text you produce: letters, business correspondence, really anything you can think of. However, we don't care about your commas and minor typos, the concerns of regular proofreaders. We're on the lookout for something more important than that. For instance, the word COCK, written in all caps. Or CUNT. Or something else in that line. Just imagine how awkward this would be: you're writing a business email, and between the lines, for no reason at all, there's the word COCK. You're writing to your boss, and at the end of the letter, after "Respectfully yours," there's DIE BITCH JERK ASSHOLE. You're writing to a woman you're trying to date, a courtly missive, and suddenly between the lines there's I'LL FUCK YOU SILLY YOU DUMB BITCH SUCK MY COCK. You may wonder, *how do things like this end up in my writing?* The answer is simple: they come from your subconscious. You don't have absolute control of the writing process, particularly if you're tired, irritated, or distracted by something. On those occasions, the word COCK, or something worse than that, breaks loose from your subconscious and ends up on the page. It's pointless to reread what you've written on your own, trying to find these outpourings of vulgarity, aggression, or repressed sexuality. You simply won't notice them; you are unable to see them. If you do come across such words and phrases in your writing, have no doubt that you'll immediately repress them again as unacceptable for your conscious mind. That's why people who value their reputations work with our agency. What we do is painstaking and laborious, and it doesn't come cheap, but perhaps it's time to stop embarrassing yourself?

Respectfully yours,
The Angel of Pure Consciousness
Proofreader of the 6th Mental Division of Interior Audits
The Takes One to Know One Agency

BRING US YOUR MONEY IDIOTS FUCKING MORONS

IV.

MEMORY OF HEAVEN

MEMORY OF HEAVEN

I was born in the center of Eden, in the Cradle of God, in Wonderland, in Dreamtime. All around me things transformed and sang—they were still indeterminate and didn't know their limits. In this state of slumber indistinguishable from waking, I spent thousands of years, and all that time I nursed at my mother's breast. No one thing was equivalent to itself, all was one and complete. Slowly, gradually, my complete, infantile world crumbled. A strange disease had found its way inside and ate away at it, and one day everything split into dreams and reality. I woke up. I left the Cradle of God and lost my bliss and my omnipotence. I was expelled from Wonderland, I was parted from my mother, I lost immortality and gained speech.

I found myself near the sea, on the shore, on Vasilyevsky Island. I was being taken for a walk in a stroller. Although I remember something even earlier than that, I remember, as a baby, pissing on an orange rubber sheet. I did it out of spite; they had just changed my diaper, and spitefully I wanted to wet the new one as soon as possible. Spite was my main motivating force:

once, at our place on the Marine Embankment, they left me in my crib and went to talk in the kitchen. I screamed in outrage, but no one paid attention to me. Then I hefted myself over the bars, fell out of the crib, and went to the kitchen on my own. There was a silent scene. I was triumphant. Later, out of spite, I learned to read when I was three years old. I had bitten my mother, and it was decided that as punishment no one would play with me for a few days. Then I picked up a book and taught myself to read so that I would depend on no one, and spent those few days having a perfectly fine time, reading.

I remember the bay, the vacant lots, the new high-rises—vast spaces with the wind blowing through them. It was windy all the time, and I caught colds—this was one of the reasons that my family decided to move. The second reason was the family room. We lived in a large, two-story apartment. On the first floor were the kitchen, the toilet, the bathroom, and an enormous family room. From that room a stair led to the second floor, where there were two bedrooms and another toilet and bathroom. Starting from the time I was born, Mama and I lived in the family room, which wasn't very convenient, since everyone had to pass through it and they woke me up, and Mama, too, wanted some privacy. I didn't want to move; I cried, I loved that apartment, and they had to trick me into coming along to our new place on Leninsky Prospekt. I was three and a half. All the best things that would happen to me were over by then; they had stayed behind in the apartment on Vasilyevsky Island.

I remember my blissful sojourn among objects, when I played in the living room and rummaged through picture books, taking them down from the lower shelf of the standard Soviet wall set with the built-in sideboard and multitude of drawers.

The way I felt then was my normal state, the normal state of a young child—bliss such as the saints feel, a quiet, causeless bliss, scattered among objects, in the atmosphere of home, in the very experience of space, the bliss of a soul contained within itself. I no longer lived in Eden as fully as I did when I was a baby, I had begun to feel the pains of exile, but it turned out that even on Earth, Eden remained partly with me and continued to live within me, there was much of it I had managed to keep. My bliss was hidden inside Mama's typewriter and sewing machine, in the way her clothes smelled in the wardrobe, and of course inside the adjustable shelf at the foot of her bed, which had a secret compartment and where in dark corners, in eternal bliss, dwelled portions of my soul. On top of the sideboard stood a box full of buttons and thread, the longed-for box, and I always wanted to play with these buttons and thread. I'm going to tell you a truth that few people can understand: nothing exists but that. People want to do one thing, another, but none of it is necessary. There is no room for anything but that bliss within God: no room for love or friendship, labor or prayer. All of the complicated, convoluted paths that people try to take to God lead nowhere. God contains only a box of buttons and thread, and nothing else. The best thing you can do is sort through the buttons, run the threads of bliss into the buttons of bliss over and over again. That is all. There is no other secret, and there can be nothing better than that. Though it's unlikely you'll understand.

I also remember how, when we lived on Vasilyevsky Island, I got a shot. My grandmother took me to the clinic, promising that they were going to give me candy there. Inside the doctor's office I stretched out my hand to the nurse and asked for candy. "Candy? Ha-ha!" said the nurse and stuck a thick needle in my arm. It was painful and unbearably insulting. My grandmother hadn't wanted to lie to me, she'd just made a mistake, but for a long time I was inconsolable.

Leninsky was a completely different kind of space, but there were high-rises, vacant lots, the wind, and the bay there, too. All through my childhood, my grandmother and I took walks in the courtyards. The courtyards behind our building and all the way to my school were one sort of courtyard: Yulka lived there, we played on the grounds of an orphanage and sometimes accidentally hit its windows, at which point nannies with brooms would scream, "Fascists!" and drag us to the juvenile section of the local police station; the courtyards behind my great-grand-mother Beba's house were different, there was a big slide there, the stadium, a pond, you passed through these on the way to the Suslovsky supermarket; there was a third set of courtyards behind the department store, and wild pears grew there; a fourth set of courtyards lay behind the old bakery, there was a round pond and a huge model of a ship, and old yellow houses with columns—the houses have since been renovated, and that area is now an elite block with outdoor lighting, cobblestone paths, and gazebos around the pond.

But my real life happened much more at the dacha than in the city. The dacha was both Eden and the memory of Eden in our world, the inner and the outer merged there: the dacha was just as much inside as it was out. It was the image of my soul, recast as nature. The space of my dacha is my innermost, secret space, the forest of my unconscious grows there, and in that forest I find lakes the depths of which you could never measure; it's no coincidence, after all, that in my dreams I'm almost always at the dacha.

Our house stood in a place where there was once forest and heather. In the 1960s, in the forests on the other side of the old Finnish border, dachas began to be built. Our house was one of the first. In the whole village there are only four four-family homes: houses with four verandas and a kitchen and a bedroom in each quarter, like a quartet of conjoined twins with melded backs. These were the houses of the very poor; most village houses were built for two families, or just one. In addition to economic considerations, there was another reason to build this kind of house: we all wanted to live together. I've said "we," but in reality I hadn't even been conceived then, and my future mother was only ten years old. They all wanted to live there, next to one another, a single group of friends: my great-grandmother Beba with her husband and younger daughter in one quarter; my grandparents and their son and daughter in another; the Kutuzovs, a married couple who were friends of my great-grandmother, in a third; in the fourth, the Bogdanovs, also friends of my great-grandmother and another married couple, along with their daughter, her husband, and their son, who was born shortly afterward. Each family had six hundred square meters, but since they all lived as one group of friends, they didn't bother building any fences on the property, so the house was surrounded by one large parcel of land measuring twenty-four hundred square meters.

Before they bought the land, my grandparents, still young then, came to have a look at the place; they sat for a while beneath the triple birch—enormous now, but then not very big at all—drank some wine, and decided: we'll take it! They bought the plot in 1965, and immediately put up our barn and the Kutuzovs' barn; in 1966 they built the house and my grandparents had a son, Alyosha, and then in 1967 they built the stoves. They cleared the heather and began to plant a little orchard among the pines, spruces, and birches, and they dug garden beds, planted apple trees. Part of the land lay on a low hill, and on top of it they built an ivy-covered gazebo, with two pines standing guard at its entrance. Next to our gate they dug a well. Beneath the triple birch they put a bench, and a second bench on the other side of the lawn in front of the house, overgrown with clover. My grandfather grew wild strawberries—there'd be enough to fill four buckets, and once for his father-in-law Nikolai Vasilyevich's birthday he brought him a bucket of strawberries. There were many different kinds of flowers: phlox, dahlias, peonies, tulips. When I was a child, my grandfather would bring cut tulips to our city apartment, and they floated aromatically in the bath. I had my own little bed of daffodils that I watered with a child's watering can. My grandfather grafted apple trees and lilacs, which he really loved, and I love lilacs, too. He got cuttings through the mail from other cities, or they had to be cut in early spring while there was still snow, before the buds began to bloom, and kept in the snow or in the refrigerator. Now our lilacs are dying and the orchard has fallen into neglect. During my childhood we always had a bounty of berries in summer: in addition to the different kinds of wild strawberries there was a wealth of raspberries, red and occasionally yellow; black currants and red currants, gooseberries. There were always onions, dill, and lettuce for the table, and in the orchard potatoes, zucchini, and cucumbers grew in a little greenhouse.

When I was very young, there was a row of stumps that ran along the lawn, left over from the forest trees that had been cut down, and I jumped from one to the next. But many trees remain: pines, birches, spruces, aspens, little oaks, and one triumphant maple by the gate. And next to the barn, at the far end of our land, by the compost piles, grows a fir that my grandfather brought back from Valaam. By the second bench at the edge of the lawn there was once a juniper, but it didn't make it. And beneath the apple tree that grew next to the path to the outhouse, which passed by an enormous jasmine shrub, sea buckthorn, black currants, and blue irises, stood my swing set. When I woke up, sunlight danced over me in little blips and sparkled in the lacy, white-gold meadowsweet flowers beneath the windows. The washbasin rang out beneath the jasmine. There were three barrels that stood by the veranda: a big one, a smaller one, and a very small one. I imagined that the biggest barrel was my grandfather, the smaller one was my grandmother, and the smallest one was me.

In our barn stood one of the most beautiful things that my family owned: an antique vanity, consisting of an enormous mirror with a carved frame and a little table and drawers of black wood, probably dating to the end of the nineteenth century. The only room was spacious and dark, with two beds, dark blue wallpaper, a brick stove, bikes, tools, and a multitude of pillows. There was also another barn, a smaller one, specifically for my grandfather's tools. In the old house there was very little space. The dinner table and stools were out on the veranda, wooden blinds hung along the glass, and some dried grasses were strung on twine from the ceiling. An old radiogram, already an antique, only picked up the Mayak radio station. Beneath the table there was once a trunk that had held all my stuff—drawings, torn, water-damaged books. The couch was piled with all kinds of junk. In the kitchen there was a gas stove, an oven, pots and pans, and a foldout bed. In the bedroom were two beds, on which my grandfather and I once slept—or sometimes my mother, when she came for the weekend—and a table, a chair, pink-and-gold wallpaper, curtains stained with the blood of murdered mosquitoes, and a black-and-white photograph of a black-and-white cat on the wall, which I told the other kids was me in my past life.

I don't remember my grandmother's stepfather, Grandpa Nikolai, at all. But my great-grandmother was close to me for the first decade of my life. When they bought the dacha, she was fifty-five years old. There are color photographs of her taken with Mama's old point-and-shoot, standing on our land a year before she died, tiny and thin, her thin gray hair dyed with golden henna, dressed in something old-lady-brown. She had been a beauty and even in her very old age kept her astounding, delicate skin. Grandma Beba was born in the year 1910 in Warsaw. What I know about her childhood is that for some reason, when she and her sister Tamara were young, they made their way through wartime checkpoints to Petrograd, and also that she seems to have studied at a French boarding school. Her father was a doctor, and her mother Anna disappeared in Warsaw during the war in mysterious circumstances: she either died of meningitis or lost her mind, we don't really know for sure.

Grandma Beba was a striking, eccentric person. A communist, an atheist, one of the pioneers of the sexual revolution: first she organized professional training courses for the heads of the Lengorispolkom, and then, after the courses were shut down, she founded Nevsky Dawns, a company that was one of the first during the Soviet period to offer family planning. She worked with the leading specialists in the field, hiring Svyadoshch, Tsyrulnikov, and some others. She was a socialite, and due to the fact that her second husband, Nikolai Vasilyevich, was the general director of theaters and palaces of culture, and later the general director of the Lensoviet Palace of Culture, she knew the theater crowd, and my grandparents had free tickets to all the plays and shows.

Nikolai Vasilyevich himself came from a village and loved to fish. He started out as a factory worker, joined the Party, was promoted to major during the war, and after the war received a higher education. For his seventieth birthday Nikolai Vasilyevich was awarded the Order of Lenin, though he had really wanted the title of Hero of the Soviet Union and was upset when he didn't get it. For the last ten years of his life he couldn't speak: he had a stroke on the day of my mother's wedding.

Grandma Beba's first husband had been Grandpa Timofey, who came from a worker's family in Tula, enrolled in a rab-fak, and became an economist. Everyone in Timofey's family had blue eyes. He had a sister, Matryona, and an aunt, Nyura, who were both folk healers. Auntie Nyura was a very powerful healer, and people came to see her from all over the country. She taught Matryona, who acquired the ability to do some things, too. Matryona had eyes of the bluest blue; she was a delinquent in her youth and spent time in prison, she really loved men, and in her old age she became devout, lived alone in Moscow, and sat outside churches, asking for alms. Grandpa Timofey loved Grandma Beba very much and kept writing her letters from Moscow, where he moved and got married again.

Grandma Beba had a story she told about how she and Grandpa Nikolai first met: they were walking somewhere, I think it was in the south, with a group of friends, and Grandma Beba saw a rose growing high up, a risky climb for anyone who wanted to pluck it. She said, "Whoever plucks that rose, that's the man I'll marry." Grandpa Nikolai plucked the rose, and Grandma Beba married him. There's a photograph of them together in which she's looking at him with the gaze of a woman who's passionately in love.

During the Siege of Leningrad, Grandma Beba and her children were evacuated to Ufa, and that's where they stayed, living nearly thirty people to a room. But my grandmother, still a child then, was happy there with a completely autonomous, childish happiness, and she made the best friend of her life, all traces of whom were afterward lost for good. To bring in some money, Grandma Beba made and sold moonshine. Later, when she was waiting for Nikolai Vasilyevich to come home from the war, she kept going out in the road to meet him in her headscarf. During the war Nikolai Vasilyevich had another family, and that other woman he lived with later wrote him letters; Grandma Beba intercepted and destroyed the letters without telling Grandpa Nikolai, saying, "He had his fun, now enough."

In my early childhood, I was sometimes taken to visit Grandma Beba and her daughter Bedya; they gave me tea with Polar wafer cake and kurabiye cookies, and I paged through children's books or old photo albums. A few years before Grandma Beba's death I was visiting the two of them, and before I left, Grandma Beba suddenly asked me, "And how is your governess?" I knew that a governess was something like a nanny, but I had never had one of those. I told her she was getting something mixed up, that I didn't have a nanny, but she didn't believe me, deciding I was fooling around the way kids do, and in the end I was unable to convince her that there was no nanny. I thought of this episode again that night, sitting on the potty, and felt a freezing horror. Before that it had seemed to me that no one would ever die, that everything would stay the same, but here was Grandma Beba, slipping suddenly into senile dementia. Later I stopped being so sensitive to this, grew used to the idea that Grandma Beba was senile, and could even laugh heartlessly at some of her ridiculous statements and oddities. The worst were those first glitches in a respected and beloved adult; compared with the horror I felt then, her actual death didn't register with me.

We went to their apartment that day and she began to die; at first I sat in another room, but at the exact moment of her death I came in. She'd been unconscious, but at that last moment she regained consciousness and said, "Save me."

In 1965, when my grandparents sat beneath that birch with the three trunks drinking wine, they were not yet thirty-five. They spent their whole lives, from the moment they met, with one another. They raised a daughter and a son, and they raised me, too. When I was born, my grandmother immediately retired and occupied herself with me. They started taking me to the dacha in the first summer of my life.

Here's one of my first childhood memories connected to the dacha: my grandparents and I are walking to our house. It's not my first summer there, but I don't yet have a grasp of a chain of events connected in time, my memory lacks continuity, and everything I do remember comes to me in separate, clipped flashes.

So, as I was saying, we had come to the dacha from the city. I don't know how old I am in this memory, maybe around three. To test my memory, Grandma and Grandpa asked me to show them how to get to our house. I discovered that I remembered the way and the dacha, and with the discovery something changed. Now the dacha was somehow different, there was a barely perceptible shift. Until then the dacha existed, but outside reflection or memory.

Another childhood remembrance that has to do with the dacha and memory is from around the same time. It may have happened the very same day. We walked onto our land, and my grandmother said she wanted to go to the Hozdvor. I already knew what that was and had been there, but when she mentioned this I felt the same strange shift as I had when remembering the way to the dacha: I remembered the Hozdvor for the first time, and in a way discovered it for myself, and, almost imperceptibly, something changed. There was a kind of split, a disconnect in the space of which the Hozdvor appeared. I remember this odd, nearly imperceptible sensation of discovery and disconnect to this day.

Until he turned eighteen, my grandfather lived in Petropavlovsk, in northern Kazakhstan. His ancestors were peasants and railroad workers from near Vyatka and Perm. Somewhere by Vyatka there's a village called Glotovo where all the villagers have the surname Darovskih, the same as my grandfather. When the war began, my grandfather and his mother and sister were strolling in the park. On the radio they announced loudly that Germany had invaded. Grandpa wasn't drafted because he was still a teenager: during the war he was between twelve and fifteen years old. But they took his cousin Volodya, who went through the war as a sapper and was killed a few days before the victory in May 1945, neither by a mine nor by a German bullet—he was shot while making rounds by his own sentry, the casualty of some absurd mistake.

During the war, it was my grandfather's responsibility to run the household: his mother worked late nights as an accountant for the railroad, and there were no men left except for him. His father died young in Alma-Ata, of cardiac arrest; he'd been sent there on a wartime mission, and his grave is somewhere unknown, while Grandpa Aleksey, who had once been the driver's assistant on the train that took the tsar's family to their deaths, died while my grandfather was still young. Grandpa's mother, Grandma Klava, sang beautifully: she took part in amateur productions and sang at the local cultural center, and I remember the songs she sang to me when she came to visit us from Petropavlovsk. There's a tape of those songs—some Russian folk, some from the repertoire of Anna German. During the war years my grandfather had a serious case of typhus. A doctor came and said, "He's surely going to die." But my grandfather heard him and thought, "Bullshit. I won't." And he didn't. He read the books that filled their attic, locked his little sister in the cellar, hung out in the street with other boys, but finished school with a medal and enrolled at Leningrad Polytechnic University to study nuclear physics.

He arrived in Leningrad wearing an overcoat and carrying a wooden suitcase. He joined the rowing team, and I think they placed third in the entire USSR. And he met my grandmother at a party thrown by some friends, to which they both happened to be invited. He saw her—a rare beauty, tiny, thin as a reed, with dark braids wound around her head—and he was a goner. A year later they were married. He worked as a research fellow in nuclear physics at a research institute and was a liquidator of the Chernobyl disaster; my grandmother, a chemical technologist, taught throughout her working life at the State Institute of Technology and worked on rubber development, for which she was awarded the title of Honored Inventor of the Soviet Union.

When she was young, my grandmother had a lot of admirers, and some went on loving her throughout their lives, but she chose my grandfather, because, as she said, "It was easy to be with him." At work she was respected, or maybe even feared. My grandmother was absolutely honest, always and with everyone. She was an associate professor and was supposed to join the Party, but she refused. I think she didn't really like to socialize. She didn't believe in God and said that probably all of that was just stories to make it less frightening to die. She was strict with her students, and once she sent the head of her department to the hospital. He was taking away her doctoral students, there was a conflict, and her Auntie Matryona, the folk healer, gave her some herbs and told her to sprinkle them in the department head's office. She sprinkled the herbs and he was immediately taken away in an ambulance.

My grandmother's entire life consisted of her family and her children. She had a difficult character. At home there was always shouting and cursing; Grandma would lament, "There's not enough evil in the world for you!" I was always very puzzled by this saying, because I thought there was plenty of it, more than enough. Mama was gentle, she never raised her voice, while Grandma yelled all the time. She was inflexible, unambiguous, intolerant. I was given over to her to bring up, and this became a nightmare. She loved us as best she knew how, and tried to do for us whatever she could. She cooked and fed us tirelessly, and she exerted control over both her adult children and me in relation to every minor thing. After she retired, she had no other interests but her family. All her life, she suffered from terrible migraines. She was always shouting in her sleep because she had dreamed about losing a child—me—in the street or at a store. She felt a terrible anxiety about her loved ones and couldn't stand it when someone was out in the evening; she demanded that we call her constantly from the street, she listened to the elevators to make sure they weren't stuck, she'd stand on a stool and watch from the window as her adult son or my mother left the house and boarded public transport. The personal lives of both of her children hadn't worked out, and Mama blamed her for this, while Grandma always said to me that Mama's life hadn't worked out because she couldn't keep house, and that I was such a slob that nobody would want to marry me, either. She kept everyone under her wing, under glass. Our family life was subject to my grandmother's emotional states. I really loved her, but I remember how I first felt, in relation to her, a torturous ambivalence. She had been screaming at me, and I was angry, but then she said or did something innocently affecting, maybe brought one of my little shovels along on our walk, I don't remember what it was exactly, but at that moment I began to feel sorry for her; I was still angry, but at the same time I felt love and pity, as though I were seeing her from above and understanding more than she did. Decades later, when we saw her at the morgue, Mama and I noted her proud forehead and bearing and the severe beauty of her face. I remember how I cried, when during a fight with my mother, Grandma shouted that I was more her child than Mama's—that after everything she had done for me she had long since earned the right to call me her child. Until a certain age, I wanted to be specifically Mama's child and was angry because it seemed that Grandma made Mama upset. As a consequence of my relationship with my grandmother, for many years I felt a powerful sense of negativity, vile thoughts came into my head and made me ashamed, and I seemed disgusting to myself. I once wrote down on a sheet of paper some vile, disgusting words about Grandma and left the piece of paper on the table. I wanted her to find it. But then I felt overwhelmingly ashamed, and I destroyed the note.

Once I put on lip gloss, and Grandma said, "How revolting everyone must think you are!" By saying things like this, Grandma provoked in me a torturous, unbearable shame; I thought that she knew something about me I didn't know, saw something inside of me that I couldn't see—and what she knew was that on the inside I really was repulsive and vile, that I should be ashamed of myself, of existing. Some of the fights between us were related to my so-called "becoming a woman." Mama tried as hard as she could to speed up the "becoming." She put make-up on my face, told me about her boyfriends and about sex; Grandma, on the other hand, couldn't stand the mention of any of that. I had to listen to her go on about "whores" and "you'll get knocked up soon enough" for all kinds of reasons. For example, once on my birthday Mama decided to curl my hair and set it in rollers. This was done with some apprehension and in secret from my grandmother, but she found out anyway, pulled out the rollers, and screamed horribly at Mama and me.

Mama and I had more of a sibling relationship. Both she and my uncle were my grandparents' grown, but not entirely grown-up, children. When I was very young, I wanted to be just like Mama in every respect: I asked her if she believed in God, she said she didn't, so I didn't, either; later she said she did, so I started believing, too. I asked her if she supported the Communists or the Democrats, she said the Democrats, so I, too, supported the Democrats. Mama was gentle and affectionate with me, she forbade me nothing. Unlike Grandma, she was warm and cuddled me, and in the mornings I climbed into her bed. Mama was a kitty cat, and I was a little kitty. We lived in the same room, and when I woke up I would say "Meow," letting her know that I was awake. In the evenings, to get me to sleep, she'd say, "Shhh." Being with Mama was bliss, and I wanted to protect her so that no one would ever yell at her. She taught me to consider everything from several points of view at once, to understand other people, to put myself in their shoes. She challenged me, posed questions that forced me to think. Very early on, I became concerned that Mama seemed unhappy. She went through breakups with boyfriends and stayed in bed all day, and she was afraid of terrifying diseases, cancer, and death in general. Sometimes I could see that Mama wasn't well, and I felt a deep pity and a sense of responsibility for her, I felt that I had to be an adult and share her suffering. Mama talked to me like a grown-up: she told me about her personal life and about human relations in general. And I understood everything like a grown-up. Mama had always wanted to be a mother who was a friend, not an authoritarian like her own mother, she wanted to be the kind of mama you could talk to about anything in the world, who'd listen and understand, somebody with whom you could talk about men and make-up. She and Grandma were polar opposites, and the balancing, stabilizing force was my grandfather.

Grandpa, the man in my life I loved most—until my son was born! In our family he was creator, protector, and voice of reason. When I was little, I called him Granper. He was one of those rare people who live in harmony with the cosmos and know where they belong within it. He never strove for power or a high social position, and he turned down a promotion at work. And he had a wonderful sense of humor, including dark humor. He played pranks on his friends, but he kept up his friendships, even those from school and university, throughout his entire life, until his death. He called me Grander. I could ask him about anything, about stars and planets, about plants, about how everything in the world works. He was also very knowledgeable about medicine and sometimes regretted not becoming a doctor. He prescribed courses of treatment and diagnosed all his acquaintances over the phone, and he was never wrong. In springtime he showed me the budding leaves. In the evenings he showed me the celestial bodies in the dark sky. Sometimes he overdid the dark humor; once he lay down and pretended to be dead, and I prodded and prodded him, but he didn't respond, and stopped playing dead only when I started crying. Grandpa was bald and always joked that it was because he was so smart—all his hair had been pushed out.

There was also Bedya, my grandmother's sister. She was said to be an unfortunate person. Bedya was fat, with snow-white hair in a bowl cut and stubble on her chin, and she had a tremor. They told me that the tremor was caused by her pills. All her life she took haloperidol and lithium. She had a kind of schizophrenia that resembled bipolar disorder: she suffered from manias and depressions, and she also heard voices in her head. It started at nineteen, when she was knocked down and assaulted by some guy on the grounds of the forestry academy where she was a student. She was miserable for a long time, thinking about what had happened to her and unable to tell anyone about it. Then she got sick. She went with other students "for potatoes" and undressed there, ran around in a state of total derangement, shouting obscene things. She was treated, and they made her into an invalid. Bedya remained an old maid, and all her life she was afraid of men while at the same time fixating on matters of sex; she thought everyone was trying to sleep with her, and if she became attracted to a man, voices immediately piped up in her head, and all her crushes had to be suppressed with haloperidol. They told me her story, and it shocked me. I believed then in the goodness of the world, and the life Bedya had led didn't fit into that schema at all. It was hard for me to understand that a person could be so unfortunate and there was nothing you could do to fix it.

Additionally, there was Uncle Alyosha, Mama's brother. We weren't close and spent very little time together. He wasn't interested in me when I was a child, and he lived his own parallel life. I was always told not to bother him.

My father appeared in my life when I was ten years old. I had been told that things hadn't worked out between him and my mother; he was a lot younger than she was, when I was born he was still a university student. They met one winter at a resort in Karelia, decided to get married, and even applied for a marriage license, but broke up before I was born, because of my mother's inability to run a household and because she didn't get on with her future mother-in-law. After I was born, my father visited a few times, bringing me a big stuffed monkey I named Kampa-Zyampa when I turned one, but then he and Mama decided that it would be better for everyone if we had no contact. When I was about to turn ten, I wrote him a letter inviting him to my birthday. He came with his mother, my other grandmother. After that we were in touch, though not often.

All through my childhood I dreamed of having a white cat. My grandmother strictly forbade any household pets. Summers at the dacha I would keep caterpillars so I could take care of them, and in the city I put spiders from the bathroom in a jar and pretended they were my pets. When I was nine I was allowed some cacti, and I was overjoyed because I now had something to tend. But my greatest wish was to have a cat. Mama and I fantasized together about a fluffy white cat; when she put me to bed, she'd say, "May you dream of a white kitty," and when I was about to turn eleven, I really did get one. Somehow Mama had persuaded my grandparents and found a white Persian kitten. We named him Peach, but no one ever called him by his name. We called him Cat or Kitty, and I gave him strange pet names, like Kitsy Lushiest, Kittygnaw, Kittenich, all kinds of names. The kitten was good and fine in every way but was possessed of a distinctively disagreeable personality. He was sweet and purred like a washing machine, but as a sign of protest he pissed on whatever we held dear. At first he pissed on the bed, then he decided this was insufficiently radical and pissed on Mama's computer, but even that wasn't enough, and he did something more original: he pissed in his own bowl. He should have stopped there, but the cat wanted to desecrate everything—God, soul, mother—and pissed on me, his beloved owner.

I too had, and continue to have, a catlike personality. It has two aspects: domestic and wild, cat and lynx. When Mama trimmed my nails and I resisted, she would tell me that at night a lynx would come and nibble on them. Once after that I did dream of a huge lynx-cat. The lynx-cat lived right on Leninsky Prospekt and wouldn't let anyone pass by. It must have wanted to nibble on my nails. I got very scared and woke up in tears. That night I underwent an initiation—I met the wild aspect of myself, my totemic animal in dream space, and from then on, in my dreams, I occasionally encounter this gigantic lynx-cat. I don't fear the lynx-cat any longer—I think the meeting is a good sign.

After Mama told me about the concept of reincarnation (which happened pretty early in my life), I started telling my friends that in my past life I had been a cat. In general, over time, I told those friends a lot of interesting things. Mama told me about an esoteric belief she'd read about somewhere, which held everything was alive, even objects. After that I told my friends that our dolls were actually alive and we had to treat them accordingly. Then my friends' parents told my grandmother, "That's all fine, let's say the dolls are alive, but it would be nice if they didn't want dinner . . . You just can't keep up. Our kids are demanding three meals a day for them and feeding them." I also told tales about a swamp dog that howled at night in the swamp on the other side of the highway, and Nadya, for one, was afraid of that dog.

My dacha friends—Anya, Nadya, Natasha—are an integral part of my childhood Eden. My every summer was spent with them: playing cards, riding bicycles, enjoying all kinds of childhood games. We caught caterpillars and fed them rose hip petals, trapped bunches of butterflies in jars and then let them all out at once, drank bitter dandelion milk, made dolls out of grass, spent evenings playing quietly on the veranda, built houses out of Lego bricks, assembled the little alligators and hippos that came inside our Kinder Surprise eggs. We played mostly in the bright summertime alleys, among bushes of blooming rose hips and the buzzing of bumblebees. I met Nadya when we dug a hole together in the alley, an engaging, slow process. We fried water in a pan and tried to hit water in the earth as we dug; we played with a lotto set and Barbie dolls; we played role-playing games, acting out scenes from shows that were on television then. We played Indians with the boys and built huts, played board games like I'm a Designer, made paper dolls and outfits for them ourselves, found birds' nests in a sandy pit and kittens in a heap of shingles. We knew a million different card games, and we used cards to tell our fortunes, asking about love. Mornings began with one of my friends coming to visit me, or right after breakfast I would rush off to see one of them. We were never bored, and it was a wonderful sort of friendship—playing together in the light-filled alleys of Heaven. It's a shame we all lost one another eventually.

I have a good memory of one of the caterpillars I had then. It was my first and my favorite. The caterpillar was fuzzy, long, and multicolored. I called it Multi. It ate rose hip leaves and pooped tiny balls that I cleaned up. Multi lived in a glass jar, but I often let it out to take a crawl-stroll along the bench or down my arm. But once I apparently kept it in the jar for too long, or something else was the matter, I didn't really understand it then, but I found Multi dead inside the jar, looking squished. I was deeply saddened by this, ashamed and scared; I didn't say anything to anyone and buried the caterpillar in the ground beneath the jasmine. Once I found another caterpillar that looked a good deal like Multi, but tiger-striped. I brought it back on my hand from the shore of the large lake in Otradnoye, where my godmother and her daughter had a dacha. We traveled to see them in the bed of a truck along a dusty rural road. There, on the lakeshore, grew a wild, humid forest, and my godmother's daughter Vika and I made believe it was a jungle.

Grandma Beba would bring me with her to get flowers from the old woman who lived in the house at the end of the street. The old woman cut some flowers for her and then for me. In our windows every morning there was the summer sun, jasmine, meadowsweet. On the clover lawn Mama showed us photos of France, which she had visited. We took walks on the village paths: Mama and I, Aunt Lena, and Natasha. We strolled during storms, wearing raincoats beneath the changing sky. We looked for frogs in the forest, the paths and the trees smelled like rain. Grandma took me to the village accountant when we had to pay for something. The accountant had the most Edenic garden imaginable. There were so many flowers there! While my grandmother waited in line I studied them, talked to them, I was small like they were, and there, in the flowers, something sparkled and shone, dew-drops, spiderwebs, the sun, little rainbows . . .

There, at the dacha, when I was four, something in my mind went wrong. As Mama was putting me to bed I glanced at the curtains and the ceiling and saw strange images. A little green ballerina was dancing on one leg, followed by animals or crea-tures of some kind. The ballerina wasn't just repulsive, she was unendurable; it was as though she were tearing the fabric of my very soul. Then I hallucinated that our barn was on fire. I didn't see an image of the fire, but it was like I knew that it was hap-pening—these were thoughts I couldn't get rid of, thoughts that were choking me. I was given some valerian drops and went to sleep, but then I woke up terrified that my mother had died. She was sleeping in the bed next to mine, and I started waking her and constantly asking whether she was fine. I wouldn't let her sleep; although I understood that she was alive, I couldn't control myself, I kept asking. I began to follow her around; I wouldn't let her go to the bathroom. This went on for some time. I was pre-scribed medication and saw a psychiatrist and a neurologist. The neurologist was a formidable red-haired woman who threatened to send me to the hospital; I was terrified of her. The psychiatrist, on the other hand, was like a sly, sweet fox; she pretended to be nice, but I didn't trust her kindness. I remember that she tried to hypnotize me. After that summer I was afraid to be alone, without my parents. In the city I'd been enrolled in an English class where kids of preschool age were taught the basics of the English lan-guage. I had gone there for a year prior to that summer, and it was going fine, but after the summer I could no longer attend. The class was only a few hours long, less than half a day, but as soon as I was brought there I would start to cry, despite all my family's reassurances that they'd come back for me. I didn't believe that they would, I was afraid I'd been abandoned. I cried every day for the duration of the class. Eventually our teacher couldn't take it and asked my mother to remove me. But the problem continued. When my grandmother wanted to enroll me in art classes, also for preschool kids, she had to be present at the lessons along with the students, though that wasn't actually allowed, because if she left I'd start sobbing. And then all of this stopped, only to return again many years later. Childhood fears, obsessions—there was no one who could accept my fear and transform it, return it to me in some kind of acceptable, tolerable form. Mama had too many anxieties of her own, she couldn't handle mine, too. I was suffocated by my thoughts, I tried to control them and I couldn't. I was losing the solid ground beneath my feet, I didn't feel confident or protected or safe, it was impossible to trust the world or my family. I was afraid that Mama would die, that my relatives would take me somewhere and leave me there—there was no rational explanation for this, I just couldn't trust anyone or anything. I was sinking into a darkness, a clinging, relentless darkness. And then the darkness receded and returned when I was already grown. Madness is a little green ballerina on one leg, and out of the corner of my eye I can always see her dancing.

That first year of English class, before I developed these issues, I actually enjoyed myself quite a bit. I became friends there with Victor Tsoi's son, Sasha Tsoi. We pretended that he was my husband, a pilot, he'd go flying while I made him dinner out of jigsaw puzzle pieces. Later, when his father died, which happened right around that time, Grandma said, "That poor boy." But I liked a different boy, I think his name was Igor, though I'm not completely sure. He wore all white and was very pristine and proper. He looked somehow unattainable, ideal, and exhibited not the slightest interest in me. And I concealed my love for him. I thought that loving someone was the greatest secret and the deepest shame. In my school years I added one more taboo to these—crying in public. No matter how much my classmates or adults upset me, after a time I never cried in front of them; I had no right to betray my tears to the world, it would have been humiliating and weak and a joy for the person who'd hurt me. I let no one inside my inner world, not even Mama, and even then I was already lonely. My inner world was separated from the outside world by an impregnable wall, and no one had access to it. It was the only way to keep it safe. As far as love went, when I fell in love with that boy, there was nothing new in it for me. I just discovered that I had always known that feeling. I had no "first love," no falling for someone for the first time. There was only recognition: oh, this is love, I've always felt this way. This love, which I had always known, I had always felt for someone: not just real boys from school or from the dacha, but many characters from books and movies. I loved Athos from *The Three Musketeers*, I loved a bunch of Soviet actors, who didn't I love! All of these were minor loves, they came and went with each new book or movie, but I had one great love for a teenage boy that lasted throughout my childhood.

He was more beautiful than anyone else I had ever seen, and they said he was an orphan and lived alone. That summer evening we were standing in a large group in the alley by my dacha. I was eight and the youngest one there, everyone else was about four years older, and the boy was there, too. It felt like everyone was waiting for something—then they nudged him, "Go on, do it already." He was nervous and broke off a raspberry cane, not knowing how to begin; finally he said, "Allochka, I love you." It was my first declaration of love. I looked around at the other kids gathered there, who in the silence that had settled over us were watching me expectantly and intently, and I said, "That's not true."

"It's true," he said.

"It isn't," I said. I was sure that they were playing a joke on me, or maybe it was a game of forfeit, or for a bet. Then Grandma called me from the dacha to come brush my teeth, and I left. That night I dreamed that this boy climbed through my window and I ran away with him. The next day one of the girls from his friend group came to see me; she'd already done some dishonest things in the past, and I was sure she had come just to continue playing this cruel joke on me. She started asking what I thought about what the boy said, apparently wanting to tell him and the others, while I didn't want anyone to ever guess that I loved him, because I was afraid they'd laugh at me, so I purposefully said to her, "I don't like him."

"Why not?" she asked. Not knowing what to say, I came up with the most absurd and unthinkable of all the impossible possibilities: "He's ugly."

Whenever I saw him my knees grew weak, I couldn't walk, and felt like I was going to faint. I was always holding on to a fence when I passed by him, or to anything else I could lean on. But even given such force of feeling I was still a child who played with toys. I remember him standing in the alley with his little dog when I was coming home from Nadya's with a toy turtle clenched in my first. I squeezed it very tight, so that he wouldn't see that

I still played with toys, and passing by I looked at him with utter disdain and indifference, all the while fighting dizziness and holding on to the fence so as not to faint from love.

Around the same time, when I was eight, I had my first orgasm. I was lying in bed, reading *The Count of Monte Cristo*, when I absentmindedly rubbed myself between my legs and suddenly discovered that it felt good; I rubbed some more and kept reading, I happened to be at the part where the Count of Monte Cristo smokes hashish and hallucinates some marble statues, their icy touch, in essence it's an erotic scene. But I'd had sexual fantasies earlier than that, beginning at a time when I was even younger; they were wild, shameful, and had more to do with psychological violence—in my imagination I was the object of the violence, I or someone I imagined myself to be—than with sex as such; after all I didn't know then what sex was or how people did it. From the beginning, these fantasies had a "contrary" basis. I didn't fantasize about what I wanted, but about what was least acceptable to me as a person, things that in reality would have been completely impossible, and which I never would have wanted to actually experience. It was somehow immediately clear to me that whatever was least acceptable to me as a person, with my elevated ideals of love, freedom, honor, and justice—that's what was sexual. It had nothing to do with love and all those elevated feelings; I had totally different fantasies about love, romantic and lofty, and I never mixed up these two spheres.

My friends and I played a few games that were "sexual." Nadya and I pretended we were psycho killers and rapists: one of us would lean against a tree and the other would pretend to rape her. Ksyusha and I had a different game; she'd tie me to a pine tree with a jump rope and whip me with stinging nettles.

Grandma Beba saw us at it and threw a fit. Lyuba asked me to give her a "massage," and promised to give me a ring for doing it. I sat on Lyuba naked, as she told me to do, and touched her where she told me to touch her, but then my grandfather came in, kicked Lyuba out, cursed terribly, and said, "That's the worst thing there can be between two women." At ten I read *The Secret Diary of Laura Palmer*, and she became my favorite heroine. I recognized myself in her: I was exactly the same as Laura. And BOB, the evil spirit who tormented her, I knew him, too—in a different way, but I knew him. Her example inspired me for many years, I compared my adolescence with hers, and at school I started pretending to snort cocaine: I'd leave class to go to the bathroom, take out a little piece of paper and pretend to do a line.

I was always reading, without any kind of system, reading everything I happened to see that caught my attention. I alternated between children's literature and adult books, fairy tales and "grown-up" novels. My grandparents had a decent home library, and I also went to the library in my neighborhood. I remember that in elementary school I read all of Balzac and Maupassant—we had their collected works at home. As a child I also read the sacred texts of various cultures and traditions, works of mysticism and philosophy—I was particularly interested in those kinds of approaches. The books that made perhaps the strongest impression on me were a children's Bible with pictures, which I knew practically by heart, Russian folklore and fairy tales, *The Legends of Ancient Greece and Rome*, and the fairy tales of the German Romantics.

For me, proof of the authenticity of my creative impulse is the memory of my favorite childhood game. I would pick up a book (preferably, but not necessarily, one with pictures), sit down, and run my finger along the lines, wearing holes in the pages while muttering strange words to myself. I was composing a text, using pictures or forging ahead without, and imagining that the text I was making up was written on those pages. Reading other people's work also inspired me to play the game. When I read something I liked, I'd pick up a book and start to compose a text in the same spirit and style as the one that had made such an impression on me. I practiced this oral artform for many years as a child, whenever I entered into a state of needing to compose in this way; it was simply an urgent need, and that is true inspiration.

What's more is that I had filled up a whole shelf with notebooks of my poems, plus a handwritten novel. The novel was written in clumsy print letters because I had not yet learned to write in cursive. All of this began when I was very small, after I asked my grandfather, "Grandpa, can anyone write a poem?"

"Of course, anyone can," my grandfather said.

"Can I?"

"Sure you can."

That very night I wrote a poem about the moon. And in the Notebook of a Young Mother kept by Mama, it's noted that I started writing poems when I was a year and nine months. These poems had no words. According to Mama's notes, my first poems were combinations of sounds that had good rhythm.

One other very important thing happened when I was a child. It was The Most Important Thing. It happened all by itself, and I don't know what to compare it to. Maybe with what lies at the very heart of poetry—a certain brief touch of the otherworldly. It wasn't continuous, it was just a brief brush that immediately faded, because it would have been impossible to hold on to it, unless maybe for just a fraction of a second. But this brief contact contained everything all at once, and the fact that it happened was the most important thing.

I was interested in living: I believed in God, I believed in magic, I believed in miracles and thought that my life and the world in general had meaning. I lost my faith at thirteen, but until then the world had been full of meaning; it was enormous, unknowable, mighty, and beautiful. But at the same time I sensed that there was a tragic part of life, a kind of painful breakage, a wound at the very heart of the world, and I understood that this wound was the most alive and the most precious, and that in some way it had something to do with me, too. At that time my mother was into all sorts of esoterica, and she got me into it. I consumed tons of dubious esoteric texts, including occasional gems that were truly worthwhile. My particular favorite back then was *Diagnostics of Karma* by Sergey Lazarev; I read all of his books, and he convinced me then that the main thing was love for God, there was nothing that could be held in higher esteem than that.

Before falling asleep, I sometimes wondered about death: would I really die, too? It was impossible to imagine. I'd ask my grandparents: "You're not going to die anytime soon, are you?" "Maybe it'll be a while," my sixty-year-old grandparents would say, "maybe we'll live another twenty years or so."

"That's fine then," I'd ascent. Twenty years was a long time.

Once on the playground a girl asked me, "How old are you?"
"I'm three," I said.
"Oh, I'm four already!"
"Too bad," I said."
"Why?" asked the girl.

"I'm not gonna tell you, you'll cry."

"No, tell me," she demanded, "tell me, tell me, tell me! I won't cry!"

"It's bad because you'll die sooner," I said.

I remember Mama introducing me to the idea that there had been a time when I didn't exist—that was my first encounter with the idea of not-being, and I just could not wrap my mind around it. "Where was I, then?" I asked her, chuckling suspiciously.

"Nowhere. You didn't exist at all."

"What do you mean at all? That's not possible, I mean, I do exist. So where was I then?"

Around the age of five, before falling asleep, I arrived independently at something like the Cartesian *cogito, ergo sum*, working out the question of what I could be really sure of and deciding that I could doubt everything except for the fact that I doubted— and, if I doubted, that meant I must exist, since after all someone must exist to have the doubt. To a five-year-old child this sounded quite convincing.

I was already thinking like a philosopher but didn't yet know how to wipe my own ass. I was so coddled, my family doing everything for me, that I only learned this skill at school, which meant that in first grade I found myself in an uncomfortable situation. I had to go to the bathroom to defecate; I asked to be excused from class, then thought, "But who is going to wipe my butt?" Walking toward me was our deputy headmistress, Vera Pavlovna, a respectable elderly woman, and I went up to her and asked, "Vera Pavlovna, could you please wipe my butt?" There was nothing she could do but oblige. I recalled this episode later, when I had won at some academic Olympiad and she congratulated me and shook my hand.

When I was ten and met my father, I was also introduced to my paternal grandfather. He was the son of a Jewish journalist who had known Yesenin, and a Russian noblewoman, the scion of two old noble families, the Podobedovs and the Kolb-Seletskys; among his distant ancestors there were Ukrainians, Serbs, Germans, French, and Poles. One of those ancestors made a significant contribution to the history of Saint Petersburg. As it turned out, Petersburg's first trolleys were the project of my great-great-grandmother's brother, Mikhail Mikhailovich Podobedov, son of my great-great-great-grandfather Mikhail Pavlovich Podobedov, an actual state councilor, a nobleman. Mikhail Mikhailovich was a graduate of the Petersburg Technological Institute and the founder of one of Russia's first electrotechnical companies. In the winter of 1895-96, he had a trolley line built across the ice of the Neva River, powered by stations owned by his company. The "ice trolley" proved popular, and in the 1910s the city government switched over to electric, rather than horse-drawn trolleys, installing lines throughout the city and importing thirteen trolley cars from a British company.

My grandfather on my father's side was said to be an interesting, original person: he'd been married five times and was a great lover of women; he was interested in art, poetry, painting, and did some writing and drawing himself. He was also fond of philosophy. We went on a walk together and he pointed at the houses, trees, and cars, and said, "Do you think all these things really exist? They only exist in your consciousness!" I was floored.

There were two other things that stayed with me throughout my entire childhood. The first is that I often had a sense of an ever-fleeting, other life—as though in the infinite infinity of the world I wasn't just living in a small bit of it, on the outskirts of Leningrad, on the eleventh floor of a high-rise, going to school and socializing with a very limited number of people—though all of this was, of course, true—but that there was also a great deal of something else, which, in contradistinction, wasn't out in the open where anyone could see it, like an inventory of objects on a tabletop, but something that existed in some other way, and in this other way I, too, was able to exist completely throughout all of infinite infinity, though for some reason this couldn't be made as clear as other, simple and given things, like today I got a score of three out of five in math, or there's an apple on the table, or there's fighting at home again. And the second thing was this: my dream or fantasy of living for a little while in every house and apartment on Earth, just for a single day and a single night, because each place must have its own smell and its own floorplan, or even in the apartments that were identical, its individual atmosphere; each of the families that lived there must have its own way of life, similar to my family's but also different, and I wanted to know what games their children played, and how I would feel if I were their child and some totally random Ivan Petrovich were my grandfather.

I also remember the impression music and singing made on me. My grandmother wanted to develop my ear for music and asked me to repeat "Chizhyk-Pyzhik" and other such melodies after her; I repeated them reluctantly and falsely, and everyone soon accepted that I couldn't carry a tune. But I remember what I felt when I heard music. It was awe and revelation; music was, for me, a pure force that did away with subjectivity and dissolved me—when I heard music, it was like I stopped being myself, passed beyond my own borders, encountered something enormous, boundless, cosmic, and it was such a powerful and personal experience that it couldn't be revealed to grown-ups. To sing back a song correctly or to sing at all would have been the same thing as a public declaration of love or crying where everyone could see me. It was a secret and a shame; Grandma couldn't be allowed to guess what emotions that music called up in me, I must not repeat these songs after her, so as not to give myself away. Plans for my musical education were quickly retired, but my first dream in the series "Who I'm Going to Be When I Grow Up" was that I would become a singer.

In those years the world was as charming as a poem written in a language you halfway know: there are some words you understand, and the unfamiliar parts of the whole are sketched in by your imagination and remain mysterious, as though shrouded in a semi-darkness onto which you project your fantasies and intuitions. And later, when you know the language better and start to understand all the words, the poem becomes too transparent, its "dark," mysterious part disappears, and it loses its charm.

There were times when I woke up at night and witnessed a little miracle: a shimmering in the air, as though a multitude of tiny fireflies was glowing there. This happened in my room; I wasn't asleep and saw it many times with my own eyes. Sometimes on the brink of sleep I was possessed by strange vibrations, as though I were swaying, and there was the feeling that I was separating from my body. Usually at that moment I became very afraid. Once it was like I was falling into a dark abyss and nearly dissolved in it. Other times I would wake up and discover that I could see the room with my eyes closed, through my eyelids, and various miracles were occurring, like the time when, within the room, near the curtains, fluttered a cross made of golden light.

I did things that made me feel ashamed. The most shameful of these I have no memory of at all, they told me about it later, many years after it happened. Mama and I were visiting Aunt Raya, a friend of Grandma Beba's. This woman was dying of cancer; she was alone and wanted to leave her apartment to my mother if my mother agreed to take care of her. Mama didn't seem too eager, but sometimes she visited this woman, and on that visit she took me with her. Aunt Raya was old and ugly, and she started fussing over me, bothering me, so I said to her, "Don't touch me, you're old and ugly." They never took me there again, and my mother didn't get the apartment. My grandmother told me about this when I was around ten, trying to show me just what a repulsive creature I was, that I was capable of such a thing. I was shaken and cried for a long time. Another time, I went with Mama to a New Year's Eve party at the Center of Management and Marketing, where she worked as a translator. Every year they threw fancy New Year's Eve parties with lots of delicious food and a bunch of children to play with. That year Mama had been asked to dress up as the Snow Maiden for the celebration. I had never believed in Father Frost, they told me early on that he didn't exist, but Mama warned me that other children did believe in him, and that I shouldn't tell anyone the Snow Maiden was my mother. But the secret turned out to be too big for me to keep to myself. I was playing with some girl, and I couldn't hold it in and bragged that the Snow Maiden was my mother. The girl cried bitterly; her mother consoled her, saying that I'd made it all up to impress her, but the girl, I think, understood.

Among my happiest memories is for some reason an unsuccessful trip Mama and I took to the Luna Park traveling amusement park. I had looked forward to it for a long time. Luna Park came every year and was located at the end of Novoizmailovsky Prospekt; I'd never been there and really wanted to go. So I convinced Mama to take me; we walked along the avenue, I expected Luna Park like a miracle, but in the end it wasn't there: either it had already come and gone or it hadn't come at all. But somehow I still remember this as a very happy outing. Perhaps if Luna Park had been there, it would have been excessively, overly happy, or the other way around, my happiness would have been diminished when my wish was fulfilled. When I was ten, Mama took me traveling with her for the first time. We traveled to Sochi, and I went to the seaside for the first time, if you don't count our cold Gulf of Finland. We stayed in the private sector of Loo, in the Armenian village, surrounded by forested mountains and beautiful southern vegetation. We hiked in the mountains, swam, lay out on the pretty pebble beach, went into Sochi, Adler, Dagomys, the Sputnik camp, sailed on the sea on a boat, ate fruit, and delighted in each other's company. I began to love traveling with Mama— on our trips we discovered the world together and rejoiced in it— and I fell in love with traveling in general.

One of my favorite games had to do with traveling, and it gave me a feeling of comfort, safety, and bliss. This was a game with a little yellow car and two tiny porcelain hedgehogs. Both the hedgehogs and the car lived under my mattress in secret from everyone; I took them out before bed and played with them under my blanket. The hedgehogs drove around the whole world in that car, and it wasn't just a car, but a trailer in which you could live. They drove the car to different places and then parked for the night, and it was good and cozy, because that meant they could travel without leaving home, and home was always with them.

At two I was talking politics with old ladies outside of our building and astounding them with my views. From my early childhood I remember long lines in the shops and ration cards, and Grandma always watching congresses on TV. I remember demonstrations and flags, and being told that the Democrats were fighting with the Communists. Mama and Grandma supported the Democrats, while Grandpa supported the Communists. I remember the August Putsch, the State Committee on the State of Emergency. Mama and I were at the dacha and heard Swan Lake, and then I sprinted barefoot down the alley, running into neighbors' houses, shouting excitedly that there had been a coup. The most surprising thing about Gorbachev was the mark on his forehead. The nineties were starting, gangs were gathering on apartment building landings, someone was methodically removing the lightbulbs from the stairwell, murderers and New Russians proliferated, kids started playing Dendy and Sega games, school uniforms were abolished when I was in second grade, there was denim everywhere, and gum, and Snickers and Mars bars, they started showing endless ads on TV, my grandfather was particularly incensed by the Tampax tampon commercials, old Soviet tape players were gradually replaced by stereos. Various religious sects grew rapidly in number, drug addiction took off, young people in leather jackets—racketeers—stalked around the markets, flea markets started up by the subways, kiosks opened in underground crossings, cassettes were sold at stands in vast quantities, and I was starting to get into them. The alcoholic neighbor on our landing was a rabid Yeltsin supporter, and for this my family nicknamed him the Yeltsinist. With time he became, like many others, a rabid denouncer of Yeltsin, but the nickname stuck, and the Yeltsinist he remained. My father, with whom I wasn't in touch then, who later became an academic internationally recognized in his branch of physics, the rector of a university, hawked umbrellas in the street. There was no money, and the factory where his mother worked as an engineer paid her in umbrellas—there was nothing left to do but try to sell them. My uncle left his medical practice and became a sales agent. At first Mama worked at the Center of Management and Marketing, but then left to be an interpreter at Baltic Bank.

In 1992 I started school. It was a regular neighborhood school with an English-language concentration. I studied without particular enthusiasm. I could write and count correctly, but my notebooks were an awful mess. By the end of primary school I was a perfect student, but this didn't happen again until after middle school. Sometimes I won at the academic Olympiads. Learning came easily to me, but the focus of my life and my interests lay completely outside of school. Out of all the subjects we had, I was really only interested in literature; I liked writing compositions. In general I was extremely lazy and willful. I was secretly convinced of the pointlessness of effort, achievements, successes, and all of that. I felt indignant when anyone tried to force me to do something; it was like I understood that I "needed" to do it, but there was still the sense that the "needed" and the "it" were a lie. And that for the sake of that lie, these vanities, they wanted me to reject something that was actually much more important: the observation of existence, mysterious and meaningless bliss, which is superior to all human doings. Going to school, going to university, working, making a life for myself—all of this was always repulsive to me. I stopped doing homework after fifth grade. Just stopped. I refused to be forced to do anything. I had two close friends at school: Yulya and Asya. They were terribly jealous of each other where I was concerned—which one did I sit with, which one had I come up to—and would take me by the hands and pull me in opposite directions. Many of my classmates didn't like me. It was like I wasn't quite the same as everyone else, and not well socialized, though I tried to hide it. But I couldn't hide it well, plus I was very shy, and from the outside sometimes this resembled arrogance. It was really hard for me to get along with the other kids and hard to exist in a disciplinary space. I thought that the other kids were mean and cruel. If they were mean to me I responded by ignoring them, but I didn't know how to stand up for myself. I couldn't hit back. There were periods when I was bullied—though this was probably later, when I was a teenager. There were a few boys, one in particular, who hated me for some reason and tried to insult and humiliate me in every possible way. I taught myself to be distant so that I wouldn't feel pain. Sometimes, deep inside, I felt a terrible shame: I thought that the people who were harassing me saw something in me that I couldn't see myself, something my grandmother, for example, could see, and that they were mean to me specifically because of who I was, because I should have been ashamed of myself, of my very essence, and if anyone saw this essence, that person's totally reasonable reaction could only be laughter and mockery. A couple of times the upperclassmen bullied me. When I was in sixth or seventh grade, there was an eighth-grade boy who over the course of an entire year called me a mop. Wherever I went, he would shout, "Hey, Mop!" In principle he was correct: I really did look like a mop—pretty tall for my age, skinny, with a long mane of tangled hair. But despite these episodes, in general being at school was pretty bearable; I could see that some other people had it much worse. School was, for me, a boring and unpleasant routine: waking early, breakfast that you tried to choke down and then hid under the bed, in secret from Grandma, walking to school with Grandma in the blue gloom as the streetlights went out one by one, the lobby, checking your change of shoes, seeing friends, alienation, boredom.

Time passed slowly; it resembled eternity. Our math teacher, a wise woman, once told us, "Time is moving slowly for you now. But later it's going to go quite fast. After university the years slipped by so quickly I lost count of them." I was surrounded then basically by the same group of people: my family, our relatives the Korablevs, who lived on the same street as we did at the dacha and who were the family of my friend and contemporary Natasha— my second cousin once removed; the Tsyupikovs, who came to visit us sometimes; Aunt Lida, Grandpa's sister, who also came sometimes, at first from Petropavlovsk and later from Novgorod; the Bogdanovs—our dacha neighbors, who shared our large plot of land. The older generation gradually died off, even the generations at the dacha shifted. At first the neighbors passed away: Alexander Georgievich, Iya Vladimirovna, Evgenia Davidovna; then Grandma Beba, then Victor Isidorich. In summer at the dacha we celebrated holidays, summer birthdays: set the table on the veranda, drank champagne, laughed, toasted, and cheered thrice: "Hooray! Hooray! Hooray!"

My childhood Eden, the very memory of it, the people and things that contained that memory, was gradually disappearing, dissolving. The toys were the first to go. When I was sixteen, Mama and Grandpa secretly threw out several boxes containing all my toys. It was unbelievable, outrageous. My kitty-bear was in one of those boxes, and Kampa-Zyampa, and Stepashka the bunny, and the pink cat, and all my dolls, which when I was a child had been my daughters or the images of a future me.

Then the cat passed. We had been together for eleven years. At six he was diagnosed with chronic kidney failure. For years I had him treated, took him to get quarterly IV infusions, spent all my pocket money on him, plus the money from one literary prize. But he became emaciated and started constantly drinking water from the tap. I took him to get his infusion, but he got even worse. The morning after the first drip he could barely walk and held his head oddly to the side, and when he lay down he'd position his head oddly and try to hide it. He started lying in the sink and the bathtub all the time and stopped drinking, eating, or going to the bathroom. We kept up the IV treatments because we couldn't just stop them, but the prognosis was not favorable; the ultrasound and various tests showed that his kidneys barely worked, his nephrons were dying, dying, there was nothing left. Then he started having seizures and nearly went into a coma; I fought until the last, but when it became clear that there was nothing more to be done, I wanted him to die on his own, without being put down. But he wouldn't die, he suffered, and then it became clear that he would die soon, but before death there would be agony. His breathing was uneven and when I was near him I saw a dark, viscous liquid come from his mouth, and a few times, quietly and painfully, he meowed. So I had him put to sleep to avoid the pain, and they told me that I should have done it earlier, but Denis, my first husband, said that I was right, because the cat had loved me, too, and had wanted to be with me as long as he could.

We buried him the following day at the dacha. Ferns and tall grass were cleared from a small plot near the barn. The shovel rose and tossed away the cool, damp earth—dark and soft at first, then hard yellow sand. It was cold and overcast. Onto the little coffin of sturdy cardboard fell the first few clumps of dirt and a handful of little wild October asters.

And all of it—Grandpa tossing earth into my cat's grave, Denis standing next to me, the wild ordinary asters, hands dirty with earth, the holey quilted jacket, and strong tea on the dark, damp veranda—seemed to me to be a picture in a book that had many pictures, and I had not initially understood that they were pictures and that there were many of them, because for a long time I'd been looking at just one picture, the one of my childhood, where everyone was near and everything seemed eternal—and a second picture, and a third, until the pages started turning faster and faster . . . And then I saw that there were many, very many of them, they were without number, like points in a line, but there's an end to the line and there's a final picture, which will be reflected by your eye at the moment when it takes in a final ray of light. And there are pictures to come of losses that will inevitably occur, that's exceedingly clear and inexorable, and there's not a chance of doing anything about it except watching, the way I watched the clumps of earth covering my cat, the pile of torn-up ferns, and the pale wild asters. I felt light and strange, as though I'd been having a lucid dream.

Animals carry within themselves a memory of Heaven. We recognize Heaven in them and remember the way we were before the fall. Before the fall, all the animals were like their young. And people were like children, too. So it was said: become as little children. Animals fell because of man, they followed man into the fallen world. If man can be saved, the animals will be saved, too, everything will be saved. Once a friend and I were out at night at the dacha and we walked through the forest to Little Borkovsky Lake, where we sat down in a spot on the beach to rest and look out at the water, and we saw that along the water something was quickly approaching. It was a silvery fish, and it threw itself out onto the shore. We couldn't understand why, and we tried to push it back neatly into the water, but the fish threw itself onto the shore again. We decided it was probably dying. Then it lay there, and we watched, and then something in the sky flashed brightly, maybe a firework someone had lit in the distance, but it was just one very bright spark, and when we looked down at the fish again, we thought its eye had gone dull, but maybe it was just an optical illusion from looking at the bright flash in the sky. We both thought the fish had died, and we were sad, it was strange, why this suicide, as though it were a message or it had wanted to tell us something. I imagined that someday, by some body of water; I would once again see a dead silvery fish by the shore, and I'd go to it, and it would flick its tail and swim away, meaning it would be alive again, and I would understand that it was the same fish, and God has forgiven me, and the world is saved, and maybe between today and the day when I meet the fish again many decades would pass, but for the fish it would have been like a momentary dream.

When I was finishing graduate school, Bedya passed. Mama found her when she came back from the dacha, in the bathtub, drowned and boiled to death in the hot water.

Grandpa lived to eighty-five. We were very close. I loved our fall trips to the dacha together, when just the two of us would go and Grandpa would fire the stoves, work on the well, solve sudoku puzzles. I rode my bike to the lakes, read sitting in the gazebo. In the evenings, before sunset, we took walks together— to "Svetlana," the part of the village on the other side of the highway, to the station, or to the nearest lake. Then Grandpa would call Grandma on his cell phone and tell her we were locking up and going to bed. On our land grew tall ground elder, celandines, yellowing ferns that had come up on our old vegetable beds. Young aspens were rising out of the earth, there were lupines with gray fuzzy pods. Apple trees that barely gave any apples, that hadn't been mulched for many years, radiated a fragile fall solitude, along with the bitter taste of unripe fruit. The earth was already swept with fallen leaves. Tajik laborers were constantly at work building something on the neighbor's land.

A long while before my grandfather's death, I had a dream. I had fallen asleep in the daytime, listening to music. In the dream Grandpa and I were going to the dacha together. We arrived, and suddenly I felt very clearly that Grandpa was seventy-five. I had a sharp, painful realization that the life of this person I loved would not go on forever, there weren't that many years left, and that later, when he died, I would forever miss him, and would never stop loving him: that's how deep, how very deep, my love went. I hugged him, we walked around the land, and I was so happy that I could still hug him, before the moment when I would never be able to do it again. Or maybe we would meet somewhere in the infinite, at our dacha, many years after he had already died and I had lived a long life without him, missing him. And the sun was setting.

Grandpa died of lymphoma. He faded away over the course of nine months, going through pointless chemotherapy, becoming acquainted with death's conveyor belt and inhumane treatment at the hospital. He had time to celebrate his eighty-fifth birthday; he invited friends and relatives, and we gathered together for the last time at our shared table—it was important to him to do that. Less than a month after his birthday he died. He fought to the end, he couldn't do otherwise. I was with him on the last day of his life, taking care of him, and in the evening I left, and he said, "Thank you!" and opened his arms for a hug. I went to him and we embraced, and for the last time I pressed myself to his beloved, slightly bristly cheek.

Grandma passed eight months after Grandpa, two days after Georgy and I were married. She couldn't go on without him. For many years she had been slowly developing dementia; she changed greatly, becoming weaker, more helpless, having trouble understanding what was going on around her, hallucinating, but with Grandpa there she had hung on and kept what she could. It was painful to see what this imperious, authoritative, self-assured person had become. After his death, she had to be cared for like a little child; we had to fasten shut the refrigerator door, keep the stove unplugged. At first she just mourned inconsolably, saying, "Sure, maybe we didn't have such an easy life, but I'd give everything to live some more the way we lived together." Gradually she became unable to speak, stopped getting up. My mother and uncle and I were with her when she died, and I told her about my wedding; she listened and seemed to understand. We washed her, moving her to do it, and then death appeared in her eyes, and she was gone.

While my grandparents were alive, my childhood lived with them. Now it lives in my mother. While she's here, I'm still almost immortal. After Grandpa's death the dacha has come to look like a ravaged Eden where the serpent crawls through the tall grass. Grandpa was the lord of the land and all things, he and Grandma were the first people on a wild, still uninhabited Earth, but the time has come for the grandchildren of the first people to bury their elders.

Once it was given to me to return to the Eden of my childhood. I was with a group of friends at a country cottage by

Zelenogorsk and I took a magical substance. At the beginning, at sunrise, I saw that a damp green spot on the gates was pulsing, breathing, which had to do with the dampness in the air, with the dew in it. And above the gates I saw steam rising from the damp, gathering in pavilions and domes. For probably an hour I watched the dawn sky, unable to look away. I saw the changing outlines of clouds, the shifting colors, the pulsing of the sky. A flock of birds flew by, and this had a surreal beauty. I saw the tiniest phenomena in the atmosphere, little rainbows and the flashing of sparks. The air stood as a solid wall, and I could see everything that was happening within it: figures and fractals. In the air before me I saw a code, something like computer code, constantly changing. Then I saw a hard surface like a very slow liquid; I saw matter down to the molecule. Then I saw Beauty, flowers. This was an insight into Beauty, eternal happiness, the exultation of the atoms. It was my lost Eden—I had returned to it. I looked at a fireweed flower, then the bellflowers in the grass. I began to cry. It was a totally soul-rending experience, breaking my heart and healing it at the same time. We all see the world this way in childhood, and then we lose the ability. It really was a lost Heaven. All of the flowers glittered, standing in drops of dew. I sobbed, but felt that it was normal, seeing the world the way I saw it then. That people deserve to always see it this way. I felt what had previously been given to me only through memories of my childhood. My consciousness was crystal clear. If I wanted to, I could have written poems or discussed complex subjects. But I just saw things the way they were. This contained all of philosophy and all of poetry. For a long time I crouched, looked at a bellflower, and cried. I was like Eve in Heaven. I went from flower to flower (in my everyday life I wouldn't have even noticed them): dew-dropped fireweed, wild grapevines on the fence, also dotted with dew, bellflowers, some extraordinarily beautiful little pink stalks covered in glittering pink-silver drops, jasmine, white basketlike flowers, simple yellow flowers, predatory-looking pink flowers with spots, extremely delicate gold-white flowers dotted with dew, little shoots. The simplest blade of grass contained an infinite world. I just saw the things that are always there, though we don't notice them. As though for the first time after eternal exile I was walking in Heaven. I understood that in this Heaven there was a place for everyone I loved, that they had all come from there. Why has man been deprived of this mercy? I was wearing a long, light-blue evening dress that reached to my ankles, and, picking up my skirt, tearfully fumbled around in the bushes and the mud. I was on familiar terms with every flower, they had ceased to be the background, ceased to be faceless, anonymous. There wasn't that sense of being torn that I always feel. There was no barrier between me and the flowers. I had never even known what a powerful barrier was always there between us and the world, but in any case now it was gone, and I understood what it was like, being without barriers. I wanted to walk though Heaven again and again, to visit every single flower, though I was so unused to so much Beauty and Life that I even thought briefly of stopping, ending the walk, plus it seemed that now, when I could SEE the world, nobody could ever take it away, and it would always be like this, but I understood that this wasn't case, that I was only allowed in Heaven for a few hours, these dawning hours—of dewdrops, of sunlight, of mists, of flowers—and I didn't want to tear myself away from what I saw. It was one of the best dawns of my life, and in reality, every dawn is like that.

Eden returns to me in the childhood of my son, whom my grandparents almost lived long enough to see. Now it's his turn to live in Wonderland, where I find myself again while at the same time seeing it from outside, as I live through his childhood with him. I'll return to my own childhood again one day, to die there. We all die as children, particularly old people. Adults hurry, they rush, they live through illusions, as though they don't understand that no matter what they do there there's only ever going to be an eternal draw. The only things that exist are childhood and death. And that's what you must carry inside of you all your life.

Every person contains two beings: the first one and the second one. The first being is born and spends her life in Wonderland. She lives in reality and in the depths. But gradually, a new form takes shape within her, a form that dwells in society and in the language with which she comes to identify. This second being, this illusory form, is actually just the first being's dream, but from that point on, a person lives inside a daydream. She forgets Wonderland. She begins to live in a dream dreamed by the first being, and then Wonderland itself seems to her to be a dream, a dream that she can't remember. In the depths of her dreams she searches for Wonderland, which for her is always in the past. But she can't return there, because she's never had anything to do with it. She never lived in Wonderland; she's trying to remember something that did not happen to her. She's only Wonderland's own dream. She is its dream; it isn't her dream, as she mistakenly supposes. She lives and always will live within a dream, that's simply her nature. She is Wonderland's dream, a dream that's trying to remember and regain Wonderland in the depths of her own deepest dream. But the being who once lived in Wonderland continues to live there. She hasn't been banished into someone else's dream. She's home.

Every person contains two beings: the being who lives in Wonderland and is always silent, and the being who has taken over everything and possesses words. The first being, the one from Wonderland, will never learn to speak the language of the second being. They have nothing to say to each other anyway. The being who considers herself the master thinks she's the only one there; she thinks the other one, the first being, is an unremembered memory, her past, a time when she didn't know herself, her dream, her unconscious, the innermost depths of her soul. She thinks of the first being as another self. But that first being, living in Wonderland and lacking language—she is really the only one who exists, and it's she (and Wonderland, from which she cannot be separated) who dreams the dream. And in that dream lives the false master of everything, the one who speaks in society, daring to do so on behalf of the first being. This illusory master of words is doomed to forever want to return to the depths where she, as it seems to her, once lived in Wonderland. It's those depths, it's that first being who lives in Wonderland, which everyone who comes to love this person wants to reach, because all lovers actually love, out of the two beings, the first one, even if they spend their whole lives in relationships with the second one. They invoke the first being while looking at the second one. When a person loves, it's as though she travels down to the very depths of the childhood dream where she thinks the first being can be found, but that's because it's not really she who loves, but the first being. The one who says "I" is in someone else's dream. The dream of the one who lives there. She seizes people's love for herself, but it isn't really she who's loved, and it isn't she who loves. The first being, who doesn't know how to say "I," lives in Wonderland and visits society and the adult world only in dreams, when the second being, who lives in society and the adult world, searches for Wonderland in the depths of her own dreams. She thinks that Wonderland is just her fantasy or an early, forgotten, formative stage, when she was not yet herself. She thinks that there's nothing more important than being a self. She thinks that there's nothing more important than saying "I" and thinking everything belongs to her. Occasionally she is able to recognize herself as a mistake, an illness. She isn't part of Wonderland, she was born and she will die, she was created and she will be destroyed, while the one who lives in Wonderland lives outside of time, in the Cradle of God.

NOTES

"It's the End of the World, My Love"

dacha: a summer home that many Russians own or rent in the countryside.

the Queen, the Witch who lights her coals in the clay pot, will never want to tell us what she knows, and which we do not know: from John Ashbery's translation of Rimbaud's "After the Flood," in *Illuminations*, published by W. W. Norton & Company, 2012.

"At the Market"

girl with a gaze sharper than a dagger's blade: a line from "Endless Suicide," a song by Survival Guide, a Soviet and Russian rock band.

got stitched: received a treatment for alcoholism involving a subcutaneous implant that makes recipients feel physically ill if they drink.

informals: *neformaly*, a general term for the various youth subcultures of the late Soviet Union and Russia.

"Tech"

tech: *PTU* refers to vocational schools that serve as an alternative to academic high schools. Nicknamed *putyagy*, these schools train students for careers rather than preparing them for higher education.

Gostiny Dvor: a Saint Petersburg landmark on the city's main thoroughfare, Nevsky Prospekt; Gostiny Dvor is a large eighteenth-century shopping arcade that's still in use today.

National Bolsheviks: a post-Soviet political party with a platform that combined nationalism and communism; the National Bolsheviks had a following among informals in the 1990s and 2000s. *Limonka* was the party newspaper.

Ostrovsky: (1823–1886) Aleksandr Nikolayevich Ostrovsky, a seminal realist playwright.

Staronevsky: literally "Old Nevsky," a nickname for the stretch of Nevsky Prospekt that runs between Resistance Square and Alexander Nevsky Square.

Katya's Garden: nickname for a Saint Petersburg public square with a statue of Catherine the Great ("Katya") at its center.

"Memories of My Forgotten Beloved"

Gumilyov: (1886–1921) Nikolay Gumilyov, Acmeist poet, traveler, army officer, and first husband of Anna Akhmatova; he was killed by the Soviet secret police.

Mayakovsky: (1893–1930) Vladimir Mayakovsky, a larger-than-life Futurist poet who praised the Revolution, had a complicated relationship with the Soviet Union, and died by suicide.

"Well, we're not stokers and we're not carpenters, but we don't have any deep regrets": the opening lines of a song from *Height*, a 1957 Soviet film about ironworkers who climb to great heights in the course of their work.

"Under the Bridge"

LITO: an abbreviation of *literaturnoye obyedinenie* (literary organization).

Lensoviet Palace of Culture: a large community center for cultural recreation on Kamennostrovsky Prospekt in Saint Petersburg. Palaces of culture were Soviet-era establishments that hosted performances, movie screenings, lectures, classes, etc. Many continue to function as cultural centers in post-Soviet countries.

Brodsky: (1940–1996) Joseph Brodsky, a Russian-American lyric poet. Brodsky's individualism was unacceptable to Soviet authorities, and he was eventually forced to leave the Soviet Union.

the Silver Age: an incredibly rich period for Russian literature and art that began at the end of the nineteenth century and lasted roughly until the Revolution.

Sestroretsk: a town on the Gulf of Finland, northwest of Saint Petersburg.

Military-Medical Academy: S. M. Kirov Military-Medical Academy, an institution that trains military medical personnel; its campus extends to the embankment of the Neva River.

Finland Station: a railway station known for being Lenin's arrival point when he returned to Russia from Europe in 1917 via German-sanctioned train.

"Before the Gates"

zapekanka: farmer's cheesecake, usually containing berries or raisins.

Boris Moiseev and Shura: pop stars who in the 1990s were widely assumed to be gay.

Assol: the heroine of Alexander Grin's beloved novella *Scarlet Sails*, a love story about a credulous young woman and a sea captain.

Father Frost: a Slavic Santa Claus who wears a long coat and wields a magic staff. His granddaughter, the Snow Maiden, helps with gift delivery.

white nights: the period in summertime when Saint Petersburg, located on the sixtieth parallel north, just south of the Arctic Circle, gets almost around-the-clock light.

Little Blue Light: a Soviet and Russian TV variety show that airs on New Year's Eve.

"we don't skip the fourth": some groups of students at the school described in this story skipped fourth grade.

"The Little Scarlet Flower": a Russian version of the fairy tale "Beauty and the Beast."

Nicholas of Cusa: a fifteenth-century German philosopher and theologian who held that the human mind can't fully comprehend the divine, which Nicholas called the Maximum; however, humans should aim to achieve "learned ignorance" through the pursuit.

"Bedya"

"for potatoes": shorthand for a Soviet-era practice of deploying certain groups of people, including students, to the countryside to help with bringing in the harvest and other agricultural work.

"Against the Law"

Bakhtin: (1895–1975) Mikhail Bakhtin, a Russian philosopher and literary critic interested in ethics and aesthetics and known for the concepts of polyphony and heteroglossia, among others.

City Day: an annual public holiday celebrating a city. Saint Petersburg's City Day is celebrated on May 27.

I have been sent by the Power: the dialogue of Maria and Sophia draws on a third- or fourth-century Coptic text (itself a translation) called "The Thunder, Perfect Mind."

"Russian Beauty"

Baba Yaga, Koschei, and the forest at night that Alenushka and Ivanushka get lost in: characters from classic Russian fairy tales. Baba Yaga is an evil old woman who lives in a house on chicken legs; Koschei is an evil old man who cannot die; Alenushka and Ivanushka are lost siblings who live in the woods.

"The Very Same Day"

Young Pioneers: a Soviet-era youth organization whose programming included summer camps.

"Lord of the Hurricane"

Philipp Kirkorov: a ubiquitous Russian pop star.

"Ivan the Boar's Knee"

Zlatovláska: a 1970s Czechoslovak movie based on a fairy tale in which an evil king and his winsome cook gain the ability to understand the languages of animals. Later, the king wants to marry a golden-haired princess, while she is, unsurprisingly, more interested in the cook.

"Memory of Heaven"

Lengorispolkom: an abbreviation of *ispolnitelny komitet Leningradskogo gorodskogo soveta deputatov trudyashchihsya* (Executive Committee of the Leningrad City Council of Workers' Deputies)

Rabfak: an abbreviation of *rabochiy fakultet* (workers' department), pre-higher-education courses that in the early Soviet period were offered to workers who wanted to attend university.

Hozdvor: an abbreviation of *hozyaistvenniy dvor* (household courtyard), a space to store household tools and groundskeeping equipment.

Victor Tsoi: (1962–1990) the beloved front man of the influential 1980s rock band Kino; Tsoi died in a car crash.

Chizhyk-Pyzhik: a folk song universally known by speakers of Russian. The lyrics address a bird, but the song is most likely about students drinking too much.

Thank you all
for your support.
We do this for you,
and could not do
it without you.

DEEP
VELLUM

PARTNERS

pixel ‖ texel

LIFE IN DEEP ELLUM

EMBREY FAMILY FOUNDATION

COMMON DESK
COWORKING

ALLRED
CAPITAL MANAGEMENT
of
RAYMOND JAMES®

ADDITIONAL DONORS, CONT'D

Mark Haber
Mary Cline
Maynard Thomson
Michael Reklis
Mike Soto
Mokhtar Ramadan
Nikki & Dennis Gibson
Patrick Kukucka
Patrick Kutcher
Rev. Elizabeth & Neil Moseley
Richard Meyer

Scott & Katy Nimmons
Sherry Perry
Sydneyann Binion
Stephen Harding
Stephen Williamson
Susan Carp
Susan Ernst
Theater Jones
Tim Perttula
Tony Thomson

SUBSCRIBERS

Margaret Terwey
Ben Fountain
Gina Rios
Elena Rush
Courtney Sheedy
Caroline West
Brian Bell
Charles Dee Mitchell
Cullen Schaar
Harvey Hix
Jeff Lierly
Elizabeth Simpson

Nicole Yurcaba
Jennifer Owen
Melanie Nicholls
Alan Glazer
Michael Doss
Matt Bucher
Katarzyna Bartoszynska
Michael Binkley
Erin Kubatzky
Martin Piñol
Michael Lighty
Joseph Rebella

Jarratt Willis
Heustis Whiteside
Samuel Herrera
Heidi McElrath
Jeffrey Parker
Carolyn Surbaugh
Stephen Fuller
Kari Mah
Matt Ammon
Elif Ağanoğlu

AVAILABLE NOW FROM DEEP VELLUM

SHANE ANDERSON • *After the Oracle* • USA

MICHÈLE AUDIN • *One Hundred Twenty-One Days* • translated by Christiana Hills • FRANCE

BAE SUAH • *Recitation* • translated by Deborah Smith • SOUTH KOREA

MARIO BELLATIN • *Mrs. Murakami's Garden* • translated by Heather Cleary • *Beauty Salon* • translated by Shook • MEXICO

EDUARDO BERTI • *The Imagined Land* • translated by Charlotte Coombe • ARGENTINA

CARMEN BOULLOSA • *Texas: The Great Theft* • translated by Samantha Schnee • *Before* • translated by Peter Bush • *Heavens on Earth* • translated by Shelby Vincent • MEXICO

CAYLIN CAPRA-THOMAS • *Iguana Iguana* • USA

MAGDA CÂRNECI • *FEM* • translated by Sean Cotter • ROMANIA

LEILA S. CHUDORI • *Home* • translated by John H. McGlynn • INDONESIA

MATHILDE WALTER CLARK • *Lone Star* • translated by Martin Aitken & K. E. Semmel • DENMARK

SARAH CLEAVE, ed. • *Banthology: Stories from Banned Nations* • IRAN, IRAQ, LIBYA, SOMALIA, SUDAN, SYRIA & YEMEN

TIM COURSEY • *Driving Lessons* • USA

LOGEN CURE • *Welcome to Midland: Poems* • USA

ANANDA DEVI • *Eve Out of Her Ruins* • translated by Jeffrey Zuckerman • *When the Night Agrees to Speak to Me* • translated by Kazim Ali MAURITIUS

DHUMKETU • *The Shehnai Virtuoso* • translated by Jenny Bhatt • INDIA

PETER DIMOCK • *Daybook from Sheep Meadow* • USA

CLAUDIA ULLOA DONOSO • *Little Bird*, translated by Lily Meyer • PERU/NORWAY

LEYLÂ ERBIL • *A Strange Woman* • translated by Nermin Menemencioğlu & Amy Marie Spangler • TURKEY

RADNA FABIAS • *Habitus* • translated by David Colmer • CURAÇAO/NETHERLANDS

ROSS FARRAR • *Ross Sings Cheree & the Animated Dark: Poems* • USA

ALISA GANIEVA • *Bride and Groom* • *The Mountain and the Wall* • translated by Carol Apollonio • RUSSIA

FERNANDA GARCÍA LAO • *Out of the Cage* • translated by Will Vanderhyden • ARGENTINA

ANNE GARRÉTA • *Sphinx* • *Not One Day* • *In Concrete* • translated by Emma Ramadan • FRANCE

NIVEN GOVINDEN • *Diary of a Film* • GREAT BRITAIN

JÓN GNARR • *The Indian* • *The Pirate* • *The Outlaw* • translated by Lytton Smith • ICELAND

GOETHE • *The Golden Goblet: Selected Poems* • *Faust, Part One* • translated by Zsuzsanna Ozsváth and Frederick Turner • GERMANY

SARA GOUDARZI • *The Almond in the Apricot* • USA

NOEMI JAFFE • *What Are the Blind Men Dreaming?* • translated by Julia Sanches & Ellen Elias-Bursac • BRAZIL

CLAUDIA SALAZAR JIMÉNEZ • *Blood of the Dawn* • translated by Elizabeth Bryer • PERU

PERGENTINO JOSÉ • *Red Ants* • MEXICO

TAISIA KITAISKAIA • *The Nightgown & Other Poems* • USA

SONG LIN • *The Gleaner Song: Selected Poems* • translated by Dong Li • CHINA

GYULA JENEI • *Always Different* • translated by Diana Senechal • HUNGARY

DIA JUBAILI • *No Windmills in Basra* • translated by Chip Rossetti • IRAQ

JUNG YOUNG MOON • *Seven Samurai Swept Away in a River* • *Vaseline Buddha* • translated by Yewon Jung • SOUTH KOREA

ELENI KEFALA • *Time Stitches* • translated by Peter Constantine • CYPRUS

UZMA ASLAM KHAN • *The Miraculous True History of Nomi Ali* • PAKISTAN

KIM YIDEUM • *Blood Sisters* • translated by Jiyoon Lee • SOUTH KOREA

JOSEFINE KLOUGART • *Of Darkness* • translated by Martin Aitken • DENMARK

ANDREY KURKOV • *Grey Bees* • translated by Boris Dralyuk • UKRAINE

YANICK LAHENS • *Moonbath* • translated by Emily Gogolak • HAITI

JORGE ENRIQUE LAGE • *Freeway: La Movie* • translated by Lourdes Molina • CUBA

FOUAD LAROUI • *The Curious Case of Dassoukine's Trousers* • translated by Emma Ramadan • MOROCCO

FORTHCOMING FROM DEEP VELLUM